Mindslip by Tony Harmsworth

Get Tony Harmsworth's Moonscape Novella FOR FREE

Sign up for the no-spam newsletter and get Moonscape and other exclusive content, all for free.
Details can be found at the end of MINDSLIP.

Copyrights and Thanks

Thanks to:

Wally Andrews, Wendy Harmsworth, Kym Miller, Annika Lewinson-Morgan, Melanie Underwood, & Wattpad

All rights reserved; no part of this publication may be reproduced or transmitted by any means, electronic, mechanical, photocopying or otherwise without the prior written permission of the author.

Also available as an ebook and audiobook.

ISBN: 9781078279741
© A G Harmsworth 2012-24
Cover ©2020 by Books Covered (Stefanie)
Image of Orion © NASA

A G Harmsworth has asserted his moral rights.

Published by:
Harmsworth Publishing Ltd
Drumnadrochit
Inverness-shire
IV63 6XJ

INDEX

Mindslip by Tony Harmsworth 1
    Get Tony Harmsworth's Moonscape Novella FOR FREE 3
    Copyrights and Thanks 5
    INDEX 7
    Author 9

1 FOURTEENTH CENTURY STARGAZER 13

2 A LIKELY SUPERNOVA 17

3 TOMORROW 21

4 AWAKENING 27

5 FALLING 35

6 UNDERSTANDING 41

7 CAPTIVE 51

8 GOVERNMENT 57

9 FASTEN YOUR SEATBELTS 63

10 SLOW PROGRESS 69

11 MAKING WAVES 77

12 ORDER FROM THE CHAOS 85

13 NO ESCAPE 101

14 HOME ALONE 109

15 SPECIAL DELIVERY 117

16 VIVE LA DIFFÉRENCE 121

17 MOUNTAIN 137

18 FACE TO FACE 141

19 LONG AND WINDING ROAD 159

20 TEN DOWNING STREET 167

21 DEADLY ASSAILANT	177
22 FAMILY	185
23 REUNITED	207
24 THE CURSE	225
25 HUMANIMAL FARM	249
26 REPATRIATION ARRIVALS	259
27 CLIVE THE PIG	271
28 TIME TO TAKE STOCK	285
29 COBRA FIELD TRIP	295
30 INEXPLICABLE SUCCESS	303
31 PHILOSOPHY OF CATASTROPHE	315
32 NIGHT CALL	325
33 NO ASTRONOMER ROYAL	331
34 A TIME FOR REFLECTION	335
35 PLUS ÇA CHANGE, PLUS C'EST LA MÊME CHOSE	343
Tony's Books	351
Reader Club	354

Author

Tony Harmsworth was born Anthony Geoffrey Harmsworth on 19th March 1948 in Brocket Hall, Hertfordshire, which was being used as a maternity hospital after the Second World War.

His father, George, came from Boxmoor, Hertfordshire, and his mother, Williamina Robertson, from Preston Pans in Scotland.

Tony was educated at Welwyn Garden City High School and Bude County Grammar School, where he decisively failed all his A and S-level subjects in Pure Maths, Applied Maths and Physics, owing, in part, to severe hay fever, although he admits not working hard enough could have contributed to the failure. His IQ was Mensa tested to 158 in his last year at school. His lifelong interest in science and astronomy has inspired his writing.

As a teenager, Tony developed a deep scepticism of religion, read both the Bible and, later, the Quran, realising that they were nothing but ancient stories without any basis in reality, and became a confirmed atheist. Don't be surprised to find this influencing some of his stories.

Leaving school without qualifications, and thrown onto his own resources, he followed his soon to become wife, Wendy, to Manchester where she read modern languages. He tried a first career in sales, and, despite his youth, he was quickly promoted from salesman to supervisor and then became part of an advance team opening new sales areas throughout the UK.

Still only nineteen, he joined Top Rank prior to Granada's takeover. Seeking improved prospects, he moved to Ridings Stores, Loyds Retailers and then the Co-op holding down department management with the latter and quickly being promoted to store management with Loyds at just twenty years of age.

Now married, they moved to Basingstoke where several firms were relocating from London. A new post was created at Wella, which involved managing an innovative computer-controlled stock system from scratch. This appealed to his mathematical leaning. With Wella, he was soon promoted to Organisation and Methods, eventually becoming general assistant to the managing director aged only twenty-five.

In 1975, he was head-hunted by the cosmetics arm of British American Tobacco – Lenthéric Morny where he introduced new systems in the industrial engineering department.

He left here when he and his wife decided to break out of the rat race and relocate to Drumnadrochit in the Highlands of Scotland in 1978.

Discovering the lack of any tourist information about Loch Ness, he conceived, researched, and staged, the Loch Ness Exhibition. It was an instant success and made Drumnadrochit the capital of the monster world.

Discovering that his share of the exhibition[1] had mysteriously evaporated, he moved on to create a manufacturing company in Fife, designed more exhibitions on Macbeth, Scottish History and Highland Heritage. In 1993 he staged Scotland's largest private heritage centre at Fort Augustus Abbey where, despite his atheism, they appointed him the first lay-bursar of any Scottish monastery.

Developing the tourism theme, he established high quality guided tours in the Highlands. In fact, his Discover

---

[1] Detailed in his non-fiction book – Loch Ness, Nessie and Me.

Loch Ness tour company was the first to achieve the maximum five stars in Scotland.

As well as having written, according to one review, 'the most comprehensive and accurate book on Loch Ness', he got the writing bug and, at the age of seventy, began a new career writing science fiction. Not the space battles, star wars variety, but near-future realistic stories in the vein of the late John Wyndham, and with an eye on the environment. Perhaps because of his age, traditional publishers shunned him. Following the theme of his life, he struck out on his own regardless. Two of his novels have become UK Kindle bestsellers in SF categories, but he writes for enjoyment rather than income.

1 FOURTEENTH CENTURY STARGAZER

Note for non-British readers – Tony writes using UK English spelling, punctuation, and grammar.

Elias loved the pristine clearness of his rural night sky. He picked out the ancient constellations with ease. The W of Cassiopeia overhead, Andromeda, with its strange smudge nearby and spectacular Orion lower in the heavens – his favourite. The five key areas were so distinctive. Betelgeuse, a bright red star at top left indicating Orion's right shoulder; two similar bright stars, Bellatrix at top right and Saiph at bottom left; plus brilliant blue-white Rigel at bottom right. In the middle of the constellation, Orion's stunning belt of three stars supported his sword which contained the pink crab nebula as if a jewel in the hilt.

As the cornfield stubble gathered its nightly moisture, Rossa kissed him, rose and departed to prepare supper. His stargazing solitude would not last much longer. The burgeoning dew would seep through his linen leggings and tunic, forcing him to abandon the mysteries of the heavens. He wondered what these sparkling jewels were, which so enthralled him?

A shooting star sped from left to right across the entire sky, its incandescence growing to a peak and then vanishing. Was this a star dying? There were too many to count. How could he ever know if one of those tiny specks of light had forever vanished in that instant?

He sat up, resting back on his outstretched arms to better see the southern horizon. Bloodshot Betelgeuse shone like a ruby. Despite all stars appearing to be no more than points of light, somehow this one gave him the impression of grandeur. Its colour and relative brightness made it stand out in the night sky.

He loved it and, with winter approaching, it would be rising earlier and earlier, giving him more opportunities to enjoy its reassuring presence. On this still, moonless night, he noticed nothing different or unusual about his prized heavenly, ruby, yet at that very instant, it was collapsing.

Elias could never know that Betelgeuse was so enormous that, if it sat at the centre of our solar system, its diameter would extend beyond the orbit of Mars. Nor could he envisage its eventual death throes. Such things were beyond his comprehension. The death of this monster would be no shooting star.

The collapse was swift and, after a brief pause, the almightiest explosion occurred. The star had gone supernova, spewing out deadly gamma rays and the heavy elements essential to life in the universe.

To Elias, there had been no change in his sky. He knew nothing of the speed of light or the concept of gamma rays, radiation and gravitational waves.

His palms, pressing against the ground, became damp. Time to go. The dew was penetrating his leggings. With reluctance, he stood and, guided only by starlight, made his way towards his nearby turf-built home. A subdued glow emanated from behind the door and shutters, accompanied by the welcome aroma of a meaty stew. He secured the chicken coop, checked the paddock gate and had a final loving glance towards his heavenly ruby.

He would never know his favourite star was already hurling its deadly emissions towards Earth. They would not arrive for more than six hundred and forty years.

2 A LIKELY SUPERNOVA

'So,' said Geoff, 'we've covered the details of type one supernovae. Now we'll look at type two.

'These are massive stars up to fifty times the mass of the sun. As we've discussed, they start to fuse heavier and heavier elements until the core of the star reaches a limit. What's the limit?'

A really bright student at the front, who'd answered lots of questions, put his hand up and I nodded.

'The Chandrasekhar limit,' he said.

'Correct... and what is it?'

'About one point four solar masses,' he said.

'Correct again. When the core of the giant star reaches that limit, it has a cataclysmic implosion taking only a few seconds. The outer regions of the star then collapse inward at around twenty per cent of the speed of light. The resultant explosion is seen as a blinding flash. If the star is close enough, it would be visible in the daylight sky and could remain so for weeks or even months before it finally dies. The core becomes an extremely dense neutron star.'

I changed the slide and waved at the projected image on the screen.

'This is the closest type two supernova progenitor. Does anyone recognise it?' I asked.

There were several calls of 'Betelgeuse', but the same young man in the front row, who'd been taking copious notes, shouted, 'Alpha Orionis.'

'Correct. All of you. In fact, the constellation of Orion has two potential supernovae – Rigel is the second – Beta Orionis. To the naked eye, variable Betelgeuse sometimes appears brighter so was designated Alpha Orionis. But, why have I chosen Betelgeuse?'

I pointed at a girl in the fifth row.

'Rigel is further away,' she said.

'Yes, it is, but that is not the main reason for my choosing Alpha Orionis.'

The young man's hand shot up once more, 'It is reaching the end of its expected life. Beta Orionis is an even younger star.'

'Yes. Betelgeuse is only six hundred and forty light years away and could go supernova tomorrow, or maybe it already did... in the mid-fourteenth century... and we'll see the result tomorrow!'

Some chuckles emanated from the audience.

'Betelgeuse would produce a type two supernova, but is so distant, it is unlikely to cause us any real harm. It might be as bright as the full moon for a few months. If it were closer to us, say, fifty instead of six hundred and forty light years, it might be more serious, bombarding us with gamma rays and other radiation.'

The student's hand shot up again and I nodded.

'Alpha Orionis has been shown to be reaching another peak luminosity recently. Is that a clue to when we might see it explode?'

'You *are* keeping up to date with my recent work. Yes, it is variable to a considerable degree, but the report you refer to is old. Over the last few months it has been dimming rapidly, rather than brightening. Just look at it one evening. You'll see that it is barely the luminosity of the belt stars. This dimming has given some scientists the hope that we might see it explode in our lifetimes, although, to be fair, it could continue to be a variable for another hundred thousand years.'

More hands shot into the air, but I'd been given the signal that time was up. 'Sorry, all, but Professor Wozniak has called time. I'll be in the lobby for a while and happy to sign my book, *The Not Quite So Big Bangs,* and answer further questions. Thank you so much for being a most interesting and attentive audience. Keep stargazing!'

Professor Wozniak joined me on the stage and took the microphone. 'Well, students, I hope you have found Dr Geoffrey Arnold's talk as interesting as I have. We are honoured to have one of Britain's foremost astronomers and astrophysicists give us this lecture on supernovae, or, should I say, the "not quite so big bangs"? Please show your appreciation in the usual way.'

Applause rang out.

3 TOMORROW

A blinding flash lit the sky.

'Geoffrey, what on earth's that?' cried Caroline as she shielded the children's eyes.

I covered my own and hastily threw a blanket from the washing-line over the family as I hurried them to the back of the house where the shade provided some protection. What could it be? A nuclear strike in the atmosphere? If so, our lives would be over in seconds. We were motionless, crouching between the coal bunker and the kitchen wall, waiting for a blast to crush us or heat wave to incinerate us. The glare penetrated the blanket.

'Daddy, what's happening?' screamed Sandra, our eight-year-old.

'Is it a war?' A deathly whisper from Wilson, two years Sandra's senior and inquisitive as hell.

'Don't know. Follow me! Keep tight to the wall!' I said, and we shuffled towards the kitchen door, keeping out of the brilliant light which washed out the colours of the garden and neighbouring properties.

'Can't be a bomb,' I said.

'You sure?'

'Yes, Cas. If it was, we'd all be dead by now. No physical blast, just the light.'

'I'm afraid, Mummy.' Sandra was in tears as I guided them through the kitchen extension to the body of the house where we'd be protected by more substantial bricks and mortar.

'Supernova comes to mind,' I said.

'But why's it still so bright? It's brighter than the sun. Aren't supernovas just a flash?'

'Can last a long time, but there should be some fading soon. We need to stay indoors for a while. Could be danger from X-rays and gamma rays. Keep the children in the hall or dining room while I make some calls.'

Caroline shepherded the children into the room and gave Sandra a drawing book and Wilson his Nintendo.

'Hello.' My boss, head of the Royal Observatory, answered my call.

'Justin, did you see it?'

'Yes, think it's in Orion.'

'Betelgeuse?'

'Almost certainly.'

'I'm going to call a few astronomers and set up a meeting at the Royal Institution for eleven tomorrow. That okay with you?'

'Yes, Geoff. Go ahead. I'll call Jodrell Bank and see if there's any data yet.'

I hung up and rang colleagues. Within the hour, I had some of the most senior astronomers in the south of England promising to attend the meeting.

'You kids stay in here. Cas, come see.' I tugged on my wife's hand. 'We'll take a look at it.'

'Can I come?' shouted Wilson.

'Not tonight, Wils. You can in the morning.'

'Aaaaw, Daaaad. It could be gone tomorrow.'

'Might be with us for weeks, but it could be dangerous for children right now. Some fade more rapidly than others, but it'll still be bright for some time. Stay with Sands for now.'

'Must I?' he moaned.

'Yes, and keep out of the light.'

'Okaaaay, Daaaad.'

I grabbed the four-inch refractor from the hall cupboard, mounted it on its tripod and Caroline and I headed to the front door, both pulling on wax jackets and hats for ultra-violet protection.

'Don't look at it directly, Cas. Keep the light off your face,' I said as I opened the door and the unearthly brightness flooded in.

Outside, I directed the telescope at the source of the light and projected the image onto a sun-viewing card. I'd done it many times before to show the kids sunspots. Unlike the sun and its visible disc, what we saw now was but a single point of incredibly bright light.

I read the tripod coordinates, 'It is Betelgeuse.'

'Amazing,' said Caroline.

She also had an interest in astronomy. It grew after we met as students in Cambridge. She was a chemist and I accused her of an interest in magical potions. She called me an astrologer because she knew how the term riled me. After a few months of trading insults, we fell hopelessly in love.

'We've all been waiting for a local supernova. To have actually witnessed it is amazing.'

'How close?'

'About six hundred and fifty light years. Must say I'm surprised at the initial brightness, but it's dropped to similar to the sun now. Any serious danger of radiation should pass soon. Better keep the kids in for the rest of the evening to be safe.'

The phone rang.

'Doctor Arnold? It's Joan Lightly.' The daughter of a friend and colleague. She sounded upset. 'Dad looked at the nova through a smoked glass. It split and we're afraid he's been blinded. Mum's at the hospital with him.'

'That's dreadful, Joan. With any luck, the blindness will be temporary.'

'He won't make the Royal Institution tomorrow.'

'Doesn't matter. Tell him not to worry. Let us know what happens. Here's Caroline.'

I handed the phone to Caroline to continue the conversation while I called Justin on my mobile.

'Tim's got himself blinded. Looked at it though a smoked glass which split.'

'Oh dear. That's dreadful news.'

'We'll miss him tomorrow.'

'Yes. Listen, Geoff, I've had Jodrell Bank on the blower. It was magnitude minus thirty-two after ten minutes so could have been up to two hundred times the brightness of the sun during that first flash. Magnitude minus twenty-four when I came off the phone, so similar to the sun.'

'Wow. Incredible. We were in the garden but took cover pretty quickly.'

'Very wise. Unexpected to be so bright at that distance.'

'Yes. By a huge factor. Did they say anything about radiation?'

'Broad spectrum but includes gamma,' said Justin.

'What? Atmospheric gamma penetration.'

'Yes. Worrying to say the least.'

'Glad we dived for cover.'

Aside, I spoke to Cas, 'No one goes out tonight. Gamma rays getting through.'

Justin and I ran through a list of the astronomers and astrophysicists who had promised to come to the meeting.

'Can you chair it for me, Geoff? I've got the press clamouring for interviews.'

'No problem. My laptop's in the office, so I'll get in early. It'll be difficult sleeping in this strange daylight, anyway. Can you get a message put out about staying under cover?'

'Already being broadcast. I was glad when the sun set. The double shadows were most disturbing. When will Orion set tomorrow?'

'I guess about eight in the morning roughly.'

Next Morning

'Excuse me, excuse me,' I repeated over and again as I weaved my way along the railway platform. Betelgeuse, bright as a hazy sun, was low to the horizon. People were still having to shield their eyes, most wearing dark glasses. Having two suns in the sky meant forever tilting your head in different directions to avoid the glare. Bizarre.

The train squealed noisily to a halt. I fought my way into the nearest carriage and took one of the few remaining seats. The rush hour trains to London were often standing room only.

The morning paper was full of the supernova. My boss, Justin Mayweather, as the Astronomer Royal, was quoted extensively.

It had been incredibly fortunate that the supernova occurred during daylight hours. Betelgeuse is a very popular telescopic object and, if it had occurred after dark, no end of people would have been looking at it through binoculars or small telescopes. They would certainly have been blinded for life. I couldn't believe how foolish Tim Lightly had been using a smoked glass. We're forever warning people not to do that to look at the sun and initially this was even brighter.

The seven forty-nine train pulled out of the station and I could answer some of the tweets and texts I'd been inundated with from observatories all over the world. Astronomers were directing radio telescopes towards the supernova, obtaining and recording enormous volumes of data.

Passengers were talking about the phenomenon and spouting nonsense about it. I kept quiet to concentrate on marshalling my thoughts and making notes for the meeting. Without my laptop, I'd had to revert to an ancient Filofax organiser from my university days. Better than the restrictive screen size on my smartphone.

The Waterloo Express accelerated through the Surrey countryside en route to the capital. With Betelgeuse and the sun being on opposite sides of the sky, the trees, hedges, buildings, and wind turbines were creating outlandish shadows. But the nova would set shortly, and the scene would return to normal.

My phone rang.

'Arnold.'

'Bill here, we're picking up growing electromagnetic output hitting the Earth. Thought you'd want to know for the meeting. If it continues to grow, it'll cause satellite problems about eight fifteen GMT. We're picking up coronal mass ejections too.'

'Thanks for the heads-up, Bill. Are the CMEs in sympathy with the nova, do you think?'

'Possibly. Leaving for London shortly, but we'll be monitoring the sun really carefully for a while.'

'Worrying if it's related.'

'Yes, quite. See you in a couple of hours, Geoff.'

'Aye,' I said and noted 8.15am in my Filofax just as my G4 connection went down. Simultaneously, Betelgeuse released an unprecedented second enormous blast of light and radiation.

In that instant, what I would later call "Mindslip", struck the Earth.

4 AWAKENING

Geoff Discovers the World Has Gone Crazy

I awoke with a pressing need to pee.

This wasn't the Waterloo train! Where the hell was I? My vision was out of focus and misty, but it gradually cleared, becoming sharper, as if I was recovering from an anaesthetic.

I was in someone's sitting room. I didn't recognise the room at all. The settee was a floral design. Why was I lying on someone else's sofa? My navy-blue-stockinged feet protruded from my suit trousers which appeared a shade darker than normal. Had the supernova affected my vision?

Odd, how I was resting. A pastel green cushion was wedged between my arm and body as if I'd been leaning upon it or cuddling it.

I tried to sit up but felt strange and dizzy so collapsed into my original position, the soft arm of the sofa supporting my head. I felt a distinct lack of orientation.

'Come on, Geoffrey Arnold, pull yourself together,' I whispered to myself as if I might be overheard, although there seemed to be no one else around.

Had someone slipped me a Mickey Finn? When? Where? Why was I here? Hadn't I just boarded the train?

Two mahogany doors with silver-coloured handles were set into the wall I was facing. The door on the left was closed.

A bookcase, full to overflowing with both hardbacks and paperbacks, hosted two framed portraits. One, the image of a young Japanese graduate girl, in mortarboard and gown, smiling at some anonymous portrait photographer; the other, depicted the head and shoulders of a pleasant-looking young man with woodland behind him. The wall was home to a series of five tall, narrow, Japanese paintings in contemporary frames. Stylish, not tacky or touristy.

Between the doors, a forty-inch television was mounted, with a cabinet beneath housing a Skybox, DVD player and music system.

Low sunlight flickered through trees beyond the bay window. In the bay, stood a circular teak table and four chairs with green seats. An ornate centrepiece glass bowl held small easy-peel tangerines, some black grapes, a pear, and a couple of apples.

I tried to sit up. Once more a disturbing sensation of nausea arose, but this time I tolerated it and swung my feet around so I sat on the edge of the settee. The slight disorientation continued. Where were my shoes?

In fact, where was I? It made no sense for me to be on a strange sofa in my suit. What the hell was going on? I was becoming annoyed with the situation and my inability to cope with it. I hated any loss of personal control.

Beside me a copy of Cosmopolitan graced a stylish glass coffee table. The unopened magazine still wore its polythene mailing sleeve. Closer to me was a Sky TV controller and beside that a pastel mauve, lady's purse. Its zip section was open revealing some banknotes. An iPhone, also mauve, lay beneath it. This must be a woman's home. I was in a strange house belonging to a woman.

My faculties were returning. The sunlight indicated morning and came from one direction. Betelgeuse must have set. The last I remembered was the second flash after boarding my morning train. I ran my hand over my chin and cheek. No stubble. It must still be early in the day for me to be so remarkably clean-shaven. I must have come here on my way to work this morning. But why? What possible reason was there for me being in this woman's home? And what about the train? What had happened between me being on the train and arriving here? Ridiculous! Why had I no memory of it?

'Is anyone there?' My voice sounded strange, as if I'd not spoken for a day and was having trouble getting the words out. There was no answer. Where was she?

Damn it! The need to pee became more insistent.

I stood, experienced dizziness and sat again. I couldn't be inebriated, yet I had all the symptoms of the almightiest hangover.

Tentatively I stood again and managed to balance myself this time. I was lightheaded and my entire body felt peculiar, unbalanced, lighter, shorter, distinctly odd.

I took a couple of steps towards the closed door, opened it and emerged into a hallway. The tiles were cold. Where the hell were my shoes?

I knocked on the nearest door. It was ajar. Out of politeness I called, 'Hello.'

No answer to my strangely feeble call. I pushed the door inwards and took a step into a very feminine bedroom. There was no sign of her, in person.

I was intruding here. In the hallway, a hat stand exhibited a beret – mauve again – a matching coat plus an anorak type garment, a baseball hat in pink, and three umbrellas. Light blue, pink, and the same mauve as the bag in the lounge and the coat and beret here. She must be a very stylish lady. A shoe stand held a pair of flat shoes, a pair with three or four-inch heels, stylish black ankle-length boots and two pairs of designer trainers – one pair pristine, the other well-used and mud-spattered. She must go running. There was another doorway. I hoped it was a bathroom. I knocked. No answer. Where was she? Maybe in the kitchen? I'd use the bathroom first, then search her out.

I pushed the door. No one inside. Once more, it was feminine with flowery curtains, a large shower cubicle, separate bath, and washbasin. The loo was on the right.

I locked the door, approached the toilet, lifted the cover and seat, pulled down my zip, reached into my underpants and got the shock of my life!

Where was it? This was mad! Where was my penis?

I reached further in. Pubic hair, but nothing else. I looked downwards, and what I saw instantly turned my blood to ice.

A graceful woman's hand, with long delicate fingers was reaching in through my fly. My whole body jumped with fright as I spun around to confront her, to ask what the hell she was playing at. When I did, I realised the hand was part of my own arm, protruding from my sleeve. How could this be? I removed it, studied it. My hand was not mine at all. It was the hand of a beautiful young woman.

I still needed to pee, and it was becoming more pressing. I guessed the act of thinking about it was making it more urgent. I reached in again. The usual device most certainly wasn't there! I had a woman's body.

A dream. That's it. It had to be a dream. I often had dreams in which I needed to pee. Usually there was a problem of some sort, but not like this. Most often the toilet wasn't private, and there were people, often women or girls staring in through glass partitions, or the toilet wasn't working. Sometimes there was a disconnected bowl or just a hole in the floor. Often there were people in the room, and I had to get them to leave somehow. But this wasn't like any of those dreams. This dream had me believing I was a woman.

If I tried to pee, I'd wet the bed. I simply had to be asleep. I'd better wake up. Why couldn't I wake up? I tugged the pubic hair. Ouch! It hurt but didn't wake me. I reached further in and felt a crease. I really was a woman. I had all the attributes.

Damn it all, the need to pee was becoming desperate. I looked around. Tried the toilet door. It was most assuredly locked. There was no one watching through the bathroom window as would occur in my toilet dreams. I closed the curtains to make sure, checked the door a third time, returned to the loo and lowered the seat.

This time I faced away from the toilet, undid an unfamiliar trouser clasp – of course, they weren't mine – lowered them and my underpants. Good grief they were a pair of ladies' designer Schulz Y-fronts. I pulled them as far as my slim, shapely hairless knees as I sat. How ridiculous was this? The Y-fronts couldn't be mine. They were far too small. The knees weren't mine, nor the silky-smooth legs. What the fuck was going on?

Now what should I do? I needed to pee. I wanted to pee. I didn't know how to pee. How did women pee, Goddammit? Did I need to hold my vulva open? I didn't want pee going everywhere. How did I know how to direct it? Did it go straight down? I'd never thought about the practicalities of how women peed.

I knew it was a dream. I knew I wouldn't really pee. It was like falling in a dream. Everyone knew if you died or peed while dreaming it also happened in real life. It was the reason why you never hit the ground if you were falling. Why hadn't I woken? What was going on? Oh, my God. I had to pee. The more I thought about it, the more frantically I needed it. I was trying to hold it in. There was an unfamiliar impulse to squeeze my legs together to stop it coming. Oh God, oh God. I had to pee. Had to pee. Must pee. Must! I was peeing!

A forceful, hissing stream of urine shot from my body downwards into the pan and I heard the cascade hitting the water below. Why hadn't I woken? It was so real, and the relief was sensational. Oh boy, I'd been desperate to go. What wonderful gratification. It continued for an age. Any second I'd wake and discover I'd wet the bed.

The stream became a trickle. Squeezing unfamiliar muscles, it reduced to nothing.

I sat still, staring at my hands. They couldn't have been more feminine or graceful. Painted nails, a diamond engagement ring on the third finger of my left hand. The fingers, the palms, the backs of my hands were young, far younger than my thirty-six years. Was I a teenager? I examined my legs, touching them. Slim, shapely. My thighs, soft, smooth, hairless. As I ran my hands over them I even felt arousal. They were amazingly sexy. If this was a dream it was unbelievably real.

My wrist was home to a tiny round-faced watch with gold bracelet strap. It showed nine fifteen. Nine fifteen! God, I had a meeting with Dr Mayweather and all those scientists at eleven. The supernova in Orion. It all flooded back. We were to meet in London. Could I get there in time?

Wait a minute – the unreality of my situation struck home. How could I go to the meeting like this? I was a woman, sitting on a toilet in a strange house. How could I think of continuing my normal routine? The whole thing, the supernova, being a woman, peeing in my sleep. It all had to be a dream, but I'd peed. I had really peed. Had I really peed?

I checked.

Yes, I had. What should I do now? What did women do? I tore off a double piece of toilet tissue and improvised.

I stood, pulled up my underwear and trousers and made myself decent. Walked to the washbasin and washed my hands.

I looked up and, yet again, almost jumped out of my skin! The most beautiful young, wide-eyed Japanese girl was staring back at me from the mirror. In fright, I leapt backwards and spun around, thinking she must be behind me as ghouls and ghosts always were in horror films. There was no one there. The room was empty. Just me. No one there to deliver the fatal heart attack, sink their fangs into my carotid artery, or slit my throat with a carving knife. Was I dead already?

Returning to the mirror, I leaned forward and examined the girl's face, touching it with her fingers. It was my face. They were my hands. How could this be? On impulse, I touched my chest. My God, I had boobs! They were small but were most certainly real.

Gorgeous, oriental, dark-brown eyes gazed back at me with reflected curiosity. I had flawless skin and the most wonderfully coloured lips. On the shelf, I saw a lipstick. I opened it. The colour matched. It was her or my lipstick. I was her. Somehow, I'd become this Japanese girl. She seemed so young, no more than eighteen or nineteen.

'Get a grip, Geoff,' I told myself, realising why my voice had been so strange – it was her voice.

I walked through to the kitchen, knocking on the door as a final courtesy, but knowing there would be no one there.

I needed to calm down and think this through, not dash straight out in this female form. I was a scientist in the prime of life. I'd be able to understand, but I needed to deal with it methodically and sensibly. Tea always helped.

While I waited for the kettle to boil, I looked at my hands, arms and legs – unreal. I touched my boobs – too real! Whatever had happened was *not* in my imagination.

5 FALLING

Meanwhile at 8:15am, Allan is on his way to meet a client near Bristol

Allan panicked, scrabbled around, trying to grasp something, anything, anything to stop himself falling. What had happened? He must have blacked out and driven off the motorway flyover.

He grabbed a handle above his head. He closed his eyes. He was still falling. Why had there been no impact? How could he be falling? He'd been driving his car a few seconds earlier. Whatever he was gripping was falling with him. Was it the grab handle above the door? Seemed too large. He opened his eyes. A wave of nausea struck him, and he resisted the need to retch. Closed his eyes. Where was he? Squinting, he saw the handle. It was white plastic. Everything around him was white or anodised aluminium. He was still falling. The car must be falling with him. No flyover was this high. Had the car fallen into a sinkhole? He'd heard of sinkholes being deep, but this was interminable. Surely it had been tens of seconds now? Bloody hell, when he hit bottom he'd be killed. He gripped the handle even more fiercely and opened his eyes again.

What he saw was all wrong. This wasn't his car by any stretch of the imagination. It was more like the interior of a van. Electronics surrounded him inside some sort of sterile room, or like the internal layout of one of those police surveillance vans in American movies, but even more chaotic. Why was he falling? Everything was white, but with cupboards and drawers and handles and wires and boxes fitted to the walls and cylinders and gauges and electronics and lights above, below, all around him. The sickness rose anew, and he screwed up his eyes. Someone was screaming somewhere. Why was someone screaming? Who was screaming? He'd been alone in his car.

The nausea settled, and he squinted through his eyelids, trying to focus on the handle, on which he still held a white-knuckle grip. Another scream and call of something which sounded like "tasketty kiddyseye, tasketty."

Ignore it! Concentrate on the handle.

Why was he still falling? Had the world ended? Was he in limbo between life and death?

'Tasukete, tasukete kudasai, tasukete!' a woman's voice called.

He tried to look but was struck by another wave of nausea and swallowed hard. He concentrated on his hand and the grab bar. He gripped it with his other hand, too, and saw someone else's watch on his wrist! Why was he wearing this watch? A big watch with dials on its face. A chronograph. He'd never owned a chronograph!

'Tasukete,' a fainter whimper this time.

Wait a minute. There was a gold signet ring on the third finger of his left hand. Blimey, they weren't his fingers. They were hairier than his and softer. Nothing like his powerful hands. More nausea and he shut his eyes, concentrating on preventing his stomach ejecting his breakfast. What on earth was happening to him?

'Tasukete, oh tasukete, tasukete, kudasai, kudasai,' the voice called.

He squinted again. The room was vaguely familiar. Where'd he seen it before? He recognised it, but from where? Why was he still falling? There was no way he'd escape this fall alive. It must be a huge hole in the ground, going on and on, impossibly deep. It must mean he was dead. This was nowhere in the real world.

'Ooh, tasukete!'

It was an elongated room, narrowing to the right and becoming a circular tunnel. A short way into the tunnel there were junctions. Two legs were sticking out, sort of floating in mid-air and kicking. He slammed his eyes shut to prevent the nausea.

When he squinted at the room again, he realised what it was. He was in the space shuttle or the space station thingy! He didn't know the name of it, but he was apparently in it. He was in free fall.

He was in space!

He settled his reflexes, allowed his impulse to spew to fade. It *was* the space station. He'd seen it in so many news bulletins. All that stuff about astronaut Tim Peake. A white tube, like a tube of toothpaste, floated past his head as if in confirmation. He tapped it and sent it spinning away. A laptop computer mounted on a strut stuck out of the wall beside him.

The legs vanished from the junction.

Above him was another handhold. He pulled it, but far too forcefully and shot forward. He twisted his body and his shoulder hit the wall painfully. *Ooh, that hurt.* He might be weightless, but he could still hurt himself by banging into things and now he'd caught his shin on a piece of equipment sticking out beneath him.

'Fuck it!'

He finally succeeded in stilling his motions, wrenching his wrist in the process.

'Hello. Who's there?' he called.

'Oh, tasukete, kudasai, tasukete, tasukete,' the tiny voice repeated.

A head and shoulders came into view. A woman with a blonde ponytail streaming out behind her. She repeated the words and promptly emptied her stomach into the air.

Out of control from seeing her vomit, the contents of his own belly joined hers and they were floating in hellish whirlpools of sick imitating the spiralling of galaxies. He retched twice more, but with little result.

He retreated to where he'd been previously, away from the spinning globs of partly digested food which were gradually drifting towards the opposite wall. Oh, the smell of vomit.

'Totemozannon,' the girl said, 'totemozannon.'

'I'm English. Do you speak English?' he asked slowly and deliberately.

'Some. Little.'

'Come over here slowly. Try not to disturb the mess. Are you okay? Will you be sick again?'

'Sick. No. Space. In space.'

'Yes. How? You astronaut?'

'No. Not astronaut. Teacher.'

'You give lessons in space?'

'No. No. Tokyo. School in Tokyo. In classroom. Now in space. You astronaut?'

'No. Salesman. Your name Taskett?'

'No, tasukete mean help. Call help.'

'Don't know how. My name Allan.'

'Me Kenta. Not girl. Man. Why girl?'

'You're not a girl?' Allan asked, assuming he'd misunderstood.

'No. I man. Man, Japanese schoolteacher. Not girl. Why I girl? Why I here?'

'No idea, mate.'

Allan pulled himself over to the end of the room away from the vomit. The vision from the porthole was mind-blowing. The Earth stretched out beneath him in all its glory.

He spewed again!

6 UNDERSTANDING

Geoff discovers his new identity

With a steaming mug of tea, I returned to the lounge, picked up the Cosmopolitan and read the name and address label.

Miss Suzy Yamata
147a Ladbroke Road
Notting Hill
London
W11 3BY

Hmm, odd. I wasn't wearing spectacles. I couldn't normally read without my glasses.

The purse contents confirmed the name. Her Visa and Mastercard both showed Ms Suzy Yamata.

The purse held seventy-five pounds in notes and a few pounds of mixed change plus some keys. A photo-booth snapshot of the young man from the bookcase portrait, together with my new incarnation, was in one of the folders. He must be her fiancé.

Her driving licence informed me I was now a twenty-four-year-old single woman instead of a thirty-six-year-old married man. Twenty-four? I didn't look twenty-four. Japanese girls must look younger than Europeans.

I switched on the Skybox and an episode of *Friends* burst into life on the screen. One of those Golden Oldie channels. I hit 501 for Sky News.

Strange. A blank screen. Nothing being broadcast. What about BBC? I tapped in 101.

Nothing. I flicked through several other channels. Live channels were blank-screened, but the entertainment channels were running shows. Must be automated programmed transmissions. Whatever was happening must be widespread.

Had the radiation from the supernova sparked a nuclear war or some other catastrophe? The instant the thought struck me, a massive explosion took place outside and the bay window cracked. I dived under the dining table for cover.

When no debris materialised, I cautiously emerged. The window was intact but with a split running diagonally across the main pane. Outside, smoke and flames were rising from several streets away, behind the houses opposite. Where the hell were my shoes? Of course, her shoes were my shoes now. I slid my feet into the flatter of the two pairs in the hall. They fitted. Taking care to put the snib up on the lock, so I wouldn't be shut out of the flat, I ran outside. Screams and shouts could be heard in the distance.

The fireball, a few streets away, was causing a huge plume of smoke, and debris was fluttering down around me. I plucked at some falling paper. It was from a budget airline magazine. Good God! The explosion was a plane crash!

There was nothing I could do to help either the passengers or those screaming a few streets away. I decided to return to Suzy's flat, turned and bumped into a middle-aged man who was standing watching the ticker tape falling around us.

'Sorry,' I said.

He seemed agitated. 'What's happening, miss?'

'There's been an air crash.'

'Yes, but what's happening to me? Why am I like this, miss?'

'Like what?'

'I'm an old man, miss.'

He was about forty. Hardly old. He wore blue jeans, trainers, and a black sweatshirt.

'How old should you be?'

'Eleven. I've just entered the big school, miss.'

'Are you a girl?'

'Don't be silly, miss. I'm a boy.'

'Best to go to your school. Someone will help you,' I said in a reassuring voice. He was an eleven-year-old boy in the body of a forty-year-old man. It wasn't just me affected.

'I can't, miss.'

'Why?' I asked sharply, cringing at him continually calling me miss.

'I don't know where I am.'

That made sense. I lived in Guildford and was now in Notting Hill – if the magazine on Suzy's table was to be believed.

'Where should you be?'

'Withington, miss.'

'Withington? Withington, *Manchester*?'

'Yes, miss. I was at school.'

He'd been plucked from his classroom and was now two hundred miles from home.

This whole situation was becoming crazier by the minute. It was obviously real. No dream lasted this long. I wasn't the only casualty. Which was worse, finding yourself in a girl's body younger than you were or being eleven and discovering you were a man approaching middle-age? Was someone in my body on the Waterloo train? Perhaps the pilot of the crashed plane was suddenly replaced by someone with no flying ability. How awful.

'Come with me. We'll see if we can discover what has happened.' I guided his arm to have him accompany me into Suzy's flat.

Inside I gave him the TV remote and asked him to flick through TV channels to see if he could find some live news.

'Would you like some tea?'

'Thanks, miss.'

'Milk and sugar?'

'Please, miss.'

'How many sugars? And you can stop calling me miss, my name's –' I could hardly say I was Geoff. I wasn't Suzy either. 'You can call me Chris.' That was unisex enough to get away with for the time being.

'Okay, Chris. I'm David. Two sugars, please.'

'Okay, David. You try to find a news programme while I make the tea.'

I joined him on the settee with our tea and some biscuits from one of the cupboards.

'Anything?' I asked. He shook his head.

My God, if this was general, what about my kids? What on earth was wrong with me? Anxiety hit me like a tsunami. A pit opened up in my stomach. This was happening countrywide.

I'd assumed the children would be safe with Caroline or in school, but now, knowing this bizarre situation might be nationwide – the worry took centre stage. They could be anywhere, like this poor lad from Manchester. I felt physically sick that I'd not thought about them.

There wasn't a landline in the flat. I picked up Suzy's phone and touched the screen in hope rather than expectation. Thank God, it wasn't locked. I dialled home.

Brrrr, brrrr… brrrr, brrrr… brrrr, brrrr… brrrr, brrrr… brrrr.

'Yes,' Caroline answered the phone. Everything must be okay.

'Cas?'

'Who?'

'Caroline, is it you?'

'No, or I might be.'

'What do you mean "you might be"?'

'My name's Jane, but I'm in someone else's body and it says, "Caroline Arnold" in her bag.'

My God. Whatever this is, it's throughout the country. Someone else was in Caroline's body. Where was Caroline?

'Are there two children there? Sandra who's eight, and Wilson ten?'

'Well. It's odd. There's a little girl who is very confused but okay, but the boy has gone out. He said – and I know this sounds stupid – but he kept saying he was a power-station engineer in the middle of an important job. He dashed out. Have you any idea what's going on?'

Wilson had been possessed by some man who'd gone off with his body. I shook my head in disbelief.

'Let me speak to Sandra.'

'Well, I can't really.'

'What do you mean, "can't"? Put her on.'

'No. You don't understand, she's acting as if she's a baby, saying things like dadda and mumma. Who are you, anyway? I don't think I like your tone, madam.'

So, Sandra's become a baby. I choked back emotion. There was no point in going to pieces over this, but I found tears building. Most unlike me.

'Sorry, Jane. So sorry, but I'm Caroline's husband and the children's father, but I'm in another town and I've become a woman.'

'Oh. You've changed sex?'

'Yes, something outlandish has happened to everyone. I presume my body is somewhere else with some other personality inside it.'

I lowered my voice and walked into the kitchen with the phone, 'I've got a middle-aged man with me who's been occupied by an eleven-year-old boy from Manchester.'

Suddenly I heard tears. She'd broken down.

'Keep calm, Jane. Can I make some suggestions?'

The sniffles eased a little, and she spoke in Caroline's voice, which was so disconcerting, 'Please.'

Caroline would be breezing through this. She was so practical and clear-thinking. She wouldn't be blubbing. I steeled myself to come to grips with the situation.

'Right. If this is widespread, we'll eventually find the underlying cause of it. We're hoping the government will make a broadcast, but nothing so far. I suggest you switch the TV onto BBC and put the kitchen radio onto Radio 4. Someone is sure to take control soon, and they'll let us know what is happening. What's your home situation?'

'I live alone and had just opened my front door to go to the shops. I should be in Ashford.'

'You're in Guildford now. I'm in Notting Hill.'

'The situation's mad!'

'Feel free to feed yourself and Sandra. Our kitchen is well stocked. If you need money, there's some in the right-hand drawer of the bureau. Not much, but enough for emergencies. Without a pin, Caroline's cards won't be much use to you. I've the same problem here.

'If Wilson comes back please give him this phone number and put it on the fridge door – you'll find magnetic numbers there.

'Also, if Sandra has a baby in her body, can I ask you to make sure she doesn't hurt herself or anything. Could you possibly look after her until Caroline or I get home, please?'

'Of course.'

'I know you'll want to sort yourself out, too, but at least you're safe where you are. If you decide to go anywhere, take Caroline's mobile. It's usually charging in the kitchen and has my number in it. Oh God, of course, it'll no longer be my number, will it?'

'I don't know.'

'Jane, can you do a 1471 now and call me back with the number?'

'Yes, sure,' she replied, and I hung up.

Seconds later Suzy's phone rang, and Jane gave me the number.

'I'll text it to Caroline's phone, Jane. The password on her mobile is "sand" all lower case. Listen. If you go out, please take the house key off Caroline's keyring and leave it behind the square planter on the porch step? I know it is a bit obvious, but burglary is the least of our worries. Use the phone as much as you need.'

'Thank you.'

'I know it sounds silly, but I'm Geoff.'

She laughed and broke down into tearful words, 'What on earth's happened to us? Please keep in touch, won't you?'

'I will. If you need the car. Caroline's keys will be in her purse. It's the red Ford parked outside.'

'Thanks. I won't go anywhere until you or your wife get back.'

I'll call you again when I have anything concrete. We'll speak later.' I hung up on the woman who sounded like the wife I loved but was clearly not her.

I sat beside David who was examining his hands. He'd aged thirty years and I'd gone back twelve. Could I do anything else to find my children? They could be anywhere, in other people's bodies. It was horrific.

All of a sudden, the television flickered into life and a stark message appeared.

PUBLIC EMERGENCY

STAY TUNED

ARMED FORCES, POLICE, POWER, TRANSPORT (train/bus) & EMERGENCY SERVICES PLEASE GO TO YOUR NEAREST PLACE OF WORK

MEDICAL STAFF REPORT URGENTLY TO THE NEAREST HOSPITAL

OTHERS PLEASE REMAIN WHERE YOU ARE OR TRAVEL HOME IF NEARBY

Well, that was pretty clear. We called David's home but there was no answer. All we could do was wait, but at least someone, somewhere was trying to keep order. However, I needed to get home and to find the new Caroline, Wilson and Sandra.

The room light flickered, and the power failed. *Spoke too soon*, I thought.

During the afternoon, David and I made our way to Notting Hill Gate on the Bayswater Road. The major thoroughfare was in chaos. Numerous pranged cars were blocking the way. There was no way I'd be able to get to Guildford if the roads were all like this. They didn't seem to be serious accidents, but the sort of crash you'd expect if someone had fallen asleep at the wheel. I guessed that if everyone had suffered from the same effect, it would've been very traumatic for drivers.

Fortunately, most of the cars were unlocked with the keys in their ignitions. We helped people drive or push vehicles to the roadside and soon cleared a section. Looking into the distance there were hundreds helping. Many were probably in the same situation as David and me – unable to get home until some organisation was restored.

We were close to the Notting Hill Gate tube entrance, and a hand-written sign was being erected. It'd been carelessly scrawled with a thick felt-tip pen.

HOPEFULLY TRAINS TOMORROW

Obviously, people were beginning to get organised.

Car clearing continued until sunset, or what should've been sunset. The supernova had risen and was almost as bright as the sun. I guessed more than magnitude minus twenty. We returned to Suzie's with hunger and thirst beginning to affect us.

As we entered the flat, power was restored. I remembered what Jane had said about my son dashing out because he was a power engineer – it must be people like him who were getting back to work.

I wondered where my real son, daughter, and wife were.

I raided Suzie's supplies and treated the two of us to fried egg, bacon, and chips in case the power failed later. We ate in front of the television which still showed its bleak message to stay tuned.

All of a sudden, the screen depicted the Thames with the Palace of Westminster, Westminster Bridge, and the London Eye. It was overlaid with a white digital clock counting down from five minutes. Someone somewhere was in control. Everyone we'd spoken to while clearing the cars, said they'd suffered the same fate – switching minds. One woman I'd spoken to had been in Australia. It must be an international problem. If so, there would be billions affected. Did the pilot of the plane suddenly become a ten-year-old? Did a hundred or more people find themselves hurtling to their deaths in an aircraft, with no knowledge of how they'd got there or why? If the original passengers also swapped minds then they'd avoided death, but only by changing identities with the condemned. Surely none of this made any sense. Could the double explosion of Betelgeuse coupled with the sun's coronal mass ejection be the cause? If so, the question which still needed answering was: how?

The clock and view of parliament faded. In an ornate office, an intense young man wearing a smart suit and neat beard, someone I'd never seen before, was looking seriously into the camera.

Who on earth was he?

7 CAPTIVE

7:15am Rome time, in an Italian field

Andrea's eyes opened. What on earth had happened? She blinked twice, shut them firmly and tried again. Apart from not recognising where she was, all the colours were eerie, subdued. She couldn't seem to move her hands to wipe her eyes. Odd!

She'd got the children off to school and relaxed with a coffee. Now, she was lying in the mud, staring at sparsely growing grass. She tried to lift her head. It was creepy. The colours were queer. The grass was blueish-green, not normal green and the trees were greyish, out of focus, washed out, as if in a poorly taken and faded colour photograph.

She must get up and out of this mud, but something was wrong. She couldn't stand.

Everything was wrong. She was unable to rise. Why couldn't she stand? She levered herself upwards using her arms, but she was still not standing. Her legs pushed, but she remained on all fours, resting on her elbows with her head and body pointing downwards. What the devil was going on?

She adjusted her position, lifted one hand out from under her and pushed, freeing the other hand, and she was now properly on all fours. Hands and feet on the ground, yet it wasn't awkward, it felt natural.

She moved forward, no matter how she tried she was unable to stand erect.

Oh God! A cow was standing beside her! It backed away as if afraid, but there were many more. The animals surrounded her, but they weren't cows, they were bullocks.

Fear struck her. One false move and these beasts could trample her to death.

There were more cattle the other way. Why on earth couldn't she stand? She turned and caught sight of her own body. It was huge, mahogany brown with a tail swinging at its rear. She was one of them – how was that possible? It had to be a nightmare. She backed away from the other animals, stood by the fence and looked around her.

She was in a large paddock with a farm building on one side. A typical area where animals would be held before being released into other fields or taken in for milking.

Although they were all cattle, not all of them were behaving like cows. One bit the side of another which ran away. A third tried to jump the fence and crunched against it. Several were rolling around on the ground, unable to stand at all. Weird.

Voices behind her spoke what sounded like Italian. She called out to them, but only managed to produce a deep bellow.

It had to be a nightmare. She stood by the fence, continuing to bellow as people passed along the lane. She heard the same language. She wasn't certain it was Italian. What about an Italian dialect? She spoke a little French and German, but not Italian. But now she couldn't speak anyway so no language would be of any help.

The animal which had bitten another decided to pester her. She butted it hard in the head and it went elsewhere. There were more people arriving and staring into the compound, particularly at the cattle which were rolling on the ground. They were certainly behaving strangely.

How long can a dream continue? The day went on and on. She passed wind and emptied her bowels. This was awful, walking around in your own excrement. On one side of the compound there was a building and she pushed against its metal doorway, but it wouldn't budge. The name on the front of the building was MACELLO.

On the other side of the paddock was a steel gate into a larger field. She studied the opening mechanism. There was a sprung-steel bar sticking up. It needed to be lifted and moved in a Z-shape. She tried several times, but there was no way her mouth could perform the task.

Now there were two suns in the sky. The real sun was setting. The crowd of people was in the dozens, but what a strange mixture. Young boys and girls, older men and women. They stared at the animals which were behaving strangely. Hay was thrown in to them. She was hungry but ignored it. A furious argument was raging between some of the people.

She ground her hoof on the earth in front of one of them and stared into his face. Three short blinks, three long blinks and three short blinks again, the code for SOS. The man simply pointed at her, laughed and prattled away to the others who came to watch. She repeated it. Several of them were speaking to her, but in a language of which she had no knowledge. They called another man over to see. She repeated the trick and he spoke slowly and very loudly to her. She couldn't understand him and, eventually, they lost interest. The sun had set. The nova lit the scene, a slightly different tonal quality, but almost as bright as day. The other cattle settled down, although those rolling on the ground continued making noises, trying to stand up and failing dismally.

Tiredness came. She sat on her haunches in the muck. It was awful. The smells were so powerful, but inevitably sleep overtook her and she fell onto her side.

«««o»»»

There were two suns again. Andrea stumbled onto all fours. Beside her, a dead animal, its sides lacerated and bloody. She looked for the culprit, the bullock which had attacked her. There it was, on the other side biting another beast which hadn't the wit to move away or fight back. There were still several cattle which were rolling strangely on the ground. It was all a big mystery.

She made her way to the gate which connected to the large field. She made several more attempts to operate the mechanism, but each time the steel bar slipped from her grasp when she tried to lift it.

Keeping one eye on the aggressive bullock, she circled the compound, seeking out any weaknesses in her prison and found none. Could she knock the door down and get into the building? She moved over to it and watched a strange assortment of people arriving and gaining access through a street entrance. If she could get inside, then this might offer an escape route. She wondered what macello meant in English. It sounded like an Italian name. Macello farm? She became more determined to get into and through the building. Knowing what macello meant might've helped. Was it a milking parlour? If it was, she wouldn't be able to get into it as a bullock, but if she could get somewhere with access to that street entrance, she was sure she could break out.

But what then? Escape to where? The only Morse code she knew was SOS. Could she scrape some words on the ground? That seemed the best possibility.

Returning to the fence with the road alongside, the grass was sparse. Using her hoof, she gouged the word "HELP" into the soil. She needed to draw people's attention to it. Most European people would know the word "help".

Noises emanated from the building. She trotted over to the doorway hoping to attract someone's attention. More noises as if equipment was being moved or arranged. Was it one of those automated milking parlours? Another bullock pushed her to one side. She held her ground to stop a second doing the same.

The door opened and the black bullock beside her forced its way inwards between some barriers. She made sure she was right behind it, but a falling barrier stopped her. A strangely dressed woman in oversized coveralls and Wellington boots, slapped the first one to encourage it along between the steel hurdles. It reached a corner and disappeared left towards the machinery noise. A gate closed off the end of the walkway. Andrea heard a bang and some clanking. Was it another door around the corner which had slammed? Were they going to separate the animals who could walk? Escape might be easier if she got access to the large field through the building.

They kept her waiting for thirty or forty seconds before the barrier in front of her was lifted. Why the delay? She walked along between the metal fencing to the corner. A gate closed behind her and she faced forward.

The scene which greeted her was horrendous. Blood was gushing from the neck of the black bullock which was hanging by its back legs. It was an abattoir! She had to get away. Panic ran through her. She tried to go back but the gate stopped her. She trumpeted an unearthly bellow and kicked out at the gate. A man came alongside her, speaking Italian. He stroked her cheek and smiled at her. Was he going to help? She flashed SOS with her eyes. Had he realised she wasn't like the others? His hand held her chin and something cold pressed against the back of her head.

What was he doing?

There was a loud bang!

8 GOVERNMENT

The nation is addressed

The young man behind the desk had a serious expression. 'Good evening fellow Britons,' he said.

'You might wonder what this…' he gazed down at his own hands and returned them to the desk, 'young person, is doing addressing you on national television. However, if you're watching this broadcast, you might already be aware of the change which has come over a large number, if not all, of the people of Great Britain… perhaps even the world.

'I am Charles Browning. Yes, I'm your Prime Minister, but my mind has been transferred from my normal body and deposited within this younger person. Similar transfers have happened to everyone with whom we've been able to make contact.

'I cannot emphasise enough, the seriousness of the situation. Many aeroplanes have crashed having lost their pilots. Other accidents have occurred throughout the country. Hospitals are in turmoil.

'We don't know *what* has happened, but we do know *when*. Whatever caused this took place at eight fifteen this morning. We are, through this broadcast and other communication channels which are gradually becoming available to us, calling upon all top astronomical scientists and theoretical physicists to come to a working conference at the South Bank for nine on Friday morning.

'I can assure everyone, we'll be trying to resolve this as soon as possible, but while the disruption continues, there are many things we need to do to ensure the safety of us all.

'I would ask you to watch the following public service film. We'll repeat my broadcast and the public service film continually, breaking into it with whatever additional news or information we can glean.

'Margaret Sutherland is the presenter. You won't recognise her, of course, as she too, has changed body. She's a transferee, as we intend to call ourselves until we can return everyone to their original bodies. Repatriation is our full intention, if it's at all possible.

'Goodbye for now, and please spread the word to tune in to this channel.'

The image of the inside of Ten Downing Street faded and the header screen of a documentary appeared with the words 'PUBLIC SERVICE FILM NUMBER ONE.'

David cried beside me. I comforted him and told him not to worry. Yet I couldn't stop my concern over the incongruity of the situation. There was me, a twenty-four-year-old woman, with my arm around this forty-year-old man who was in tears. Meanwhile, my wife and two children had vanished.

'Don't cry, David,' I said. 'They'll soon sort it out.' I wished I felt as confident as I sounded.

A young woman, in her mid-twenties, with long black hair and immaculately dressed appeared on the screen.

'Hello.

'I'm Margaret Sutherland. I used to be in my fifties, and many of you will be familiar with me in my original incarnation. I'm now in the body of a younger woman. I'm telling you, so you are aware this is literally an old head on young shoulders.'

A photograph of her original face appeared in the corner of the screen labelled, "The presenter is Margaret Sutherland.".

'There are many serious dangers in our current situation.

'The Prime Minister has mentioned aircraft disasters. There've been other accidents too. Many hundreds of vehicle crashes, caused by the fact everyone seems to have become unconscious for a period of a few seconds up to two hours, although most blackouts seem to have been thirty minutes or so. Anyone transferred into a vehicle when it occurred inevitably had an accident, some with serious injuries and fatalities on faster roads. A website is being prepared which will list the identities of all the bodies, but you must understand that the personalities from those people will not have died with them. The ramifications of this are considerable.

'Common sense has helped in many situations. Ships, trains, submarines et cetera have been safely stopped despite being crewed by novices. We know of deaths in hospitals where surgeons blacked-out during operations and awoke as ordinary members of the public.

'It's a priority to bring things back to normality as quickly as possible and the government wishes to do this in two phases.

'Phase one is to consolidate the situation. Phase two will be the reversal of the body transfer. For those interested in the technicalities, early information suggests the Earth passed through a severe electromagnetic storm which might have been connected to the recent supernova. This storm seems to have triggered the event. If it happened once there might be a way to reverse it.

'Initially, however, we need the country working properly and to achieve that, hospitals, power stations, fire stations, and the police force need their original employees.

'So, while many responsible people have already taken up their old duties, we need to ask everyone, *all of you*, to find your way to your usual work. We need things back to normal as soon as possible, but particularly the emergency services, transport services, army, and anyone else who carries out a critical function.

'Can you help in other ways? Roads are blocked by abandoned and crashed cars. Please help clear your own streets so vehicles can get through. If you'd like to volunteer to join one of the vehicle-recovery squads, please go to your local police station. Allow time for them to get organised – tomorrow morning would be fine.

'Power workers are desperately needed at their power stations if we're to avoid more cuts. Also, would anyone who normally works on the railway or underground, please get back to work urgently so we can get some form of transport up and running quickly. This is extremely important. Allowing people to move from place to place is the quickest way to bring order from the chaos. We know many of you are now tens, hundreds and, in some cases, thousands of miles from your home or work.

'If you are a bus driver please help the vehicle-recovery squads clear the roads and try to get back to work tomorrow. Taxi drivers please get back to work as soon as you're able and the roads are clear in your area.

'Please cooperate with the following plan.

'One. Be aware babies have been, in some instances, transferred into the bodies of older children and adults. They can harm themselves and others. Be aware. Be helpful.

'Two. People from prisons and mental institutions are now among the public. Beware the dangers of befriending what might have been a mass murderer, rapist or paedophile. Protection is best in numbers. Stay together with others if you can. We don't mean to scare you unnecessarily, but the dangers are real.

'Three. While we need you all to help bring the country back to some sense of normality, please be careful. You might have lost skills you normally rely upon. If you're in a child's body or the opposite sex – yes, some people have changed sex – take care operating heavy machinery or advanced technology. We've unskilled people doing the best they can in Accident and Emergency, so if you've ever worked in those areas, please offer your help. Particularly doctors and nurses as A and E is in crisis *right now. People are dying* **right now!**

'Four. If you're a long way from home or work, you can go to train stations, perhaps as soon as tomorrow, for free travel to wherever you need to get to. Allow time for this to be up and running. We're calling on all railway workers to get to their places of work as a priority to ensure this wholesale transport of people happens quickly and efficiently. Others, please keep any unnecessary travel to a bare minimum.

'Those are the main points. Town halls will become information centres, so if you have questions, head to your place of local government for help and advice but make allowances for the time this will take to set up and the difficulty obtaining information. Remember, all the people needed at work also have their own personal and family problems to deal with, so make allowance for delays. This is a time for sympathetic tolerance and patience.

'Visit the website showing on the screen for more information and updates on the travel situation. Keep tuned to this channel for news. If you're in a strange body, please be careful with it. It belongs to someone else and might not be capable of what you ask it to do. Particularly lifting or carrying out heavy work.

'Thank you for your attention. Please tell everyone you meet about this channel.'

I sat back into the settee. I needed to get to the Royal Institution in the morning and prepare to get to the South Bank conference for Friday. What about David? I'd better see if I could get him on a train to Manchester first thing.

What about Sandra, Wilson, Caroline? I hadn't the first idea how to start to seek them out. I knew I tended to be cool, calm and collected by nature, but inside there was a raging fear, verging on panic, that I'd not only lost my family, but also that I had no idea how to find whatever new bodies they inhabited. All three were clever. I was sure Caroline would quickly make contact. Wilson was an intelligent lad and would find his way home. Sandra was my biggest worry. How would she cope if deposited inside an old man or any adult for that matter?

We lost the power again later in the evening. I found a couple of torches and told David to sleep on the sofa while I used Suzy's bedroom. I felt uncomfortable about undressing so just lay on top of the covers with a blanket pulled over me. After the exertions of the day, sleep found me pretty well instantly.

9 FASTEN YOUR SEATBELTS

8:15am Mindslip morning, in north east Scotland

The Aberdeen to Edinburgh express charged through the Highland countryside. Peter and George rehearsed their PowerPoint presentation.

Peter would have preferred to be flying. He flew small planes, gliders, and was training for his helicopter licence. With four friends, he part-owned a small Cessna. They kept it at the Aberdeen airport flying club. He loved to fly to the Hebrides at the weekends and often stayed B and B with his wife on the outer islands.

Today he was heading to a conference in Edinburgh with colleagues from the Aberdeen City Council. Sadly, he wasn't permitted to use his aeroplane on council business, even though it would have got them there far more quickly and at a similar cost. They boarded the 7:30 am train to the Scottish capital instead.

When Mindslip struck, Peter and his assistant were running through their PowerPoint presentation in hushed whispers. The very next second he was recovering from an unexpected blackout, in a far smaller seat and his laptop had vanished, replaced by some handheld gaming machine which was playing the *Funeral March* and proudly announced, *"You are dead!"*.

Uncanny.

He gripped the seat arm as he came back into wakefulness. What had made him pass out? The sounds around him and proximity of the seat in front was all wrong. Outside, in place of the rural Aberdeen-shire countryside, was a mass of cumulonimbus far beneath him. Good grief! He was in a plane, surrounded by a growing hubbub of raised voices, many becoming panicky. Still more people were asleep or unconscious.

Peter was in row three. It appeared to be a 737 aircraft and the orange colour-scheme left him in no doubt it was one of the budget airlines.

The cockpit door opened, and the first officer emerged with a puzzled expression, then, bizarrely, cried out loudly in distress and tears streamed down his face. What on earth was going on? Professional pilots did not behave like this.

A second person, the captain, peered into the cabin from the open cockpit doorway. He seemed similarly confused and disturbed at finding a plane full of passengers.

He switched his gaze several times from the cockpit to the passenger compartment. He stood in the doorway, staring down the fuselage as if seeking out someone to help him.

Peter watched in horror as the captain stepped out of the cockpit and the door began to swing shut.

Peter leapt up and screamed at the top of his voice, '***Don't let the door close!***'.

The captain put his hand into the opening while trying to find the source of the shout.

Peter stood, wriggled past an unconscious middle-aged couple sitting next to him, extracted himself from the row, and moved to the front.

'I'm a pilot,' Peter announced, looking up at the incredibly tall man in the captain's uniform. 'God, you're huge!'

'You sure you're a pilot?' the man said looking down at him.

'Course I'm bloody sure. Can you fly?'

'No. I'm a joiner, but how can you be a pilot?'

'I've been flying for ten years.'

'With respect, son, you're not much older than that.'

What!? What did he mean? He looked at his hands. He was barely a teenager, perhaps eleven or twelve. No wonder the captain seemed so enormous!

'Don't know what's happened to us, but I'm a qualified pilot, aged forty-two. I'm in a boy's body, but I *am* a pilot.'

He must have made his statement with real authority as the captain stood back, keeping his hand in the door.

'I'm Peter. By the way, if you'd allowed the cockpit door to shut, we'd have all been dead as there's no way through those doors without a button inside being pressed to allow entry.'

'Shit!' the man in the uniform exclaimed, his face paling in shock, 'I could've doomed us! I simply woke in the pilot's seat. I'm Joe. Thank fuck you were quick enough to stop me.'

Behind them a lot of people were standing up and coming forward.

'Quick,' Peter said pushing past him. 'Into the cockpit. Come with me.'

They shut the door. 'I'm worried about panic,' Peter said, 'Will you help me?'

'Yes, but I know nowt about planes.'

Peter sat in the captain's seat and checked the status. Autopilot on. Level flight. Thirty thousand feet.

'Everything's fine. We're on autopilot so we've time to sort this out. This is what we're going to do. I'm going to write some announcements and you can make them over the PA system.'

'No, I can't. I'm a carpenter. I've never done anything like that. I can't tell people what to do.'

'Well, I can't. My voice is too young.'

There was a minute's silence while Joe gradually came to realise there was no alternative. Peter left him to his thought processes while he checked the rest of the systems.

'Okay, I'll try… You really are a pilot?'

'Yes. Really. We need to stop panic.'

While Joe rehearsed the announcements, Peter watched the CCTV with growing concern. A lot of people were gathering outside the cockpit. There was banging on the door.

'Now or never, Joe. Stay calm. Speak with authority.'

Peter passed the microphone. 'Hold in the red button.'

'Ladies and gentlemen. This is the captain speaking. Will you please listen to what I have to say and return to your seats as the plane is in danger of becoming unbalanced with so many people in the front of the aircraft.'

Joe released the button and they watched the screen. People exchanged puzzled glances with each other and most quickly returned to their seats.

Time for the second message.

'Something has happened to all of us. We're all disorientated or have switched into different bodies, but we're fortunate to have an experienced pilot on board. He's flying the plane so we're all safe. Please return to your seats and fasten your safety belts because there might be some turbulence.'

He released the button. Peter praised Joe for the fine job he was doing. The monitor showed the gradual retreat of what was in danger of becoming a mob.

Now the third message.

'We do need some help. We'd like a co-pilot to assist the pilot. Would anyone with flying experience please come to the front of the plane.'

For a few minutes no one came forward, but eventually a woman in a red dress and an old man in tweeds approached the front of the cabin.

Joe opened the door and asked them to come inside quickly. He firmly closed the door behind them.

'Christ, it's only a kid at the controls,' gasped the woman.

'Don't let appearances deceive. I can fly,' Peter said with concealed apprehension. He'd flown single and twin-engine light aircraft, not sophisticated airliners. He was better than nothing, but full of trepidation about having to land this huge machine on his own. Nevertheless, he realised confidence could be everything in a situation like this.

He examined the newcomers, 'Who are you and what experience?'

The woman said, 'I'm Jack Greaves, Royal Air Force air crew, years ago. Want to be useful. I've flown jump-seat in Hercules many times.'

'Good grief, you've changed sex,' exclaimed Joe.

'Yes, and I should be retired. I'm a sixty-year-old man, not a woman in her thirties,' she said.

'And you?' Peter asked of the tweed-clad gentleman.

'Harry Kass. I'm twenty-eight and I've been learning to fly these with BA.'

'Harry, I'm delighted to hear it because you and I are going to have to land this thing. I've only flown single and twin-engine Cessna aircraft. We're on autopilot at thirty thousand. Jack, you might be useful back in the cabin to keep people calm. Act as chief steward. There should be a phone on the port side wall by the steward's jump-seat.'

'Sounds good,' she said.

'I'll take the pilot's seat. You take the captain's,' said Harry.

'What about me?' asked Joe.

'Your uniform will help keep the passengers calm so go with Jack. I'll write some more announcements for you first,' Peter said.

Harry said, 'Tell them I'm going to make some simple manoeuvres, so they don't panic. Say I'm used to a bigger version of this plane and want to get to know the controls.'

Peter wrote the announcements. He was still bemused but coming to grips with the fact that they could, perhaps, get out of this alive. What on earth had happened to the world?

10 SLOW PROGRESS

Geoff finds the streets of London are still in chaos

The next morning, I wrote a detailed note for Suzy, apologising for taking most of her cash. Intending to go home tonight, I didn't take any of her clothing or personal belongings as I could probably use Caroline's. The mild, dry weather meant I wouldn't need her coat over the trouser suit. I'd have felt stupid in the light mauve colour anyway. Over breakfast, I rang Jane and she said there'd been no calls from my family. I said I'd call again later.

David and I left the flat by seven in the morning. I hid the key under a flowerpot.

Betelgeuse was still relatively high in the sky and when the sun rose, we found the streets strangely lit by the two stars. The effect on shadows was quite disconcerting. We walked through the streets to the Notting Hill Gate tube station. The sign promising trains tomorrow was still there. We'd have to walk the three or four miles to Euston, so set off eastwards at a brisk pace.

On the Bayswater Road, many crashed and abandoned vehicles still littered the road, although most had been pushed to the side now. We saw a mechanical digger moving a damaged lorry and bus out of the carriageway. None of the taxis were for hire so there was no alternative to walking.

At Marble Arch, there were ambulances and people being treated in the street where there had been a multiple pile-up, presumably this morning. An abandoned red double-decker bus lay on its side nearby.

Several times we saw people scurrying around on all fours. What the devil was causing that? David laughed when one of them, an elderly, naked woman stopped in front of us and looked up into our faces as if trying to find someone. She wasn't quite naked. I noticed she had one long sock hanging half-off her foot, a loose belt around her waist and wore an earring and a wristwatch. The ear without an earring and her cheek were covered in dried blood! Bizarre. She made a 'hugnn' sound, shook herself and scampered off across the road, being narrowly missed by a breakdown vehicle. Very puzzling.

Forced to continue on foot, we cut through behind Selfridges and on towards Euston. Large crowds waited on the approach to the station.

I asked a man at the back, 'Do you know if any trains are running?'

He nodded. 'You just missed a guy with a megaphone who said a train left for the northeast at seven forty and one is just leaving for the northwest. He said there'd be more but couldn't give times.'

'Thanks,' I said.

'He also told us rail workers are trying to organise things inside the station and we should wait.'

'Yes. Imagine it'll be a logistical nightmare. Trains in the wrong locations and many abandoned in the countryside. There might have been crashes too.'

'Dead man's handles should have prevented crashes,' he said.

'Yes. Suppose so.'

The crowd moved forward, and I guessed it meant another train was being boarded.

People were quiet. No one had friends. We were all alone within our unfamiliar bodies. Men were straightening their ties and adjusting their belts. Some of the women were uncomfortable, hoisting up their skirts and tottering in heels. The symptoms of men, women and children adapting to unexpected bodies amused and I had to suppress a laugh. Thankfully, I was in a trouser suit and tried to stop my body falling into the natural standing position of a woman. I was in control of voluntary muscular actions, but Suzy's subconscious looked after automatic functions like breathing, heartbeat, how I stood, walked and used my hands. At one point, I found myself biting my nails, a habit I never had as Geoff Arnold. Was an internal battle for possession of Suzy's body taking place?

A giant video screen above the station entrance was showing the government information film with subtitles. I guessed most exterior monitors in the capital would be utilised in the same way.

In the crowd, I was becoming aware of glances from both sexes. Suzy was undoubtedly very attractive, but some, including children, were ogling me and I guessed these had been men prior to the "event". I ignored them. David was fidgety and his gaze darted in all directions.

'Might be a bit of a wait here, David,' I said. Despite his middle-aged appearance, this was a young boy who'd suffered a serious trauma.

I checked Suzy's phone for the umpteenth time – still no contact from the family. There was little I could do. The police would be no help in this situation.

Now at Euston, I could get David onto a train back to Manchester. Leaving him worried me. He was, after all, still a child. Presumably someone in Manchester would ensure he got back to Withington. There was still no answer on his home phone.

I intended to wait until I got him onto a train, but this queue was taking forever. I needed to get to the Royal Institution to collect some material and my laptop to be prepared for the South Bank meeting. I was also desperate to get home and as soon as I had my laptop I could head homewards. Anxious thoughts of my family in trouble were growing. I rang Jane again.

'You're still there?'

'Yes. Problems with your daughter, I'm afraid,' said Caroline's voice.

'What? What's happened? Is she okay?'

'She messed herself.'

'What?'

'I improvised some nappies out of towels. I think she's quite a young baby inside.'

'God, sorry you've had to deal with that. Can you drive?'

'Yes. What're you thinking?'

'The best thing would be to take Sandra to Guildford Hospital and tell them I'll contact them later. Then you can sort yourself out.'

'Yes, I could do that.'

'Take Caroline's car and leave it at the hospital. Leave the keys in A and E. You can walk through to the station from there. It looks as if some trains are now running and you might be able to get home, although the London stations are heaving.'

'You don't mind?'

'No, not at all. Have you checked our answerphone?'

'Yes. I heard a few calls being recorded. One was about the Friday meeting and there were several about a meeting yesterday saying they couldn't get there because of what had happened. Presumed you'd guessed that.'

'Thanks. Yes, the meeting never happened because of this. No family calls though?'

'No, sorry.'

The whole situation was such a goddamned mess. How could it ever be corrected?

An image of Caroline crossed my mind, but Jane was now in my wife's body. Would my Caroline still be in her thirties? Would she be male or female? Perhaps she'd be an old woman, a man or a child. Could love transcend such boundaries? I was decidedly heterosexual. How would sex work? What would I do if she was male or if we were both female for that matter? She hadn't rung home or her own mobile so was she even alive? She could've transferred into a baby. Would a baby transferee be able to speak? She might have transferred into one of the people who died in a plane crash. No, I didn't want to go down that route for there, surely, lay madness!

I put the myriad family implications out of my head. It served no purpose while stuck in this queue.

The crowd was trying to get back to homes in the north via the mainline services. For such a large mass of humankind, the lack of noisy conversation, laughter, and loutish behaviour was unusual. There was sobbing. Many were trying to come to terms with what had happened to them and lots would not even have seen the television broadcast until now.

Individuals were asking others what had happened and how it could be put right. People's insecurity meant they were talking in hushed tones. It was eerie to say the least.

Time was marching on as we waited in this creeping sea of humanity. I needed to go. How could I leave David? His eyes were spinning in all directions, trying to make sense of the chaos which had beset him. I felt a responsibility for him but couldn't stay much longer.

As time passed, the noise levels changed as if patience was expiring. Sporadic fights began. People were losing their tempers over perceived injustices in the queuing procedure. Many shouted at their neighbours in the heaving mass and more were in tears, sobbing their hearts out. Sound levels grew. It was all very distressing for David.

A motley assortment of individuals approached from the west. They were carrying placards with badly composed messages such as "OVERTHRO THE GOVERNMENT"; "ITS A WIKED TORY PLOT"; "TORYS OUT", and the like. It was irrational to blame the government for whatever had happened, but people will be people. One or two disgruntled individuals joined their ranks and the poorly organised throng headed south towards Westminster.

It was almost nine thirty when David and I reached the top of a broad stairway. The crowd followed as one. More arrived every minute. I wasn't going to get him onto a train for hours.

I cupped my hands and shouted, 'Anyone going to Manchester who can take care of someone until they get there?'

Dozens of blank faces stared at me as if I were mad, but a man in his thirties eventually came over. 'I'm heading to Manchester. Need company?'

'No. Not me. This man here has got an eleven-year-old child within him and he needs to get back to Withington. If someone could accompany him to Manchester, he'd be okay from there.'

'I can get a bus from Piccadilly Station,' David growled in his middle-aged voice.

The man undressed me with his eyes. 'No, thanks. Thought it was you, love. I'd have taken you anywhere!' He left.

I was dumbfounded. I resisted the impulse to swear at him. He'd been trying to pick me up. Evil sod. The British people in a crisis usually pulled together. Where was the Dunkirk spirit in this nightmarish station?

Another man, a little older in appearance, eased his way through the crush. 'I heard what you said. You want me to make sure he gets there?'

'Yes, please. He's disorientated and lonely and needs help. He's eleven, yet inside this older man. His name's David.'

'Hello, David. Would you be happy to come with me on the train to Manchester?'

The whole scene was incongruous. There I was, mid-twenties and pretty, trying to get a middle-aged eleven-year-old to go with another man who might be any age or sex.

'Okay, sir,' he said.

The newcomer raised his eyes at me in surprise at the response.

'Takes some getting used to,' I said. 'He's been calling me miss as if I'm a teacher. He seems to be a nice lad caught in a dreadful… situation.'

I'd almost said, "caught in a dreadful body", but prevented myself just in time. David couldn't help what he looked like, and it might have upset him.

'Okay, David. You stick with me, and we'll get to Manchester as soon as we can,' the man said.

'You are okay with this? Sorry, I don't know your name. Can you tell me a bit about yourself? David's not a relation of mine, but I do feel a little responsible for him.'

'Yes. Fine. I'm Jessica. I was dying of cancer in the Manchester Royal Infirmary when this happened. Helping someone else is a small price to pay. Some other poor soul has changed places with me and has only days to live. We're the lucky ones.'

I laughed, then said quietly, 'It's an ill wind… Thanks, Jessica. Well I'm Geoff and was in my mid-thirties. A shock for me, too. I'm an astronomical physicist so hoping to be at the South Bank conference tomorrow and I've a lot to do this afternoon.'

'Will they ever sort this out?'

'No idea. Frankly, I don't know how. It was all so random.'

Jessica squeezed my hand with hers, 'You go. I'll take care of David.' We exchanged mobile numbers, and I gave her David's home number and explained why he thought my name was Chris.

'David, you've got my number in your pocket. Give me a call when you get home, won't you?'

'Yes, Chris.'

I thanked Jessica and wished them both well, with not a little concern for David's well-being, but Jessica seemed trustworthy.

As I descended the steps, I heard David ask, 'Why're you called Jeska? It's a *giirrll's* name,' but I didn't hang around to hear the reply. Interesting times for sure.

I hurried down the steps. I wasn't going to be able to get the tube, so I'd another two miles to walk to the Royal Institution.

11 MAKING WAVES

Back to Mindslip morning. The commuter express thunders towards Paddington.

Returning to consciousness, lying on his back in some wooden structure with clouds skidding across the sky above him when, minutes earlier, he had been on the regular 7:45 am express to Paddington would be likely to confuse someone with the most even temperament. Garth didn't possess such a thing. He wasn't at all amused. How did this happen to him? In fact, what *had* happened to him?

He levered himself into a sitting position. Wow, he thought, that was far too easy. He couldn't believe how effortlessly he'd moved his considerable bulk.

More disturbing was how the wooden thing moved as he sat up. What the… he was in a boat! His position suggested he'd fallen off one of the seats. There were oars. He sat up further. There was another seat and a second person flat on his back with his legs similarly folded over the seat in front of his. This fellow was out cold. Beyond was the bow which also formed a low cabin area with a sealed doorway.

At the rear was a larger cabin, probably eight feet long with the opening facing him. He was in a long rowboat, perhaps twenty-five to thirty feet in length.

He decided to get up properly but didn't want to fall overboard. Owing to his weight, he could easily overbalance. Where was his crutch? Where was his walking stick? He couldn't see either. He wouldn't be able to stand without one or the other. Nevertheless, he attempted to lever himself into a kneeling position. Again, it was far too easy. Glancing down he saw his legs. Not possible! How could he see his legs? He hadn't seen his legs for years – feet yes, but legs – not for ages. Not only could he see them, but they were in some sort of Lycra. He surveyed his body. Damn it all, he was rippling with muscles. His exposed flesh tanned and hairy, the hair dark, not grey as it should be. He was fit and athletic, yet minutes before, his twenty-five stone[2] body was occupying two seats on the Paddington train. He flexed his muscles and stood. The sooner he got ashore to find out what was going on, the better.

To the left, or should he say, "port side" there was ocean as far as the eye could see. Calm and glassy with the tiniest swell. Quickly turning to starboard he expected to find a harbour wall or marina, but no. Again, the water extended to the horizon. How could he be at sea? He did a one eighty turn to be sure. What the devil was going on? It was strange enough seeing that nova sun beginning to set and shining as brightly as the real sun, but to be out in the ocean, too, was frightening.

Garth climbed over his own seat. His crewmate was an equally fit specimen of manhood. He stepped over the second seat and opened the forward cabin. Electronics. No wonder it had a spring-loaded, waterproof door. There was a computer monitor, echo sounder, radio, keyboard, and various other items he didn't recognise. Behind those were boxes of food. He shut the door and climbed back along the boat. Oh, how wonderful to be able to perform this simple task. Since he'd passed his fiftieth birthday, he'd had trouble even boarding trains and used one crutch plus a sturdy walking stick just for walking. Moving freely like this along a cluttered boat was a dream come true.

He reached the rear cabin. Behind another door were two beds with sleeping bags on either side, some sort of stove and more boxes of provisions. Without doubt, the boat was well equipped but what was he doing here?

---

[2] 350lbs or 160kg

He thought back. Had anything unusual happened during his train journey? The supernova was causing weird shadows, he remembered that. He'd been reading the *Financial Times*. He'd checked some of his major holdings and noticed two of his funds were down, but it hadn't worried him. They'd come back up. All the uncertainty over the oil price seemed to be the cause, but the stocks he'd selected mitigated the fall in oil revenues. He'd been wondering if this supernova thing was going to affect the FTSE share index. Two people with coffee had been sitting opposite him. No one sat beside him because, frankly, there wasn't room. He really did occupy two seats on these modern trains. Nothing had seemed out of the ordinary. He hadn't even been dozing. He'd checked the share prices, there was a second flash in the sky, and he'd woken up here. None of it made any sense.

He closed the cabin door, returned to the other crew member and gave him a few nudges. Still out cold. Hopefully, he'd be able to call for help and get them off this boat.

He pulled the oars into the craft so they wouldn't be washed overboard. He assumed his current body had been rowing when whatever it was had occurred. Whilst pulling in the oars, he found there were chains holding them to rowlocks on the boat side anyway, so he was probably worrying unnecessarily, but he was always a careful man when it came to safety.

He thanked his lucky stars it was calm, sat on the rowing seat and pondered his options. The other man was still unconscious. He decided he'd better wait until he awoke as he wouldn't like Garth playing around with the radio or other equipment which might be specially tuned-in or set.

He scanned the horizon. Nothing. Only the almost glassy surface with a gentle swell. The now overcast sky was featureless and, occasionally, a light breeze turned the craft left or right. Each time he used an oar to direct it back to what he assumed was the west. It would hold its position for a while until the next wisp disturbed it anew. A seagull circled the boat for a few minutes then flew towards the horizon. Did seagulls mean he might be close to land? He knew too little about the ways of the ocean to be sure.

Something odd had clearly happened to him. He'd shed his huge bulk and was now in this young, fit, and clearly muscular man's body. It had to be something to do with rowing, perhaps the Atlantic or Pacific. It was a godsend not being so heavy. There was no labouring to breathe. No fighting with his weight to stand up or move around. It was, in fact, miraculous.

His shipmate groaned. Garth tapped his shoulder with his trainer. He moaned again and rolled over, his legs falling from the seat into the bilge area. Deep, steely-blue, wild-looking eyes opened and stared at him. Garth put on a friendly expression and said, with a rising lilt, 'Morning.'

His fellow crewmember opened his mouth and let out a scream of earth-shattering proportions. It was so loud, Garth fell back off the seat into the bottom of the boat. Another scream. Garth moved onto his side and regarded the man.

'Shut up!'

He screamed again and let out a stream of guttural sounds in some foreign language. Almost bestial.

'Oi, shut up, you! What's wrong with you?'

The noise stopped. The man regarded his own hands and legs in a mystified manner.

'I'm Garth. Who are you?'

He produced another deafening stream of meaningless sounds, rolled over and tried to get up, but with no coordination whatsoever. Garth leaned over and tried to help him.

Now, Garth was screaming even louder than his crewmate.

This moron had sunk his teeth into Garth's hand. Not a quick nip and release but a vicious, deep bite which drew blood and caused Garth to have to yank his hand free creating more damage. The action made him take a step backwards, he tripped and fell overboard.

He tried to grab a breath, but too late. He took in a lungful of water. In seconds, he surfaced, coughing and spluttering. He thanked heaven for the lightweight life jacket, which was keeping him the right way up, because he couldn't swim.

He examined his hand as he bobbed up and down in the water. He was bleeding. Something in the back of his mind told him it was not a good idea to be bleeding while swimming in the ocean. There were tooth marks in a neat circle across his palm but the blood was coming from the back of his hand, between his thumb and wrist. He guessed it would soon heal up, but it was bleeding profusely now.

Ignoring his hand for a moment, he sought the boat. No sign of it. Must be behind him. He'd never learned to swim but the lifejacket made up for his inability. He swished the water with his good hand and gradually spun around.

Heavens! The boat seemed a long way off. The light breeze had strengthened and as there was more of the boat above the surface than him, it was drifting away.

Panic set in. Supposing he didn't catch it? He'd be left, floating in the ocean. Sharks. *Sharks!* Sharks were the reason you shouldn't bleed in the ocean. He'd seen a documentary which said a shark could detect blood several miles away. He struck out towards the boat, flailing inexpertly, pulling himself through the water with his good hand while trying to keep the bleeding hand above the surface.

Despite his efforts, the boat wasn't getting any closer. He saw his crewmate lean over the gunwale, eyes flicking madly from side to side.

'Help me. *Help me!*' Garth screamed at him, but the fellow stared at him blankly before dropping back into the hull.

Blood was still dripping from his hand into the sea. Holding it aloft wasn't helping and Garth decided getting back to the boat quickly was more important than keeping it dry. If the breeze continued to strengthen, he'd be eaten alive.

He struck out with both arms and hands. Finally, he seemed to be making some progress, but it was slow, and he was cold. More effort, stronger strokes. He was gaining upon it. Now four or five yards away.

His crewmate appeared again, peering over the gunwale, not at him, but at the water surface.

'Help me, you fucking moron! Throw me a line.'

His shout drew the attention of the man. He looked directly at Garth and climbed further over the side.

'Careful you idiot or you'll fall in too!'

The man wriggled himself side to side, up and down as if trying to get out of the vessel. Was he mad? He was deliberately climbing overboard. There was a splash and he disappeared beneath the surface.

What was the idiot playing at? Despite his lifejacket, he hadn't surfaced. How could he not come back to the surface?

There was a swirling to his side and he saw the man surface, coughing and spluttering. He surged towards Garth and tried to bite his arm. What the hell was it with this guy? Garth twisted in the water and kicked him square in the face. He let out a shriek and floated off away from both him and the boat.

Garth was horrified to discover the boat had opened the distance again. He recommenced his inexpert flailing, trying to recover the lost ground. The cold was affecting him. He needed to get out of this water, and quick.

He was making progress. It was now only three yards away, but the effort was taking it out of him. If this had been Garth as he was before this crazy change, he'd have been dead. Only the muscles and fitness of his new body offered any chance of saving himself.

Something hit him in the midriff. What was it? The man in the lifejacket was way over to his left so it wasn't him. Shark. Sharks. It had to be a shark. He redoubled his effort to reach the boat.

The boat was inches from his grasp. Again, something brushed against him and the shapely, triangle of a dorsal fin was moving away. He needed to get onto the boat now, now, *now*!

Glancing momentarily to his left the shark was now about three boat lengths away, heading towards his crewmate. In horror, he watched as the lifejacket submerged in a maelstrom of thrashing grey bodies.

What was that? Something else had touched him, but it was only the side of the boat. If he'd been himself, he'd never have been able to hoist his body back into the craft. He grabbed the lip of the boat and heaved.

He'd almost made it when something pulled on his leg. He was slipping back into the ocean! His body spun around and he saw the second shark just as it bit his midriff.

His scream was stifled to silence as he was dragged into the depths.

The empty boat drifted onwards.

12 ORDER FROM THE CHAOS

Geoff finally gets to the Royal Institution

I saw little traffic. Black cabs passed me, but either occupied or not for hire. Others tried to hail them. I walked hurriedly onwards, thankful Betelgeuse had set and the illumination was now from only one direction.

At the grand old Royal Institution building, I marched straight over to the man sitting behind the reception desk. He was fiftyish, dressed in a blazer, white shirt, and a colourful diagonally striped tie. The blazer incongruously proclaimed MCC[3].

He looked up from his desk, 'And you are?'

'Doctor Geoffrey Arnold. I'm going up to Doctor Mayweather's office where I'm on secondment from the Royal Observatory.'

'Good grief, Geoff! You've had an interesting swap,' the man said with a laugh, looking me up and down admiringly.

I smiled, puzzled. 'You have me at a disadvantage.'

'Diane. Diane Major.'

'Blimey, Diane, you've changed sex too!'

Diane was a lady approaching retirement, who'd run the reception team for as long as I remembered.

'Yes. He's not very healthy, but if I work at it, I'll soon whip him into shape,' and she chuckled, deeply.

Diane was always slim and wiry, so this hefty, overweight man must have been a real shock to her.

'Is Justin in?'

'No, you won't believe this. When I finally got in and got the phones manned yesterday, he called from Nigeria.

---

[3] Marylebone Cricket Club – a famous cricketing institution responsible for the laws of the game.

He is now a twenty-five-year-old black African and he is trying to negotiate to leave the country. It is total chaos over there, and it took me ages to get Foreign Office support. He's hoping to fly back today or tomorrow but warned me it might be longer. It was only because of the Betelgeuse thing and him being Astronomer Royal that they pulled their fingers out.'

'Amazing, thousands of miles away. Male?'

'Yes. Michael's in. He's in your office, but I should warn you he's a lot older. He's still a he, but I'd guess at mid-seventies, so he's lost thirty or more years.'

'They might find a way to swap us back.'

Diane made a sudden ducking motion. 'Lots of flying pigs around today, Geoff,' she said gruffly.

I laughed. 'Yes, not hopeful, is it?'

'You going tomorrow? I left a message on your answerphone.'

'Yes, it's why I'm here. I need my laptop. I've not been home yet. I presume whoever got my body at eight fifteen yesterday morning, would have arrived at Waterloo.'

'Not turned up here, although Doctor Whitaker and Professor Peabody did for your meeting. They understood when I said I hadn't heard from you. Doctor Whitaker was a four-year-old toddler.'

'But had all his faculties?'

'Apparently.'

'Sorry, Diane, I should've rung in. They'll know about tomorrow's conference by now. Well, if my body does turn up, get him to call this number,' and I wrote Suzy's number on one of Diane's notelets.

'Will do. Have you heard from Caroline and, oh dear, what's happened to your kids? You poor man.'

I explained what I knew.

'Nothing at all from Caroline?'

'No. She's not rung here?'

'No.'

'It's an odd situation, Diane. I feel as if I should be doing more to find them but can't think of anything practical to do. Getting home would be good. I can re-record my answerphone message with something more appropriate including my new mobile number.'

'Don't worry too much yet, Geoff.'

'Give Caroline my number if she makes contact. I must get up to the office, Diane. We'll chat again later,' and I squeezed her gnarled, chubby male fingers. Weird, and I was sure it would get weirder. We both laughed at the odd situation and quickly released our limbs.

Thankful to be wearing trousers rather than a skirt, I bounded up the grand staircase two at a time, down the side corridor and up two more flights to our office. Suzy seemed to be much fitter than me. I keyed my PIN into the electronic lock and it clicked open.

Inside the vaulted, timber-clad room were three workstations. One a classic oak desk with green inlaid leather where Justin normally worked. My own desk, a cluttered, plain, two pedestal modern type. A second similar desk was at the other end of the room, behind which sat a haggard old man with thinning silver hair and half-moon spectacles. He was wearing a pin-striped suit with an open-necked shirt and a loosely hanging tie. He frowned as I entered, removed his spectacles and smiled with appreciation as his eyes undressed me and his eyebrows rose.

'Michael?' I asked with trepidation.

'Yes. I know you're not Justin – he's now black as coal apparently, so through my masterful powers of deduction you must be Geoff. Think you got a better deal than me,' he said in a trembling voice.

'Yes, it's me. Oh, Michael, you have drawn the short straw.'

'Ha. Finally, I've a colleague who is worthy of my very best sexual passes, and I'm too old to take advantage. You don't fancy me by any chance?'

'Not a chance, Michael.'

He laughed. 'Probably no bad thing. I suspect a good fuck would kill me! Only just made it up all those stairs. I'll use the lift next time. Was worried about power cuts with hardly anyone in the building.'

'It's strange, I've been studying people while walking across London and I'm certainly male from my own perspective. I still like looking at girls and cringe about the possibility of a relationship with a man. Always been decidedly heterosexual.'

'Maybe you're now a dyke. You look female enough from the way you are standing. Any news of your wife and family?'

I had one buttock resting against the corner of my desk, one leg wrapped around the other with a hand on my hip. I changed my posture, straightened myself and stood with my legs apart while I repeated the story I'd told Diane, but by the time I'd finished I was again in a more feminine pose. Suzy was definitely influencing my subconscious actions.

'Damn it. The host seems to affect my mannerisms. My wallet shows I have a fiancé too,' I said, flashing my ring finger.

Michael laughed. 'Might be bisexual! My body has some strange mannerisms too. I'm not acting like myself at all. I suppose I must laugh or I might cry. The brain is okay, by the way. It's only the body which is decrepit.'

He stood up and, using a stick, made his way painfully across the office. 'Waterworks not so good,' he said and looked at me intently. 'Fuck me, you're beautiful, Geoff. Sexy as hell!' He ran his hand over my behind as he left the office.

We had toilets along the corridor. I, too, had a need. The need was different as Suzy. More internal but obvious.

At my desk, I collected everything I needed and packed it all into my briefcase and laptop case. I also opened a large, glass-fronted, antique bookcase and took out a book on electromagnetic radiation and another work on coronal mass ejections. I had it in mind to compile a list of references which might be useful. Michael returned, this time running his hand across my hip as he passed me. I slapped it away. He laughed and I went to pay my own visit.

The corridors on this floor were a uniform magnolia and each of the doors was ornate, reflecting the age of the building. The passageways were certainly impressive. Just before the grand stairs, were the toilets. Modern, functional black doors. No ostentatious timber for the entrances to the loos. The doors were labelled GENTS and LADIES. Which should I use?

I supposed I should use the ladies, not the gents, but it seemed fraudulent. I was decidedly heterosexual but would be sharing the toilets with the opposite sex. In fact, the same sex. How confusing. Well, I needed to avoid confrontation, so I opened the LADIES door. It didn't matter too much while the building was deserted.

I'd been co-opted to work at the Royal Institution for several years and the ladies' lavatories were probably among the few rooms I'd never visited. Inside, the difference was obvious. The walls were half-tiled and wallpapered with birds and flowers. In the gents, they were plain and the decoration far more tired.

The mirrors were larger, but something else stopped me in my tracks. I stood, stock still and stared at the sanitary product machine.

My God. Tampons? Periods!

Back at Suzy's apartment, I'd rifled through her bag and seen a long ornately decorated tube, like a lipstick but longer. It was a rather lovely object, encrusted with presumably fake jewels and gold filigree. I'd opened it out of curiosity and a couple of tampons had fallen out. I'd poked them back into the container and left them in her bag. The fact I might need them never crossed my mind. How did you know when it was happening or about to happen? I knew Caroline was sometimes unwell the first day, but was that before it started or after? How was I meant to know? Was the tube of tampons her emergency supply or was I in the middle of a period right now? Surely, I'd know or be leaking or something after more than twenty-four hours.

I used the cubicle and checked. Nothing of any description dangling! What a relief.

I washed my hands and read the instructions on the machine.

I'd transferred Suzy's loose change to the trouser suit pockets rather than use her purse. A pound coin supplied me with a couple of tampons in a paper container. I was now prepared for the inevitable shock when it happened. What other aspects of my change might I encounter? Periods seemed the most life changing. I hoped Suzy wasn't pregnant as that would be even worse. I shook myself out of my consternation as I re-entered the office.

'You going tomorrow?' I asked.

'No. When I've tidied up here, I'm leaving. Here's this body's mobile number,' he passed me a note.

We both updated our phones.

'Frankly, Geoff, I'm so tired, despite how little I've done. I might go back to the home and let them care for me for a second night. It's a bit "help yourself" but there are some volunteers helping and it's better than climbing three flights to my bachelor flat.'

'What's going to happen about money?'

'Don't know. Access will be difficult and there's sure to be some people who'll find their accounts cleared out,' he said.

'God. I suppose so.'

'How will you prove who you are to your bank?'

'Jesus. No idea. Details on old bank statements, I s'pose.'

We both sat in silence trying to think it through, although the way Michael's eyes were fixed upon the junction of my thighs, I guessed he was having other thoughts too.

'I bet there's some pretty pissed-off millionaires out there,' I said and laughed.

'What a goddamned mess!'

'Stock markets will go into freefall.'

'No. All trading's been suspended.'

'How do you know?'

'Latest bulletin. You can watch it on my laptop.'

I walked around and stood behind Michael. I felt a hand feeling the outline of my buttock and slapped it away.

'Fuck off, Michael. Not funny!' I said.

'I wasn't trying to be amusing.'

'Seriously. Don't!'

The hand slid slowly down the back of my thigh and reappeared on the keyboard in front of him. He called up the replay of the latest news, skipped Charles Browning's general message, and Margaret Sutherland's new voice came as the scene changed.

'Those of you who've not seen earlier messages can find them on the website shown at the bottom of your screen,' she said and gave the usual introduction of who she was.

'Firstly, some warnings. There have been instances of theft, rape, assault, and even murder. Criminal activity is being conducted by prisoner transferees as well as some people who are being opportunistic. Do remain on your guard and stay with others if possible.

'Secondly, although seemingly not as common, there are instances of transferees entering animals.'

'God, I saw some people on all fours. One was naked and actually came and stared at me as if looking for its master,' I told Michael.

Margaret Sutherland continued, 'There are two immediate consequences of this – one, a wild animal in a human body could cause a lot of damage. Police already have a number in custody. Two – please be helpful to any animal which seems to be trying to communicate as it could have a human mind within it. Farmers are reporting many instances of animals behaving strangely. Human to animal transfer and vice versa appears to be unusual, but it has been happening and isn't rare. We must assume there have been inter-animal transfers, and these also offer some danger to the public. A rat in a cat, perhaps, or wolf in a dog.

'Thirdly, ensure your physical condition does not make you a danger to yourself or others when operating machinery. For example, tiny children should not attempt to drive cars or operate heavy plant. Common sense is the interim solution to this.

'Some worse news is the large number of casualties and fatalities. See the website for a list of the dead but bear in mind they are transferors. We know of more than two million to date, but the figure is growing continually. Better news shows the people of Britain are rallying around and trying to get things back to normal. All mainline stations in London are now manned and providing a skeleton service to get people home. The Underground network should be partially operational tomorrow. More doctors and nurses are arriving at hospitals every minute.

'Our government has agreed with all governments with whom we've been able to establish communications to close stock exchanges until things have normalised. Many small to medium-sized enterprises are having problems with staffing and even getting their doors open so if you're a manager or owner of a small business, please try to get to it as soon as you can and discuss with your staff how you might best be able to operate.

'In the same vein, there's no problem with pensions and salaries although it is going to become important to correctly assess who is working for whom and to formulate a system of property ownership. For the time being you can withdraw a maximum of five hundred pounds a week from your bank account. The restricted withdrawals should protect the person you inhabit from your actions and protect you from the person inhabiting your body. Terminology is now being applied to these situations to avoid confusion. You are the transferee and the body you used to inhabit is your transferor. Please try to use these terms as and when things normalise. The transferee is the owner of the transferor's assets, so please treat them with respect and do not abuse the situation in which you find yourself. Any fraudulent action against either's assets or cash will be a criminal offence and the relevant individual will be prosecuted. Parliament will be passing emergency legislation as required.

'During the crisis, the government will ensure no one suffers from the inability to obtain enough cash to live. Credit and debit card use is a problem as the holders of those cards are not in possession of the PIN. You can get new cards from your bank after answering personal questions. All wages and salaries are frozen until methods have been determined to ensure the correct person gets the money. Go to the website for more information.

'What has happened to us as individuals? It has become increasingly clear the higher functions of our individuality have slipped into another body and mind. It seems to be a worldwide phenomenon caused by an electromagnetic storm through which the Earth passed at eight fifteen am yesterday. Automatic bodily functions like breathing, heart beating, the way we walk, our right or left-handedness all remain as it was for the body we inhabit, which explains why you need to take care in your current body.

'However, our thoughts, memories, physical and mental abilities have transferred with us apart from a few exceptions. Some motor functions didn't transfer well. Surgeons have reported they're finding they're having to re-learn skills and the same applies in some other professions. The moral is to be careful before attempting anything dangerous or difficult, however confident you are you have always been able to do it.

'The scientists from various disciplines attending the working conferences at the Royal Festival Hall on the South Bank tomorrow will be assessing all these matters, including how the effect occurred, its likelihood of recurring, and the possibilities of reversing it.

'The final message is to be patient with others. There have been far too many instances of people shouting and screaming, and even attacking the police and emergency services. Panic serves no purpose and will only delay attempts to get back to normal. Please restrain your anger at your new situation – no one is responsible for it. Treat everyone with respect. Care for those who are no longer able to look after themselves. Think of the consequences whenever you do anything until you better understand your host. If you can get to your place of employment, please do so as soon as possible. This will help your employer sort out your identity for salary. We need to get everything back to normal as soon as possible and it's really your own responsibility to try to do that.

'If you're trying to return to your usual place of work or home, the transport services have been asked to assist you to do so free of charge. There will be queues. There will be delays. Please be patient. If you're a critically important employee, such as an NHS worker, policeman, military or emergency worker, please let the transport staff know and they'll try to expedite your travel. Please don't abuse their help, it is in everyone's interests for genuine emergency personnel get to work quickly.

'Please try to minimise power consumption and be prepared for power cuts at peak usage times.

'This ends Update Number Two. We recommend you tune back to BBC One, ITN or Sky News regularly.' The screen faded back to the text.

'God. Depressing isn't it?' I said.

'Worse for some than others.'

I had been incredibly lucky compared with Michael, a single virile thirty-something, used to dating a string of girlfriends, suddenly in his mid-seventies.

'Yes. Sorry. Wasn't thinking.'

'Oh, it's not your fault, Geoff. My problem is I'm so tired.'

My mobile, or Suzy's to be more accurate, rang. Would it be Cas or one of the children? I fumbled, trying to answer the unfamiliar device.

'Geoff Arnold on Suzy Yamata's phone.'

'I'm Suzy,' said a young woman. Disappointment struck me – it wasn't Caroline.

'I was hoping you'd call. I left everything at your flat neat and tidy. The key is under the flowerpot.'

'Oh, thanks. I was stuck on a ferry in the North Sea, had no identification on me and didn't know which my cabin was until after we'd berthed.'

'Sounds difficult.'

'We were kept outside the harbour for ages until a pilot came on board. You're speaking with my accent. The stand-in crew were amazing and saved all our lives.'

'Glad to hear you're safe.' I could hear the strain in her voice and went out into the corridor for privacy.

'This is the eighth number I've called. I couldn't remember my own number correctly! It is unreal hearing my own voice speaking to me.'

'Must be. When will you get home?'

She sounded desperate.

'This is a pay-as-you-go phone I've bought. I've taken the transferor's stuff, but her phone was locked. I'm waiting to get a train from Hull to home.'

'I'm in London and about to head home to Guildford.'

'You said your name was Geoff. You're not a man, are you?'

'Yes. My change has been somewhat challenging.'

'Oh. Yes. I suppose so. Not sure I know what to say. You're a man and in my body. Don't know quite how to deal with that information.'

I couldn't imagine what she was going through, hearing her own voice coming from me. 'I'm wearing your trouser suit.'

'Yes, I was about to leave for work when it happened. Has anyone else called you? My mum or Gerald, my fiancé?' I could hear her sobbing again.

'No. Sorry. Not yet. I'll put your new phone number into your phone and give it to them if they ring. I had to take your phone and your cash, but your credit cards are still in your purse on the coffee table. I'll get the money and phone back to you when I can.'

'Thanks. Gerald will be shocked if he rings.'

'I'll be careful what I say. How is your new body?'

'On the verge of overweight and thirty according to the driving licence.' She sounded more composed now.

'What size clothes do you wear? I'll have to get something other than this trouser suit.'

'Oh. I suppose so. If this situation continues you could have some of mine, maybe.'

'Thanks.'

There was no sound, so I continued, 'Anything serious about you of which I should be aware? Allergies or the like?'

'Not much. I get hay fever and have a reaction to crab – come out in blotches.'

I heard more sobbing at the other end of the phone.

'Don't cry, Suzy. With any luck, they'll soon have this sorted. I'm going to this conference tomorrow. I'm an astronomical physicist although I'm not sure how much I can help. I'll let you know if I hear anything.'

She seemed to compose herself quickly enough and responded, 'Right. You can post me a cheque for the money.' She had an afterthought, 'I'm on the pill Microgynon 30. It might be a good idea to continue it to save side-effects. I take them each morning. Try to get some as you should have taken one this morning.'

'Hardly likely to need them.'

'Well it could play havoc with your cycle.'

'Cycle?'

'Menstrual cycle!'

'Oh, God. I was going to ask when you're due. I saw a machine in the toilets here.'

'I'm due on twentieth this month. Wear a towel the night before. Poor man. You're in for a shock. However, if you don't take today's pill by about two pm it could trigger a period.'

I looked at Suzy's watch. It was nearly midday.

'Okay, thanks. I'll try to find an open chemist. I won't be able to get back to your place in time.'

'Make a note, I'm dress size eight and shoe size five. My measurements are thirty-three, twenty-four, thirty-five.'

'God. I wouldn't have the nerve to wear a dress or skirt. It is so weird simply being female,' I said as I made notes.

She laughed, at last seeming more relaxed. 'It'll give you a chance to experience harassment!'

'Already have! I'll be careful how I deal with Gerald and your mum.'

'Thank you.'

'Suzy, I need to go as I have to find a chemist and get back to Guildford. I took your charger as well and will ensure I keep the phone charged. Don't forget the key is under the flowerpot.'

'Okay, Geoff. Do let me know if you hear anything positive about reversing this thing. I must admit I'm not hopeful.'

'I'll keep in touch. Have a safe journey. Bye.'

Returning to the office, I told Mike, 'My transferor. Ended up on a ferry in the North Sea and they've just docked in Hull. Sounds nice.'

'Looks nice, too,' he laughed. 'Are you standing sexily deliberately?'

'What? How was I standing?' It was making me feel self-conscious.

'Well, you've changed position now, but you were standing in a delightfully feminine way with one foot behind your other leg and your hand on your hip. Oh, and how long have you been biting your nails?'

I pulled my hand away from my mouth and chuckled. 'I'd better go, Michael. Do you need anything?'

'A blow-job if you like!'

I ignored his habitual crudeness, 'Seriously, Michael. Can I get you anything?'

'No. I'll head back to the retirement home for tonight and let them feed me. I'll try going home in the morning when I've got some energy. Call me if you need me... or fancy a cuddle.'

I rolled my eyes, and, with briefcase and laptop, I left the office. After my conversation with Suzy, I paid another visit to the loo and purchased a pack of two towels. The twentieth was only a week away and I doubted the chemist would give me her pills without a prescription.

Diane was alone at her desk in the lobby.

'How are you getting on in the toilet?' I asked and laughed.

'Harrumph,' she pulled a face and gesticulated, 'I have issues with having to handle it, but I'm managing. You?'

'Was a huge shock discovering something I'd had all my life had vanished but managing okay. My transferor rang and I need to get a drug she takes. Have you seen a chemist open?'

'Yes. On the corner towards the river.'

'Thanks. I won't be in tomorrow, Diane. I'm going to this conference at the South Bank. You've got my number. Ask Justin to call me if he gets in.'

'No problem. Good luck.'

The streets of London were as quiet as the middle of the night. Would Waterloo be as busy as Euston? I hoped not or I'd have trouble reaching home until late. I found the open chemist and managed to obtain a pack of Suzy's pills and instructions when to take the last one for the month. They were very helpful and I popped one, a few minutes before two o'clock.

There were no taxis, so I walked the two miles to Waterloo briskly. My feet were already hurting. I wondered if that was because of Suzy's shoes or my unusual gait within them.

13 NO ESCAPE

Meanwhile, on Mindslip morning in a house in Hertfordshire

A dog. How could she be a dog?

At first, she thought it was a weird nightmare, then spent an hour walking aimlessly around the house, shouting for help, which came out as barks. She became increasingly alarmed she'd never escape the place. She'd no idea how she'd become a dog. She tried to think it through, but to no avail. There was no logical explanation.

Someone would come home eventually. There was both food and water in the kitchen. How she could have been about to take the kids to school and end up in a strange house in the body of a dog was simply unbelievable. Such things just did not happen!

A further hour's pacing and thinking didn't help. Logic and intelligence weren't helping her. A mirror in the hallway allowed her to see herself. A greyhound! She was quite a slight dog and her muzzle, head and ears were silver grey. She lay down and checked what she could see of her body. She was female.

Cleverly, she opened internal doors by pressing down on the handles. Too late she saw the bedroom door swing closed behind her. That isolated her from food and water. Her imprisonment had become critical. She tried and tried to get the door to open, but although she could press the handle down, she couldn't get her paw or muzzle into the gap before it shut. What was she to do? She needed something to push into the gap.

A frantic search of the bedroom produced a wooden backscratcher. She propped it up so when she pressed the handle and pushed against the door, it rebounded inward an inch or so before closing. On the third attempt, the backscratcher fell into the space and propped the door open. She'd been lucky and resolved to be far more careful with other doors.

She returned to the kitchen and the beanbag, on which she'd awoken. Across from it was a bowl of water and she lapped at it. She was clumsy, but enough went into her mouth to quench her thirst. A bowl of dog food sat beside it. She smelled it – God no! The smell was too powerful. She was not eating that! Another bowl held some biscuits in beige, brown, yellow and red, although the colours were strangely muted. She crunched a few. Yes. Okay. That would do for now, and she spotted a large bag of them leaning by the wall. Food wouldn't be an immediate problem. She was also sure she could work something out with the taps in the sink for water. No life-threatening problems as long as she was careful with doors.

What was that? Good gracious, it was a dog-flap. How could she not have noticed the dog-flap in the door? Could she escape?

She examined the flap and gave it a shove to be sure it would allow her to return, then pushed it open and made her way out into a gravelled backyard. A wooden fence surrounded her to a height of about six feet. Too high to jump over. It was just another prison compound. There were suitcases in the spare room which she could climb upon, but unless she could open the back door to get them into the yard, they were useless. She noticed there was only one sun now, so Betelgeuse must have set. The nova had to be the cause of all of this.

Back in the kitchen, she sat and puzzled over what to do next. Whatever had happened occurred sometime earlier in the day. How it had happened was a mystery, but she recognised something must have caused it. The previous night's supernova was the prime suspect. She wondered what had happened to the children. There was nothing she could do to resolve that question.

She trotted through to the lounge, knocked the television remote control onto the floor and turned it to point at the television. She pressed the red button. Nothing.

Perhaps she'd pressed the wrong one. Her snout got in the way of seeing. She lined it up again and pressed. Nothing. She walked around to the set and checked the plug socket. It was off. Carefully she managed to press the socket switch and a red LED illuminated. A light also appeared on the television. Her eyesight was subtly different. She'd had no idea dogs had such indistinct vision.

Once again, she pressed the red button on the remote.

The screen was grey with a stark message upon it in white.

PUBLIC EMERGENCY

STAY TUNED

ARMED FORCES, POLICE, POWER, TRANSPORT (train/bus) & EMERGENCY SERVICES PLEASE GO TO YOUR NEAREST PLACE OF WORK

MEDICAL STAFF REPORT URGENTLY TO THE NEAREST HOSPITAL

OTHERS PLEASE REMAIN WHERE YOU ARE OR TRAVEL HOME IF NEARBY

What on earth, she thought. Something serious must've happened. Her becoming a greyhound had to be part of it. Her hearing was excellent. She heard hums from the television and refrigerator, so she was confident she'd hear if the channel started broadcasting.

She needed to get home. Where was she? The street outside wasn't familiar. She went through into a small study and jumped onto the chair to examine the papers on the desk. Her eyesight was so bad it was difficult to read the address on the credit card statement. It looked like Hatfield. Hatfield? Hertfordshire. Twenty miles north of London. It must be fifty miles from her home. As a dog, she was sure she could walk the distance, but how to get out of the house? She ran back to the lounge.

Telephone. She tried to work the small radiophone but kept pressing the wrong buttons. They were too close together, but she'd seen a phone with large buttons on the desk. Back in the study she jumped onto the chair a second time, knocked the phone off the cradle and heard the dialling tone. Her hearing certainly made up for her poor eyesight.

She carefully dialled the eleven numbers of home, making mistakes several times and having to obtain a fresh dial tone on each occasion. This was so time-consuming.

Her husband's voice was on the answerphone, but when she tried to leave a message, no words would come out, only some whining sounds. Hopeless. She'd have to think of something else. Not putting the phone back on the cradle properly, she jumped down again and ran through to the television. Nothing new.

She returned to the front door. The small, oval, brass knob of the Yale lock near the top of the door needed rotating. She couldn't reach it well enough to get a grip.

The lounge coffee table would provide a platform. Magazines spilled off it as she dragged it into the hallway. She ran into the bedroom, bringing the backscratcher, and positioning it so that it would stop the door closing if she could open it even an inch.

Now she jumped onto the table and tried to turn the knob with her teeth. They wouldn't grip the shiny brass tightly enough to rotate it. Thirty minutes she wasted upon the attempt.

The back door was deadlocked, but it led nowhere anyway. Damn it, damn it, damn it!

She examined each of the ground floor windows, but they all had catch-locks.

It was now five o'clock. She guessed someone would return to the house soon and she could make her escape. But would someone come? What if her master, she was sure it was a man, never returned? She could be stranded here until she died. No. She could always dial 999 and leave the phone off the hook. Someone would come to investigate. She hoped someone would. No point worrying about it yet. She ate some more biscuits and drank her fill.

Wandering back to the front door, she had a new idea, ran into the study and brought out a roll of masking tape. She managed to free the end of the tape and tried to wrap it around the brass knob. Again, she tried to rotate the knob, but still it slipped through her grasp and, on the third attempt, the tape stuck to her teeth.

It wouldn't come off. She ran through to the hard floor of the kitchen where she could press the tape to the floor. She managed to get a paw onto the end of the tape and pulled her teeth away, leaving the tape stuck to the kitchen floor. She abandoned the attempt for the time being. Tiredness overcame her. She curled up on the beanbag to await developments.

She awoke with a start when noises came from the front hall. Up in a single bound, she was through to the hallway just too late to run outside. A man stood in the hallway staring at the coffee table.

'Hello, Bunty, at least you're all right. How did you move the coffee table, girl? Almost stopped me getting in,' he said, putting out a hand tentatively as if worried she might react strangely. She allowed him to stroke her head and he eased his hand around her ears and along her back.

Of course, he mightn't be in his normal body either, so he'd be cautious when first stroking her.

'Good job I had a hidden key under the gnome or I wouldn't have been able to get in to you without forcing the door. Someone else must have my keys and the car,' he said, telling her his woes.

He carried the coffee table through into the lounge, and she followed him.

'What've you been up to, Bunty? Remote on the floor and the telly on. Magazines everywhere. Coffee table in the hall. How did you move it?'

She sat down and tried to appear obedient.

He went to the kitchen.

'Ooh. Gone off your food, girl?' He picked up the dog food dish and smelled it, 'I'll give you some fresh. What's this tape doing on the floor. You been playing?'

She ran through to the hallway, stood by the front door and whined. He followed her.

'What's up, Bunty? Want your walk early?'

She ran back and forth between him and the door.

'Okay, girl, give me a minute,' the man said, put his coat back on and, oh no, he took a lead off the coatrack! She was wearing a choker collar. If he put a lead on her it would make escape more difficult. She didn't want to be running any distance dragging a dog lead.

In a second or two, he'd clipped the lead to her collar and the door was open. She was outside. Now she had to get free. Surely, she'd get an opportunity.

14 HOME ALONE

Geoff finds home a lonely place

I queued for a frustrating two hours to get a train for Guildford, and it was standing room only. I was desperate to get home to collect what messages there might be on the answerphone.

The Surrey countryside flew past. Betelgeuse had risen, creating the unworldly and disturbing duplicate shadows once more.

En route, I rang Jane, but there was still no sign of Caroline and the conversation was disturbing with her speaking with the voice of the woman I loved. The sooner I got home the better.

The phone rang.

'Geoff Arnold on Suzy Yamata's phone.'

'Is that really you, Geoff?' said a strange man with a strong African accent.

'Yes, I've become a woman. Who are you?'

'It's Justin. Embassy's given me a phone. In Abuja airport awaiting a flight. Chaos here. What news with you?'

I filled him in on the current situation and we started to talk about the slipping of minds.

'Don't see how it can be reversed en masse.'

'No. Any method would have to be piecemeal. Complications are frightening. To return to my body I'd need the actual body, Suzy's body and Suzy's new body. They could swap me back and Suzy too, but what about Suzy's host and the person currently in my body? It'd still leave two people in the wrong bodies.'

'My situ is likely to be even more complex. Even if a process is found, rolling it out to cover the population of the world would seem too great a task.'

'Don't forget there'd also be cases where people transferred into bodies which had perished in the numerous plane crashes and other accidents. The news is of millions having died.'

'There've been plane crashes?'

'Dozens. A blanket mass transfer is out of the question.'

'Awful! Never thought about the pilots vanishing.'

'Justin, there are terminally ill people too. I met one at Euston who was in her last few days. Now she's in a young healthy body. Did Diane tell you about Michael?'

'Yes. Lost a huge part of his life.'

'And would his transferee want to change back?'

'Lawyers will have a field day, Geoff.'

'For sure, and if a method *is* found, the wealthy and powerful would want to transfer into younger bodies!'

'Whole thing's a total mess. World will never be the same again.'

'There's a meeting of astronomers, astrophysicists and the like tomorrow in London, Justin. I'll be attending.'

'Yes. Diane told me. Let me know how it goes.'

'We're pulling into Guildford. I've put your number in my phone. Call me when you get back to the UK.'

'Will do.'

I disembarked onto Guildford station and a nice-looking young man stepped aside to let me pass. Two steps later, I came to an abrupt halt, causing someone to walk into the back of me. I apologised and looked back at the young man who was still standing by the carriage.

He *was* nice-looking! I'd even thought, "cor" when I saw him. What was *that* all about? Why would I think a guy was "nice-looking" in *that* way? Was Suzy's personality battling with mine for possession of her sexual orientation?

This new turn of events disturbed me. As I walked, I studied all the women I saw. Two of them were girls in their mid-twenties. Yes, they were lovely and impinged upon my mind as sexually desirable, but the young man's torso had also seemed to be of interest. Suzy's mind was certainly influencing me, even if she couldn't take me over entirely.

Fear struck me!

Perhaps the transferred personality would slowly lose its grip on the host mind. Could the original owner become increasingly dominant over time? Would my memories progressively fade? Was the transfer only temporary? Would my personality eventually face eviction? If so, would my own mind in my body recover its ownership?

Dare I even fall asleep? She might take possession while I slept! I reassured myself that nothing happened last night.

I hurried from the station into Walnut Tree Close and, within ten minutes, I was standing at the gate. Everything was so ordinary. The gate shut. No lights inside. My car still where I'd parked at the weekend. Caroline's would be at the hospital.

I fished the house key out from behind the planter, where Jane had left it.

Inside, the lounge and dining room looked fine. I put my laptop on the kitchen counter. Thank God, I'd left it at the Royal Institution on Tuesday night or I'd have lost it and its contents. A red light was flashing on the telephone docking station. Frantic for news of my family, I pressed *Play*. The first message was Diane telling me about the South Bank meeting. The next five messages were from voices I didn't recognise saying that they were people I knew well. Their messages said they were assuming I'd cancelled my morning meeting and might see me the next day at the South Bank.

Message seven was from a young woman with a French accent, 'Daddy, it'z me. I'm all grown up and don't know ver I am. Can you come and get me?'

How distressing. Was it Sandra or Wilson? Both called me Daddy. I had no way of knowing. It was a woman's voice, but I supposed it could easily be Wilson transferred into a woman. There was no return number. The French accent might mean he or she was in a French body. Damn her, damn her, damn her for not giving a return number. How the hell could I find her?

The next message was a series of strange sounds and breathing noises. Weird.

The final message was the French woman again. Definitely one of my children. 'Daddy. Vot's happening? I'm in a place called Toolong. Zey're all foreigners. Please come and get me.'

Damn it all, he or she is in France, perhaps Toulon, and again no number. I guessed it was Sandra owing to the juvenility of the sentences. Wilson, I'm sure, would have left a number.

I dialled 1471. The system hadn't recorded the caller's number, so it must have been international or withheld. What an awful situation. One of my children is in distress and I've no idea where, or how to contact them.

I telephoned the police to see if they would be able to find the number for me, but they were swamped with work and couldn't look at anything which wasn't a current emergency. Frankly, they were annoyed at my call. I supposed millions were in my situation. I must try to be more logical.

I sat. My heart was thumping and I was breathing heavily. I needed to settle myself down. I took off my jacket and kicked off Suzy's shoes – no point looking for my slippers, they'd be too huge. I made some tea and sat in the lounge to watch the news.

After a while I felt more human and recorded a new message, 'This is the telephone of Geoff and Caroline Arnold. Important – Sandra, Wilson, if you call please say your name and leave your number so we can call you back. The mobile is 06787-450198. Please speak after the tone.'

It took me four attempts. I ruined the first two by saying I was Geoff Arnold when I was clearly speaking with a girl's voice. Didn't want to freak the children out. The third was the need to add the extra message for the kids.

Once that was done, I visited the government website. There was an indexed list of people who had died in accidents.

With great trepidation, I searched out Caroline Arnold and there was nothing. Then I realised how stupid I was. If she were dead the name would mean nothing because all we'd get was the transferor's name, and it wouldn't be Caroline. Jane was in Caroline's body, of course. I wasn't thinking straight. Caroline couldn't possibly be on the list if Jane was inside her body.

I checked my own name, and I wasn't listed either, which was a relief. Why had the transferee in my body not rung home or the Royal Institution? Was I inhabited by a child or someone who spoke no English or, heaven forbid, an animal? I mentally slapped my face. Of course, he wouldn't be able to use my phone because it was password protected. Was there even anything on my person which said where I worked? My driving licence would have given my home address, but as we were ex-directory, he wouldn't be able to access the home phone number. The ancient Filofax wouldn't have helped either. Maybe it was not so surprising there had been no contact after all. Where was he? Would he head here or to his own home? I surmised a trip to Guildford would have no meaning for him any more than Suzy's Notting Hill flat was of interest to me. The person occupying my body, like me, would only be interested in getting home and locating his or her own family.

What should I do about the baby Sandra in Guildford Hospital? It would look like her, but not be her inside. Should I go to see her? What purpose would it serve? I decided to wait a day or two for Caroline to return. We could go and see her together then.

The BBC was full of news about people who'd transferred into animals and more warnings about animals in human bodies being potentially dangerous. It said most were not standing upright. A human figure on all fours wasn't particularly fast or agile. I remembered I'd seen the naked woman on all fours near Marble Arch. Must have been an animal inside her. The military were establishing camps to care for them "until a reversal process was found" but, as a short chaotic, news sequence showed, it was a challenge getting them to eat and behave amongst each other.

Farms were housing humans whose minds were in animals. An increasing number were being identified. It was much more common than first thought.

At eight, I cooked a meal, but the whisky I poured tasted vile. I poured a vodka and tonic which went down well enough. Suzy must still be in control of her taste buds.

Later, I tried on some of Caroline's clothes, as I couldn't live in this trouser suit indefinitely. Caroline's jeans were a little long, but I could turn up the legs. They were also baggy as Suzy was a much smaller size. I decided not to try on any skirts as I wouldn't have the confidence to wear them. Caroline's blouses were all on the large size but usable. Suzy would likely not be impressed with my fashion sense. Caroline's shoes were too large. I found a couple of pairs of slacks but again the legs were too long. I'd have to do some shopping. Underwear was all too large. Damn it. How would I shop for women's clothes? I ought to ask Suzy if I could borrow some of hers.

The power failed, and fatigue was setting in.

The nova was still very bright, but I decided on an early night. I used the bathroom, brushed Suzy's teeth and undressed in the slightly unworldly diffuse light, coming through the net curtains. I spent more time than I should admiring my incredible naked body in the full-length mirror, stretching and turning from side to side. Suzy was absolutely stunning. A real beauty.

I climbed into bed and sleep arrived instantly.

15 SPECIAL DELIVERY

Mindslip morning in the Queen Elizabeth II hospital

Angus released a scream of sheer agony.

What the hell was hurting? 'Oh fuck, oh fuck, oh fuck!' he thought.

He screamed again, a high-pitched scream of distress. Something in his stomach, in the bottom of his stomach. Had his ulcer burst? For more than thirty years, his ulcer had grumbled, but never hurt him like this. Now he was in his sixties and retired with lower stress levels, it bothered him less. But how was he here? He'd been on a flight to Madeira for a vacation. How'd he get to hospital? He didn't remember any of it. Had he passed out?

The wave of pain diminished giving him time to look around. It was certainly a hospital. A blood pressure monitor on a trolley stood beside the wall, and hospital curtains and rails were around two sides of him. Had he been in a plane crash? Why couldn't he remember?

Two puzzled looking nurses were jabbering away to each other as if lost or somewhere they weren't expecting to be, one didn't seem too fluent in English. A doctor stared at him as if in a trance, and a man in casual dress was sitting beside his bed examining his own hands. It was a crazy situation. No one seemed to know what was going on – least of all, Angus.

Another doctor was lying slumped against the wall as if he'd fainted, and a third nurse was lying in a crumpled heap by the door. It was like the Mad Hatter's tea party with him at its centre. In fact, they appeared to be more confused than him, if that were possible. Had there been a terrorist attack? Even that wouldn't explain how he'd got here from the plane. Who was this man sitting beside him? Was he undergoing an operation? He must be undergoing an operation. He remembered, years ago, someone sitting beside him when they put a camera up his backside. Were they doing the same again? But this was much more painful. Agonising and too low in his body for his ulcer.

The doctor approached, peered at him and said, 'I think she's close.' What an odd thing to say.

He walked over to the two conscious nurses, 'Get a grip, you two. Heaven knows what's happened, but this woman needs our help.'

He shook the shoulder of the man sitting beside Angus, 'Come on you, hold her hand or do something. Could be any moment.'

The man grasped Angus's hand. *What the fuck?* He tried to pull the man's hand away, but he was holding too tightly.

'It's all right, dear,' said the man.

Dear? Why was he calling him dear? The pain grew once more and built to a crescendo of suffering. He released another long drawn out cry of torment as something seemed to rip through his lower torso. Had they forgotten the anaesthetic or something? Had he been in a plane crash? Whatever they were doing to him was excruciatingly painful.

The doctor shouted at the two nurses, 'Stop bickering, you two, and look after her! I don't know how we got here, but we've a situation to deal with!'

They turned towards Angus and stared at him.

'Soon, soon, I promise. Bear down, dear,' the doctor said.

Bear down? What was this? He cried out, 'Help me, help me, I can't stand it!'

The older nurse looked intently at the lower part of the bed and sympathetically back at him and exclaimed, 'I saw the head! Another big push at the next contraction.'

Contraction? Push? They were talking to him as if he were having a baby. Madness. Who had brought him here? He'd sue their bollocks off. He heard the other nurse asking the older one why they were there. They didn't know where they were either. Was everyone delusional?

The man shouted round at them, 'For fuck's sake you two. Stop fucking arguing about it and help! She needs help!'

She? Did he mean him? She? What the hell had happened?

Oh God, here it came again. Agony, agony, he couldn't stand it. He released another strangely high-pitched scream.

The older nurse shouted, 'Yes, there it is. Here it comes!'

She dived between his legs and the blessed relief of the tearing, stretching, agonising pain rapidly faded. He was sweating profusely, and the sitting man wiped his brow and face.

'It's a boy,' the nurse called, a massive grin upon her face. She hoisted a bloody mass of grizzle and gore from beneath his abdomen, swaddled it in a small sheet and carried it around to him. God, it was a baby! He'd had a baby. A real baby! She lowered it into his arms, and a strange reflex action made him take it and grasp it to him. He couldn't help it.

'Congratulations,' the nurse said, 'you've a lovely baby boy.'

Angus looked at each of them in turn and beamed at the infant. He couldn't help the smile either. It seemed so natural.

The baby boy opened his eyes, struggled to focus, looked around and back at Angus. A look of shock came over his little face. It turned into an expression of anger. He opened his toothless mouth and, in the tiniest, angry, whining, barely comprehensible voice, shouted, 'Where the fuck am I?'

16 VIVE LA DIFFÉRENCE

Geoff's moral dilemma

I awoke early, about four, relieved that I still knew who I was. I'd worried that Suzy might take me over while I slept, but I was still me.

I was lying on my right side in the foetal position and cuddling one of the spare pillows. Must be Suzy's preferred sleeping position. I always sleep au naturel and lifted my hand to my breast and checked I were still female. I was. My touch was good and gentle squeezes caused a warmth to grow within my breast, a sensation the like of which I'd never experienced before. How wonderful for women to have this incredible erogenous zone!

I'd the most beautiful female body, and I wanted to know what other feelings it could provide. I had lost none of my male interest in the female form. I investigated myself intimately, enjoying sensations I'd only guessed at previously. So different. Totally novel. Amazingly exciting to enjoy both the exploration by my fingers from my male perspective and the thrill of their touches and caresses from my female point of view. Double the pleasure.

Was I being unfaithful to Caroline? My thoughts churned. God, was I abusing Suzy? I stopped.

Was I abusing my host body?

She wouldn't have wanted me to be doing this. Or would she? I wasn't sure. Maybe she did it all the time. Maybe not. But it was me feeling it, not her. She'd never know. But I'd know!

I lay quietly, the sexual tingle fading, and the warmth seeping from my breast now I'd released it. Should I do this? Why shouldn't I do it? Like all men, I masturbated occasionally and knew most women did too. Why not as

Suzy? I told myself Suzy would never know. What harm could it do? That was the crucial question. Could I do any harm to her if I had some personal fun? No, I didn't think I could harm her. But it was her body, not mine. But I was in it… I was living in her now. I so wanted to continue but wasn't entitled. Damn, damn, damn!

But the arousal I'd experienced had now vanished. How annoying. I'd heard about women's arousal being temperamental. Was this it? Could they really go off the boil so quickly and so completely? This was the opportunity of a lifetime, to experience sexual arousal from the viewpoint of the opposite sex. I'd always wondered what Caroline felt during foreplay and lovemaking. I'd made a mess of it. For some time, I lay awake staring at the ceiling, chewing over my moral dilemma.

I turned over and did my best to fall asleep. At least, the concern about losing my identity overnight had evaporated, but there'd be pressing concerns in the morning. My two children were lost and in distress somewhere in the world. At least one had tried to make contact. I could only guess at the terror they might be feeling, consigned to some other body goodness knows where in the world, and I couldn't do anything about it. Why had I heard nothing from Caroline? Two whole days had passed.

Eventually sleep surprised me.

The alarm sounded at six fifteen, and I sat on the side of the bed, examining myself in the wardrobe mirror. What a beautiful girl. Amazing how sexy she was – I was – we were. Which should I say? Another conundrum.

Looking at myself was compulsive. I was obsessed with Suzy's beauty. Her legs, her waist and tummy, her breasts, arms, face, hair, lips, fingers, and that mesmerising black triangle. Surely this was only because I was a man. Girls didn't all look at themselves like this and become aroused. That wasn't possible. As a man, I saw nothing in myself as a man, to arouse me. It meant this was most certainly different. She was so lovely. I vowed to ensure I would not miss the opportunity if I became aroused again. After all, right now it was *my* body and, if I didn't physically harm it, I had the right to live normally within it. Another time. For now, I needed to get up and dressed.

I stepped out of the shower, towelling myself dry. I almost slapped on my aftershave lotion, but it wouldn't be suitable for this body. I was shocked to see my hair in the mirror. I'd no idea whatsoever how to style it. It had seemed ordinary before. Pretty, not elaborate, but had a lot of body to it. Now it lay damp and limply against my head. I'd never used a hairdryer on my hair as a man, but obviously needed to now. Even more problematical, I'd need to brush or comb it back into shape. How the hell was I supposed to style it?

I sat in front of Caroline's dressing table mirror. Betelgeuse was shining more directly into the bedroom now, casting its otherworldly light. I shut the curtain. Normally I'd have dressed straight away, grabbed breakfast and left. I waved the hairdryer randomly around my head while combing through Suzy's hair. After about fifteen minutes it was dry and had plumped up a little. It looked nowhere near as nice as it had yesterday. It would do. I'd a lot to learn. I picked up Caroline's Chanel No 5 spray perfume and gave some sprays across my abdomen and either side of my neck, as I'd seen her do. At least I'd smell feminine even with my cack-handed hairstyling.

I had to press Suzy's Schulz Y-fronts into a third day's use. Not ideal. I used the same socks and bra but with one of Caroline's smaller tops. Suzy's trouser suit now concealed a multitude of sins. At least I was comfortable in the trousers.

I had Suzy's size details, so I could buy something different. Ideally, I should come to an arrangement to buy her clothes from her. I didn't look as smart as yesterday and it bothered me, which was strange. My Geoff self wouldn't have cared, as long as he was tidy. The mirror said I *was* tidy, but not like yesterday. Suzy's mind was nagging me. Damn it all. I ignored my lack of fashion sense and headed downstairs.

BBC One had its Breakfast programme running as normal today, but with the latest updates repeated every fifteen minutes. None of the Breakfast presenters were recognisable, but they still had the same names. It was simply that the names did not match the faces. I made a few notes about electromagnetic radiation, which an American scientist was mentioning on the programme. I'd check the facts later. The news about myriad accidental deaths was frightening. House fires, car crashes, suicides – millions were known to have died already. I continued to write ideas in my notebook when they covered anything serious, but far too much of the news was sensationalised tales of disaster or miraculous escapes from it. More than eight hundred planes had crashed, but with Air Traffic Control's help, novices had landed even more. Thank goodness modern aircraft had almost automatic landing systems.

The lack of new messages on the answerphone was depressing. I tried my own mobile again and there was no answer. I tried it twice more in case my transferee couldn't answer it immediately, but still no answer. Even though it had a password, whoever had it would've been able to answer an incoming call. Curious. If a kid or baby inhabited me, I supposed it would remain unanswered.

I wrote a couple of notes for Caroline and pinned a message to the front door with Suzy's phone number, so I could tell Caroline or the children where to find the key. I left for London.

Guildford station was nowhere near as busy as normal. While waiting for the train, many men ogled me. It was clear Suzy was beautiful despite my best endeavours to mess up her hair. The most annoying aspect to the ogling was that when I returned the gaze, they continued to stare, even raising eyebrows and winking. There was no embarrassment. They wanted me to know they were enjoying looking. Were they hoping there might be a spark in return? All it made me want to do was to never catch any of their eyes again. I consciously ignored men's gazes.

Was this "eyeing" part of male harassment? I now understood how a girl might feel uncomfortable because of the unwanted attention. I remembered how it was before the event, how I'd be walking along and a pretty girl would pass. They were always gazing straight ahead or past you and never caught your eye. Was this the result of years of unwelcome stares? It now made sense. By determinedly not catching men's eyes, girls weren't having to deal with the ogling. Or was I imagining this? Had my change of sex made me hypersensitive to the glances of others?

I was lucky to step straight onto a train and the trip to Waterloo was uneventful even with standing room only. I examined each of the passengers in a different light since discovering my occasional, but worrying, change of interest in the appearance or appeal of men. Women continued to be attractive to me and any attraction to the men was peripheral, although there was no denying it was there. Once more there was little conversation. Had there been during journeys before the event? Was there any more conversation before? Was the quiet more noticeable now because I was observing it?

At a crowded Waterloo, there were still hordes of people wanting to head to the south and west of the country. I was glad to be arriving and strode out of the station towards the nearby Festival Hall. Large queues were forming. I resigned myself to a great deal of waiting around this morning. Betelgeuse was just setting. It was about a quarter of the sun's brightness today.

The queuing people were talking to each other, discussing the "effect" and how to reverse it. The physical make-up of the crowd was no different to that of a football match, but the children were hosts to some brilliant minds while others inhabited bodies ancient before their time.

When I reached the head of the queue, an official gave me a badge, which announced that I was Dr Geoffrey Arnold of the Royal Observatory. How did the badge equate with the body of an attractive young Japanese woman?

Each badge was large with the name in huge letters. Normally, at conferences people had a good idea who would be there and would recognise them. Now you couldn't recognise anyone at all so the large badge, six inches by three inches, was a brilliant idea. At least here, there had been some joined-up thinking in preparation for the event.

The photocopied sheet of events and workshops allocated me to the Queen Elizabeth Hall. Our workshop's brief was to brainstorm the situation without portfolio. They wanted us to think and work laterally through multiple disciplines.

A five-minute walk away, the Queen Elizabeth Hall sported a large builders' sign announcing, 'CLOSED FOR

REFURBISHMENT', but a temporary sign by the door announced 'MULTI-DISCIPLINE SCIENCE GROUP'.

A stout security officer stood outside. He had no uniform but did have a military cap which proclaimed "SECURITY". Was it his own hat, the only remaining piece of his uniform which fitted him after Mindslip? A handful of police in variously ill-fitting uniforms were preventing a demonstration from getting too close to the hall.

Their placards called for the government to resign, and there was that annoying rhythmic chant of "What do we want…? Browning out…! When do we want it…? Now!" Whatever made them think the government was the cause of Mindslip? It was an opportunistic excuse to protest.

The queuing and registration had taken very little time, so, around nine, I telephoned Caroline's mobile and had a word with Jane who told me there had been no calls to that phone. I thanked her for leaving the house so tidy, and we chatted about our situations.

Secondly, I phoned Suzy, who took a while to answer.

'I didn't wake you?' I asked, knowing she'd been travelling back from Hull.

'No. Literally arrived home this minute. Nothing to eat en route so making a rare cooked breakfast before crashing out, so I'm glad you rang now. Has Gerald rung?'

'No one has rung your telephone, I'm afraid. You got in okay?'

'Yes. Thanks for thinking about the key. My neighbour, also a sex-change transferee, had to break a window to get into his apartment. Whoever was in his original body didn't think things through.'

'Oh. I think I might know why, Suzy. Was he middle-aged and overweight with thinning hair?'

'Yes, sounds like him.'

'He'd been occupied by an eleven-year-old boy called David Baker from Manchester. I never asked which house he'd come from, but he was standing there when I went out after the explosion. It was an air crash a few streets from you.'

'Oh, how awful! I wondered why there was debris everywhere, shredded clothing and paper.'

'Tell your neighbour, I left David at Euston with someone called Jessica who was going to ensure he got to Manchester Piccadilly. David said he'd be able to get a bus to Withington from there. I have his home phone number too. I'll text it to you.'

'I'll tell him, sorry, her. Oh, this is so confusing.'

'Tell me about it. Listen, Suzy, when I got up this morning, I tried on some of Caroline's clothes. All her trousers are too long and oversized for me, I mean you – well – us, anyway.' I laughed at my inability to express myself. 'So, I was going to try to buy some clothes, but you mentioned your current body is a different size from your new body. Can I borrow or buy some of your outfits? Would you mind? Say no, if it will freak you out, meeting me – er, yourself.'

The phone went silent for a while.

'Are you still there, Suzy?'

'Yes, sorry. It's weird hearing you talking to me with my voice. Did you know you have my accent?'

Did I have a Japanese accent? Whichever of my children left the answerphone message had a French accent. Accents must stay with the body. It hadn't registered with me until now.

'No, hadn't realised. I suppose so, now you mention it. It really doesn't matter about the clothes if you don't want to meet. I can soon buy some.'

'No, let's be practical about it, Geoff. When would you want to come?'

'How about if I drive over tonight? I'm in Guildford after this conference today. I could be with you in an hour or so by car after I get home, subject to the roads, but I would've hoped the main A3 into London would be reasonably clear by this evening. Could give you an update on the situation. I'd ring first. I could return your telephone if I'm able to buy another and repay the seventy-five pounds.'

'Yes. Sounds a plan. We're not going to ever change back, are we?' Strain in her voice again.

'Well, changing back is what these conferences are about. To be frank, I don't think there will be any instant solution, but now we know a mind *can* transfer, I'm sure we'll find a way to do it. The problem comes with the fact that the transfers were so random. It's a nightmare situation. We'll have to improvise, but whatever happens, it won't be soon. I'd say years, and it's likely to result in myriad legal cases. Do we own our own bodies?'

'Well, yes. I was thinking along the same lines. Okay, Geoff. When you come bring a few suitcases. We might as well ensure you have plenty. You can always give them back when or if we change back. I'm becoming resigned to this being a permanent change and nothing will fit my new body.'

'Thanks, Suzy. Bear in mind, this conference may finish late, so it mightn't even be tonight. I'm resigned to being female. You are an extremely beautiful female, I should add,' I said, and chuckled.

'Oh, thank you. I've got some real work to do with this lady. After this fry-up breakfast and a proper sleep, I intend to get her fit. Any sign of your wife and children?'

'Yes. Either my son or my daughter is in Toulon. He or she rang with a woman's voice but didn't leave a number. No sign of the other child or my wife.'

'Oh. I'm sorry. I'm worried about Gerald not having made contact at all, nor my mum. After I've had some sleep, I'm going to her house.'

'Okay, Suzy. I'd better get into this conference. I'll let you know if I can make it to Notting Hill tonight.'

'Right. I was thinking, Geoff, I'll need to buy clothes for my new body, so it'd really help me if you bought my outfits instead of me loaning them to you. Would buying them be a possibility?'

'Yes, I'm happy to buy them if I can get my bank sorted out during lunch. I'll need clothes anyway and your taste is likely to be far better than mine and I'll know they fit, so I'm sure we can come to an agreement.'

'Okay, see you later, hopefully.'

'I'll call you first.'

I entered the hall contemplating my new priorities – I needed a phone, must sort my bank, credit and debit cards and be prepared to drop everything if my family made contact from some far-flung location.

Inside the building, sheets shrouded the walls. Stacks of disassembled seats leaned against them as part of the refurbishment programme.

About thirty people stood near the stage, talking. The agenda had us headed by Dr James Meredith from Oxford University. I'd met him before, which, of course, wouldn't help me identify him today.

There was a low-level buzz of conversation. As I approached, people peered at me and then at my badge.

'Good God, Geoff. I could almost fancy you!' a tall gangly youth said and laughed. I examined the name badge.

'Ha, Pete Watson. What's it like to no longer be a short-arse?' I retorted to this once diminutive friend from my university days.

A middle-aged, balding man stepped forward and offered his hand, 'Dr Arnold. Glad – glad to meet you again.'

'Dr Meredith. The pleasure's all mine.' He didn't look too dissimilar to his original self.

'We're getting to know each other and, with one thing and another, I intend – intend to formalise things around eleven when we should have a good number of our complement,' he said

'Right. Any current ideas flying around?' I asked.

'General opinion is we'll be unable – unable to find a way for a mass reversal, and we'll be in the hands of the medical and psychoanalysts for some sort of personal solution in some – some circumstances. We should be trying to figure out exactly what caused the effect, whether it's likely to recur, and what we can do to stop – stop it happening in the future.'

'Yes, and the effect on people has been dreadful,' I said.

'It's been distressing for everyone involved. Breaking up families, and it'll, no doubt, destroy relationships. My own wife is in the body of a man my age. How am I able to respond – respond to her or the situation? She's still the person I love, but in a form I could never love.'

'Yes. I've been thinking along similar lines. I've not managed to find my own wife and both of my children are missing. One, only nine, went walkabout saying he was an engineer and must get to work. A baby occupied the other one and is now at Guildford hospital.'

'No?'

'It's a dreadful situation. I've been agonising over visiting her. Waiting until I find Caroline, I suppose,' I said and discovered I had tears welling up in my eyes. I must hide my feelings better.

'A shame. Right. Right. Make yourself familiar with our little group of geniuses. We'll talk – talk again soon,' Dr Meredith said and went off to talk to another new arrival.

I made my way into the group of scientists and picked up on conversations, throwing in my three ha'pence worth when appropriate.

By midday, they'd elected me deputy to James Meredith and we had broken up into groups of five or six to discuss various aspects of the scientific part of the problem. James and I moved between the groups contributing occasionally, teasing out interesting threads and passing them to other groups.

Our total complement was about fifty. Many names from the original list were missing. Our most bizarre attendee was Dr Kenneth Michaelson, a brilliant quantum physicist who was originally over seventy, but now occupied the body of a five-year-old boy. It was strange listening to him enunciating the most amazing ideas about quantum physics.

One drawback to his change was his forgetting terminology. It didn't damage our comprehension of what he was saying but it was becoming most frustrating for him. We thought it might be that the boy's actual brain size was insufficient, so there had been overspill when Mindslip occurred. We made notes about anything along those lines which had arisen in our conversations and a clerk entered them into our computer. We continually entered, indexed, and reformatted these notes. The hastily designed, computer programme was intended to help us keep track of everything. It securely shared the information with workshops and conferences elsewhere on the South Bank over an intranet. Very impressive, given they'd only had a day or so to develop the system.

My word "Mindslip" soon replaced "event" or "effect" and would probably immortalise me.

Were we making progress? Impossible to tell. A group of systems analysts were linking common threads and firing back questions about their interrelationships via the intranet computers.

We had a full hour's break at lunch to clear our minds. I set off briskly to Waterloo Road where I purchased an iPhone. That I chose a pastel green phone proved Suzy's gender was still in control of non-specific decisions.

It took the rest of my lunch hour to organise new credit and debit cards. The security questions needed a real knowledge of the historic management of my bank account.

Running back to Queen Elizabeth Hall showed me that Suzy was much fitter than the old Geoff. I wasn't even out of breath.

Fresh ideas dried up. The morning session had come up with the best. At four o'clock, James called us all into a single group around the stage and we summarised the situation as we saw it. Our main findings were:

- Electromagnetic radiation from the supernova's unexpected second blast, accompanied by coronal mass ejections from the sun probably caused Mindslip. The conclusion was that the chance of any repeat of the event was vanishingly small.
- No one had the slightest idea what had caused the second supernova flash. Nothing in known science explained it.
- The International Space Station might have recorded the radiation types, and we sent NASA requests for data. If the ISS hadn't got the

information, we'd be hard-pressed to find it elsewhere.
- We considered the chance of mass reversal of the phenomenon to be absolute zero. No one dissented from this view. We'd remain in our new bodies unless we found an innovative method to transfer minds on a piecemeal basis. The few medical doctors and consultants in our group considered any such possibility to be remote.
- We had sent questions to selected universities to investigate if there'd been exposure to more dangerous radiations. Were we doomed through some other form of radiation poisoning? Our own consensus was no, but it needed checking.
- We flagged up security issues, particularly life insurance, banking, assets, shareholding, and property ownership. These were not within our brief, but they'd asked us to think laterally, and we intended to do so with latitude.

It seemed we'd not made a lot of progress. The next afternoon, James Meredith and I would be attending a conference of workshop heads and deputies. We'd decide on the reconstitution of groups for further brainstorming. Distinct project work would also be allocated.

When we finished our session, I agreed to meet up with James for lunch at the Festival Hall restaurant the next day. As we parted, he moved to kiss my cheek and I jumped back.

'God, sorry, Geoff. It seemed, seemed so natural,' he apologised.

'I suppose I ought to get used to it.'

We laughed, shook hands and parted. If our findings were correct, I'd be a woman for the rest of my life. I must adjust to it being my reality. I thought about Caroline. Would she be male or female? I loved her, but could love transcend whatever differences we might have when we found each other again? What about sex? It was one of our great pleasures – would we ever make love again in our new forms?

As if to emphasise to me how much my life would change, in the extended underground walkway to the station a grubby man came up alongside me and said, 'Goin' my way, darlin'?'

I ignored him.

'Come on, luv. I'll show yer a good time. The worl's endin', yer know.'

I stopped and faced him. God, he was huge, and I was tiny in comparison. I thought better of what I was going to say and strode towards the station.

'Come on! Yer know yer want it! A quick fuck'd make us both feel better.'

Over my shoulder, I said, 'Listen, mate, I'm a kickboxer in a woman's body, and if you don't leave me alone, I'll crush your balls and you won't stand for a week. I'm trying to keep my temper!' I hurried onwards.

It had the desired effect. He stopped following me, but my heart was racing and I was scared. I'd not known fear like it since a gang beat me up as a teenager.

Further on, another man wolf-whistled me and, as I reached the blessed relief of the station, another called out, 'Love yer legs, bitch!'

This was a shock. I'd heard about harassment from Caroline but hadn't imagined anything this aggressive or the blatant catcalling. Maybe it was because people were no longer themselves and could behave as if anonymous. Inside the station, I stood quietly and recovered my composure. Once my breathing and heart rate had stabilised, I managed to squeeze aboard a train to Guildford. Standing room only and I had to force myself into a corner by the door to stop a man who was trying to rub the front of himself against my behind. I was certainly getting a crash course in harassment.

I arrived home safely and went straight to the answerphone.

17 MOUNTAIN

In Austria on the morning of Mindslip

Wind whipped the canvas of the tent into a frenzy as the howling gale struck. How had she ended up in this noisy, flapping, multi-coloured shelter? She was ensconced in a sleeping bag; her cheeks and nose were freezing. A strange man, his face almost concealed by a beanie and quilt, lay opposite. His eyes were closed. Who was he?

She had no idea how this had happened. Surely it must be a dream. Pregnancy was tiring. She'd been enjoying a well-earned lie-in at home and woken up here. Not possible. A particularly strong gust of wind rocked the flimsy structure.

'Excuse me,' she said. More than her location had changed. She was speaking with a man's voice.

She brought her hand to her face. What a shock! She touched a beard, short hair, and saw the rough chapped fingers. Gradually it sank home she'd become a man. It must be a dream but so real.

The eyes opposite opened, piercing grey irises gave a surprised stare, 'Who the hell are you?' the man said.

'I don't know. I was Karen, now I'm in this tent with you... and I'm a man. Where are we?'

'What the fuck is the howling noise?'

'We're in a tent in a storm. Who are you?'

'Greg. Greg Ramsey. This is crazy.'

'I know. I'm a housewife. I'm eight months pregnant. I live in Southampton.'

'Listen, mate, you're not pregnant. You're a man and this isn't Southport or Norwich which is where I was. Blimey, it's cold.'

Karen reached down the sleeping bag. No bulge. She wasn't pregnant. She reached down further... and withdrew her hand in horror. She definitely wasn't a woman!

'I was in Southampton, not Southport. Where are we? What has happened?'

'How the hell am I meant to know?'

'No need to be nasty.'

He stared at the flapping nylon material. 'No, sorry.'

Greg unzipped his bag and extricated himself. He was fully dressed, as was she. He stood, although bent double with the lack of head clearance, and made his way to the opening. He raised the zip and a blast of icy air entered the tent causing them to be surrounded by an incoming flurry of snow in imitation of a shaken snow globe. He peered outside.

'Damn it all. We're on a fucking mountain!' He rapidly withdrew his head and shoulders and zipped up the entrance as the cutting gale tried to balloon inside the tent and lift it into the air.

Greg sat, cross-legged on his sleeping bag, rubbing snow out of his beard, 'This isn't possible. You say you were sleeping in Southport?'

'Southampton!'

'And I was in my car on the way to work in Norwich. This isn't real.'

'I thought I was dreaming. It isn't a dream though, is it?'

'No. It isn't, and I was only twenty-five before. My hands are older.'

'I'd say you're more like forty,' Karen said.

'Damn it. What's happened to us?'

Karen opened her sleeping bag and they both rummaged around in the tent. She found a mobile phone and a map.

'Give me the map,' he demanded, and she handed it over while she fiddled with the mobile.

'It's locked,' she said in despair, 'and it's not mine. I don't know the password.'

Greg turned the map over and studied it. 'Damn it, we're in Austria and, if these marks are correct, we're somewhere on the Großglockner mountain in the eastern Alps. We're also in the middle of a storm so we're stuck in here for a while. That's for sure.'

'Are you a climber?'

'Well, I've done some hill-walking in Scotland and Wales, but not this stuff. I know what *not* to do, though.'

'And what do we *not* do?'

'In this blizzard, we don't do anything. We stay put until this storm blows over.'

18 FACE TO FACE

Geoff finds a message at home

The red answerphone light flashed. I pressed the button.

'Daddy. Daddy it'z Zandra.'

The voice changed to a man with a heavy French accent, 'Mrs Arnold. I am François Damay. Your daughter is in our daughter's flesh. She seems young, maybe under ten years. My daughter was twenty-two. We are putting Sandra on train to Paris. My brother meet her. His number 92-56-46-60. She arrive four this après-midday. You call him, yes? Oui, you call him please. Sandra safe. Not to worry. My number 94-36-44-41. You call me, oui, so I know you get this? Yes?'

Sandra came back on, 'Love you Daddy, Mummy. Zee you soon.'

The second message was from the brother.

'Mrs Arnold. Jean Damay is how I am called. I have Sandra. Please call 92-56-46-60. We can put her on Eurostar but must know you will meet her. Call me, yes?'

I rang François first. Thanked him for all his efforts and asked about his daughter's address, details, and if she'd any allergies, took any drugs or had any illnesses. She was a fit, healthy, twenty-two-year-old. Poor Sandra had lost a great chunk of her childhood.

Next, I contacted Jean Damay and arranged for him to put her on the Eurostar first thing Saturday, and I'd meet her at St Pancras. He told me he'd call with the expected arrival time once he'd seen the train depart. He asked me if I would like to talk to Sandra, and I explained I was actually Mr Arnold in a woman's body, and I didn't want to freak Sandra out. We agreed it might not be a good idea to tell her yet.

So, Sandra is safe. Now where are Caroline and Wilson?

I updated the answerphone message and entered my contacts into my new iPhone, also texting each of them with its number. Finally, I called Suzy to say I'd be with her by eight thirty.

The roads were quiet. Volunteer squads had pushed most abandoned vehicles and wrecks to the side of the road. Despite zigzagging around a few badly located vehicles, I arrived at Suzy's flat in ninety minutes. This would doubtless be traumatic for her. I rang the doorbell.

A very attractive woman, a few years older, a little taller and not quite so slim as myself, opened the door. She instantly put her hand to her mouth as she came face-to-face with herself.

'Oh dear. What a shock! Thought I was prepared.'

'Hi. I'm Geoff.'

'Yes. Right. You'd better come in,' she said, staring up and down my body as I passed. 'Go into the lounge.'

'Sorry about the shock,' I said, placing her mobile phone, charger and seventy-five pounds on the coffee table. She was still staring intently at me, her hand covering her mouth and I could see it shaking with emotional tension.

'Thank you. I can't get over the fact I'm standing here looking at myself and you're a man.'

'Yes, it must be freaky.'

'It is much more than that.'

'How do you mean?'

'You wouldn't want to know.'

'Tell me, Suzy. I do want to know.'

'I'm furious.'

'Yes,' I agreed, almost a whisper.

'You've stolen my body. Stolen years of my life. I'm angry – really, really angry. I know it's not your fault, but there you are… you're standing there. You're me. It is not fair. Really not fair,' she'd balled her fists and her colour had risen. I could see how annoyed she was.

'I guess I'd feel the same if I found my own body. I'd hate the person who is inside it,' I said, trying to keep my voice and manner as steady and reasonable as possible.

'How dare this happen to us? How stupid. I feel like screaming at God. I know it's been a couple of days now, but I still feel it is some dreadful nightmare which will end sometime.'

I answered in a quiet, soothing voice, 'Sorry. Think we're both stuck with the situation.'

She stood, silently. She was trying to calm down but having real trouble.

All of a sudden, she slumped onto the sofa and burst into tears – real wracking, sobbing tears. I quickly skirted the coffee table, sat tightly beside her and put my arm around her shoulders. She leaned into me, shaking with anguish, a contagious misery which found me joining her sadness, tears running freely down my cheeks. Stoical Geoff crying like a baby – I couldn't remember being so miserable in my life.

'It's so unfair,' she sobbed.

'Yes. Yes. Yes,' was all I could say. I couldn't believe I was reacting like this. It was certainly not my normal self.

It continued, the two of us sobbing inconsolably, rocking back and forth, locked in our embrace, each of us hanging tightly on to the other.

My Geoff-self finally managed to regain some self-control, but I dared not release her. I continued to envelop her as she clung tightly to me in her despair. I needed to let it run its course.

After many minutes, she pulled back from me, her eyes red, her cheeks streaked with mascara.

She reached for a tissue and blew her nose, leaned back and looked at me. She said, 'That was embarrassing, sorry.'

'No. Not at all. Think nothing of it,' I said.

She studied me, or more accurately, studied my hair, then burst into a semi-forced, nervous laugh, as surprising and emotional as her tears. 'What *have* you done to my hair?'

I saw an opportunity to lighten the mood. 'Whoops! I showered and didn't know what to do to put it back as it was.'

She laughed again, dabbing her eyes with another tissue and passing one to me. 'You've got a lot to learn as a female.'

'Well, it's a bit trivial in the circumstances. More important things to worry about.'

'You can't walk around making *me* appear untidy. Give me a minute,' she said, heading for the bathroom.

She emerged, looking much better and stood, looking down at me. 'For goodness sake, you look awful! The only way I can make sense of this is to, at least, show you how to look presentable.'

'I'll probably get a short hairstyle when I can get to a barber.'

'*What?* Don't you dare!'

'Even if we eventually swap back, it is going to be a long time before it happens.'

'Yes, but I'd be awful with short hair. Don't you want to be nice-looking… and smart?'

'I suppose so, but there are more pressing matters to deal with.'

'Yes. I know, but do you have something *"pressing"* to do tonight? This very moment?'

'Well, not really. Why?' I felt trapped.

'Let me give you some lessons. At least you'll be presentable. How much respect would you give to someone who dressed in a slovenly manner and didn't care about their appearance?'

I wasn't sure how to answer. Being neat and tidy was all I usually paid attention to. Was I slovenly? I hadn't thought so.

'I suppose knowing how to do my hair better would be useful.'

'It's more than your hair. Let me make use of what might be our only meeting and give you some tips.'

She'd cornered me. I had no more valid excuses, 'Okay.'

'Come with me,' she said. I followed her into the bedroom.

About forty minutes later, she'd shown me how to do my hair and, despite my protests, how to add mascara, lipstick and even a little rouge. I had to admit it all made me look fabulous.

'Thank you, Suzy. Much appreciated.'

'Did you bring suitcases?'

'Yes. In the car. Shall I bring them in?'

'Yes. Are you sure you're okay to buy my outfits? They were moderately expensive. I've always dressed well.'

'Well, as long as there aren't any thousand-pound designer dresses,' I said and laughed.

'No, I don't dress *that* well! Most of my suits were under two hundred. Fetch the cases in.'

I was soon back with two large and two smaller suitcases.

'Can you give me whatever trouser suits you have? I'm too worried about wearing a skirt.'

'Don't be silly. Skirts are nice and cool to wear, especially in summer and most of my professional outfits are skirt suits. They suit my figure, sorry, your figure. You'll look brilliant in them. You're embarrassed because you are thinking of yourself as a man. As far as anyone meeting you is concerned, you're a woman. Come on. Take the trousers off and I'll show you how to wear a skirt.'

What? She wanted me to undress in front of her? No, no, no! 'You serious? You want me to undress?' I asked in shock.

'For goodness sake, Geoff. You are me. I know you intimately. Certainly better than you know yourself. What's to hide?'

She was right, but it was so strange. Did I want to undress in front of another person, a woman? It was a stupid situation. I was in her body. She knew every hair and pimple on it, but I was still embarrassed.

I plucked up courage and stepped out of the trousers.

'Okay. If you are wearing a skirt you will want to wear tights, not socks and slight heels are better than those flats. Those are more for wearing with jeans or slacks. Try this on.'

She handed me a straight grey skirt. I undid the clasp and the zip, stepped into it and pulled it up to my waist.

'How high up? It's not like trousers where there is a crotch.'

'Pull it up as far as you think it should go.'

I took it up to my waist and fastened the clasp and zip.

'About here?'

'How is it?'

'A bit tight.'

'Okay, pull it up further until the waist is comfortable.'
I adjusted it, 'Here?'
'Is it comfortable?'
'Yes. It is now.'
'Because it is in the right place. It's not brain surgery, Geoff. Good clothes are worn comfortably. If it feels right, it probably is right. Look in the mirror,' she said pointing at the mirror on the far wall. It was full length.
'Looks good,' I admitted.
'Better than good. Terrific! You'd better not damage my body, Geoff Arnold. It took time and exercise getting it to look so good.'
'Yes. I'll be careful. I don't smoke or drink to excess.'
'The blouse isn't one of mine,' she said.
'No. It's Caroline's.'
'Far too big. Take it off.'
Again, it was strange taking my top off in front of her. Once more I felt stupid for worrying about it and took off the jacket and blouse.
'Try this on,' she handed me a skinny cotton top.
As I pulled it on, there was a frantic shout of 'STOP!'
'Mind your hair and make-up!' she shouted.
I was pulling it on roughly as would a man. I took more care and combed my hair back into shape where I'd mussed it.
'Here's a jacket which goes with the skirt. Try it on.'
I slipped into it and looked at myself in the mirror. God, not bad.
'Not perfect. Have you noticed what's wrong?' she asked.
No. What had I got wrong? I looked again.
'No, what? Apart from the socks.'

'Not the socks, they actually look a bit "punk" if you like that sort of thing. The skirt is twisted. The pleat isn't central.'

Oh yes. The pleat was offset to the left by several inches. It meant nothing to me. I pulled the waist around to the right and centralised it.

'Much better. Zips are always central, either back, front or side,' she said.

'Yes, I see what you mean.'

Suzy put one white, one black and two flesh-coloured skirt slips into a case followed by two full-length slips for dresses. 'Slips are worn under some skirts and dresses to make them move better and to remove transparency.'

'I don't think I'll wear dresses, Suzy,' I protested.

'Nonsense. Bet you'll be wearing them within a few weeks. Don't you want to make a good impression?'

'Well, after today's harassment I don't think so.'

'Ha! Fact of life as a girl! And don't imagine for a single moment that being dowdy will stop it. In fact, the more professional you look, the less harassment you attract. Smartness intimidates.'

Six dresses were put into the cases, followed by half a dozen skirts, four suits, a dozen blouses and several t-shirts and sweatshirt tops, plus skinny tops and vest-like tops. I saw the cost adding up with each item. I didn't mind the cost, I suppose, but thought I'd rarely wear many of the clothes. I might want to look good, but not sexy and many of these clothes were beautiful.

Next were three pairs of jeans in different colours, a couple of dozen pairs of briefs and panties, many so skimpy I was sure I would never dare to wear them. She added half a dozen bras, a few pairs of tights in different tones and colours, a couple of dozen pairs of socks, mainly ankle length but some longer, and a couple of sexy, brightly coloured, jazzy, over-knee long socks, probably thigh length. She passed me a black slip, pair of briefs and some tights.

'Put those on. You can't wear those Schulz Y-fronts under a skirt.'

'I'm going to change back into the trouser suit,' I said flatly.

She laughed. 'Not a chance. You're wearing this outfit home.'

'Not on your life,' I said firmly.

'Geoff. You are going to have to learn, so best if I can see what I look like – sorry – *you* look like!'

Extremely embarrassed, I reached up under my skirt, pulled off the Y-fronts and slipped off the socks. One leg at a time I pulled on the briefs, having to lift the skirt up to my waist.

'Much easier to put your knickers and tights on before the skirt when you are dressing normally, of course. Why're you so shy?'

'You're a girl. I can't help it.'

'I hate to state the obvious, Geoff, but so are you!'

She filled the corner of the case with tights and briefs.

'Come on, Geoff, take off your skirt, get your underwear comfy and add your tights and slip, okay? You're not showing me anything I don't know about. Finally, put your skirt back on,' she said as she put the Schulz Y-fronts, Caroline's blouse and the used socks into a polythene bag which she tucked into the side of the biggest case.

'Sorry. I keep thinking of myself as a man,' I said while struggling with the tights.

She laughed and put some sweaters into the other case, a couple of cardigans, some jackets and two fleeces. She added some accessories including three handbags which she said she didn't like any more, two pairs of trainers, some more shoes including some with heels, although no stilettos – thank God, two pairs of long pyjamas, two short and three long cotton nightdresses. The cases were now almost overflowing. She was going to put in a longer slinky nightdress but put it back in the wardrobe.

'Gerald bought me the nightdress when we went away for a weekend. I can't give it to you.' I saw tears welling up in her eyes.

'No problem, Suzy, and if you want any of it back for any reason call me.'

'Right… Thanks,' she sobbed. I put my arms around her and pulled her to me in a sympathetic hug. It was very natural. She was warm and smelled lovely. I could never hold a strange woman in such an embrace as Geoff. Even sympathy tears strangely developed in me. Most un-Geoff-like.

'Where can he be? It's such a nightmare,' she said.

'Yes. Really is.' I was always one of those men who didn't cry, yet here I was, close to tears. In fact, more than close. I went to wipe my eye with a finger but she grabbed my arm.

'Dab with a tissue or you'll smudge your make-up,' she scolded, handing me a tissue.

I dabbed my eyes and she did hers, checking her own make-up in the dressing table mirror before standing up again.

'Well,' she said, 'check yours! Is it okay? Got to think about these things, Geoff.'

I checked. My eyes were okay. I might not wear make-up after tonight. I didn't want to have to be worrying about my appearance continually.

She'd pulled herself together, put two coats into the expandable sections of the third and fourth cases and said, 'I can't give you any jewellery, purses or scarves et cetera as I will still be able to use those, but you can take the coat and beret off the hall stand. I'll get those other pairs of shoes, too,' and she popped into the hallway to bring them back in.

She asked me to turn around. I'd fully dressed now.

'Skirt's not straight again, and also higher on the left. Look at it. Just *look*, for heaven's sake!' she chided.

'Yes, must have twisted it when I pulled up the tights.'

'I know, but you have to remember to *look* at yourself when you do anything with your clothes. It's the reason we have mirrors!'

Her voice was much more powerful than her own – mine – and I had been decidedly told off. I said, 'Sorry.'

She laughed and said, 'No. I'm sorry, Geoff. I'm simply trying to make the best of this situation and I don't fancy you walking around making *me* look a mess,' and she laughed again. I joined in the laughter, but she was quickly in tears once more and I was joining her in that too. Damn it, damn it, damn it!

'Want a coffee?' she asked, regaining her composure.

'Please. That would be good.'

She looked at me strangely. 'Amazing you have my accent!'

'Yes, suppose so. Shame a knowledge of the language didn't transfer with it.' I laughed.

'Okay. Do up those cases, put them in the hall and come through.'

She left the bedroom. I tried on the shoes with the two-inch heels. Yes, I looked good. I closed the cases, moved them to the hall and made my way, gingerly in the heels, through to the lounge where Suzy had two steaming mugs of coffee waiting for us.

We sat and I gave her a breakdown of what the conference had been about, including the bad news that we didn't believe there would be any early return of minds to correct bodies.

'How much do you want for the clothes?' I asked.

'Difficult question, Geoff. I've always dressed well so this wardrobe was expensive.'

'I guessed from the quality of the trouser suit. So how much are we talking?'

'You honestly think we'll never be able to transfer back?'

'Well, never is a long time, but it's not going to be soon,' I said.

'So, we've got to live in the bodies we have?'

'Yes. It would be foolhardy to think otherwise.'

'Well, it means I have to dress my new body, so I can't give my clothes to you.'

'No, I'd never have expected you to. Suzy, I'm not rich, but neither am I poor. I am going to have to look tidy, if not smart, man or woman, so tell me a fair price.'

'I work for a PR company, so the suits were expensive, but they look terrific... *if* you check they are on straight! What you have in the suitcases probably cost more than six or seven thousand spread over three years.'

It was quite a lot more than I expected, but I knew good women's clothes were costly. 'Would four thousand be fair?'

'It seems such a lot in one lump. Three thousand,' she suggested.

'Suzy. If it's fair, nothing else matters. I have savings and if I'm going to remain a young woman I'm going to need everything you've given me. You really think I will wear the skirts and dresses?'

'I'm sure you will, once you get used to being a girl. You just need the confidence. Three thousand is fine, if I can get them back for the same amount if ever we change back.'

I'd left my cheque book in the jacket, so found where she'd packed it and extracted it. 'No problem, but don't cash it until next Monday as I'll have to transfer some money into the account,' I said and wrote the cheque for three thousand five hundred. She'd been so good about this, I didn't want to appear ungenerous. I handed over the cheque.

'Thank you, Geoff. Do call me if you need help or advice from a real female until you find your wife.'

She examined the cheque and thanked me for the extra. She returned to the bedroom. I heard some fumbling around going on and she brought out a holdall.

'I've put my gym gear in there. Tracksuit, running shorts and vests, sports bra, et cetera. If you want to keep me fit, you should go to the gym at least once a week, and I usually run a couple of miles on Saturday or Sunday. Now you've got the gear, there's no excuse.'

'I'll set up a regime.'

'Do. You won't fit in my clothes for long if you pile on the weight. Also, do hang the skirts and dresses up when you get home.'

'So kind of you, Suzy. I will. I'm not sure what it'll be like loving Caroline and being a young woman. I foresee problems for many people. At the moment, I have no idea what form she might take, if she's even alive.'

'It is so dreadful, the not knowing. I've still had no word from my mum or Gerald.'

I leaned forward to pick up my coffee.

All of a sudden, she looked horrified and said, 'Don't move a muscle, Geoff. Sit absolutely still.'

I froze. My God! Was there a tarantula or something climbing over me? Suzy ran out of the room to the bedroom and came back with a portable wall mirror.

'Don't move,' she said and held the mirror so I saw my reflection.

'What?' What was I doing wrong now?

'Your legs! You're sitting like a man. Put your knees together, damn it!'

I looked in the mirror and could see, instantly, that it was so wrong. It looked like a man in drag. Really wrong! I quickly snapped my knees shut. My God, it looked so dreadful.

'Uncanny, Suzy. I'm sure your body was trying to make me sit more decorously, but I consciously forced my legs apart for some reason as I sat forward to get the coffee.'

'Well, *nice* girls do not sit with their legs apart in skirts and dresses. You had better remember or you'll give me a bad name, and other women will talk about you. Not in a nice way, either.'

We both laughed after her scolding of me, and as I sat back on the sofa, my natural inclination was to keep my legs together to one side. This time I let it happen. It was easier as a girl, too. No tackle in the way, in fact I crossed my legs and found it comfortable either side. Once more, it seemed the natural reflexes of the transferor were able to dominate subconscious movements and characteristics. I must learn not to resist their inclination unnecessarily. I'd seen my gait was female when I saw myself in shop windows at lunchtime.

The doorbell rang.

'I should go anyway,' I said and stood up, following her into the hallway.

She opened the door and there was an explosion of sound. '*SUZY!*' a man shouted, pushed Suzy out of the way, dashed towards me, lifted me off the ground by the buttocks and hugged me tightly as he swung me around. I fought my way out of the embrace uttering some choice swearwords.

'It's me, Suzy. Gerald!' he said, puzzled at my reaction when I pulled away from him and straightened my arms to stop him coming at me a second time.

I looked at Suzy. I could see that controlled fury was hovering just beneath the surface. She looked at him and said, 'Gerry, she is not me.'

'What do you mean? It is you. No, not you. What the hell is going on?'

I had seen Gerald in photographs on Suzy's phone. He was early twenties, tall, short dark hair, good-looking (there I was again, talking about good-looking men). This man, this reincarnation of Suzy's Gerald was in his early thirties, still handsome though, perhaps more so, but not as tall or as fit.

I decided to clarify things, 'Gerald. I am not Suzy.'

He studied me carefully.

'I know I am physically her, but I am only in her body. I am not her. This lady is Suzy. Not me. You do know what has happened, don't you, and that you don't look like you anymore?'

Suzy was now in floods of tears. He moved to her, opened his arms and the two of them embraced warmly.

'Is it true, Suze?'

'Yes. I'm me. Why didn't you call me? I've been so worried. Where were you?'

'I was in Belfast, didn't have my phone and couldn't remember your number. I had it on autodial.'

They held each other in the embrace, rocking and kissing. I was so pleased for them. The love was shining through the Mindslip.

'Suzy,' I said. Gerald looked me up and down suspiciously, 'I'd forgotten to give this back to you,' and I slid the engagement ring off my finger and gave it to her.

Gerald took it from her and tried to slide it onto her finger but it was too small, 'We'll get it adjusted,' he said.

'You still love me?'

'Oh, yes. It's you I love, and you're inside this woman.'

They embraced again.

I took the mauve coat and put it on but left the beret on the hat stand. I wouldn't wear it.

'Gerald, Suzy. Let me get off and leave you to catch up. I'll get back home. Busy day tomorrow and my daughter will be home on Saturday.'

Gerald came over to me and kissed me on both cheeks. He stared into my eyes and kissed me full on the lips, not passionately, but warmly, lovingly, pressing hard against me. I didn't pull away but couldn't respond. It wouldn't be right to do either. He'd get enough of a shock when Suzy told him I was a man.

I picked up the first case and holdall, Gerald took the other cases and helped me out to the car, Suzy chasing after me with the beret which she laid on my head at a jaunty angle. She came around to the driver's side and gave me a terrific hug, pressing her cheek hard against mine and whispered, 'Keep in touch. Stay friends.'

I promised I would, climbed into the driving seat and set off.

Driving in heels and a skirt was odd, but I managed and was proud of myself when I turned off the A3 into Guildford.

When I arrived home, however, I was bursting. While a man would simply have stopped and had a leak behind a hedge or the car door, my new persona couldn't. I had to hold it and, even breaking the speed limit towards the end, only just got to the loo in time, the tights, skirt, slip and panties almost causing an accident. I wouldn't allow it to happen again. I resolved to always make sure I peed before a journey in future. I was learning some of the less obvious disadvantages of being a woman.

19 LONG AND WINDING ROAD

How is the greyhound's escape plan progressing?

The man opened the door and she walked through it on her choker lead. He was around thirty and seemed to truly love her, continually reaching down and scratching her neck and behind her ear which felt unexpectedly good.

They set off along the path.

'Strange times, Bunty, strange times. Do you recognise me, I wonder?' his monologue continued as they reached the gate.

They made a right into a street of semi-detached houses. She guessed he was a bachelor or widower and lonely too. What did he do for a living?

'Nice being young again. Must say. What do you think, Bunty?' and he gave her a pat on the head as she walked to heel, trying to give the impression she was obedient until the opportunity to flee arose.

'Everyone's changed. Weird, Bunty, the woman in the newsagent's is now a ten-year-old boy. Had to laugh. She was always so nasty to the ten-year-old boys who shoplifted.' He laughed out loud.

She seemed to be his companion and confidante. She liked his monologue.

'I was driving to work when it happened. All of a sudden, I was this man at a check-out in the supermarket. Rushed to work 'cos I had to finish a fridge repair for delivery this morning. I was nearly two miles away from the workshop.'

They stepped out around an abandoned car.

'Only four others turned up for work and no boss. Mrs Ireland had to let me in, and she was only a teenager. The delivery van didn't come so the fridge was still there tonight. Undelivered. Did my bit, though. I didn't let anyone down.'

A crow dashed out of the hedge and attacked his shoe. Very strange behaviour. He kicked it gently away and it half ran, half flew across the road, narrowly being missed by a car.

'See that, Bunt? Why'd it do that? Don't know what's happening to things. Kept fumbling with my tools. Bloody government's fault – all this.'

She was his sounding board for all things fair and foul. She would be hurting him when she ran.

'You are being good, Bunty, no pulling. Have you changed places with some better trained dog? Ha-ha. Wish they could have given you a younger body, Bunt.'

So, she was not young, which explained the pain in her hip and the fluttering in her chest. She pulled on the lead to sniff the hedge. God, everything smelled so strong. She'd done it to give the impression she wasn't too obedient. She didn't want to raise suspicions of her harbouring a higher intelligence.

'We'll get you to the vet on Monday, Bunt. Want to check the sore on your front leg. How'd you do that?'

What sore? She counted to twenty to be sure he wouldn't know it was a reaction to what he'd said, stopped and checked her front legs. Oh yes, the right one had a raw patch. Had she done it during the day, jumping up and down? She hadn't noticed anything. She licked it and they walked on.

'Sit,' he snapped as they came to the major road and she, almost automatically, sat back on her haunches. Was Bunty the dog influencing her subconscious? She re-examined the sore on her leg. It was raw and, now she was aware of it, it was hurting.

A few cars passed by and the odd lorry. There were lots of cars on the pavement and several had obviously been involved in crashes. Others weaved their way between them. A blurred but readable sign in the distance said, "Welwyn Garden City" and "Hitchin" straight on and "Hertford" to the right.

Hitchin was north of Hatfield, so, when she got free, she'd need to come back here and follow the road south.

'Come on, Bunt, wake up, old girl,' he said and yanked on the lead to make her rise and walk at his side across the road. He directed her to the right where they had to walk into the road to skirt a Ford Focus which had crashed into a lamppost, almost knocking it over. She needed to keep herself orientated. The sun was behind her to the left so southwest with it being evening. The road was roughly south-north which would be right. The nova, which had risen again, confused her senses. She wanted to go the other way. They stepped out around another crashed vehicle.

'Don't know what they're going to do with all these abandoned cars, Bunty. Tried to find mine on the way home, but it wasn't where I was when this thing happened. Someone must have it.'

On the far side of the road, there was an ambulance and people were lifting someone from a wreck. It was a body. She looked the other way.

'Not long now, Bunt,' he said enthusiastically. What did that mean?

At the next corner, they went left towards the real sun and walked at a leisurely pace. How could she break free? He had the end of the lead wrapped three times around his hand. She wouldn't be able to yank herself free and any failed attempt at escape would make a second attempt impossible. Patience, she cautioned herself, patience. Wait for the certain escape opportunity and go for it.

After another two to three hundred yards they took a left into an area of parkland. She couldn't be this lucky. Was he going to let her run free? She hoped so, desperately.

Once inside the boundary of the park, he led her over to the side of the grass to a hedged area.

'Okay, Bunt. Do your business, girl.'

God, was he serious? He wanted her to crap here? Strangely she did want to go. Was this her regular trip to the ablutions? She mustn't cause any suspicion. She took an almost sitting posture, separated her back legs and peed. So embarrassing. She stood again.

'Not ready yet, old girl?' He led her on slowly along the park boundary.

She knew, to him, she was a dog. It was bad enough having to relieve her bladder in front of him, but the "other" – could she do it with him watching? She was human. Every fibre of her being didn't want to have to pass a motion in front of him.

'Come on, Bunty. Can't play with your ball until you've done, girl.'

Ball. Ball meant throwing and chasing and catching and he'd have to release her. She pulled him closer to the hedge and faced him. Was it better to face him or away from him? She reluctantly adopted the position and strained to force the bowel movement. It took less than a minute and it was done. She walked away from it and he picked it up with his hand inside a bag, turned it inside out, knotted it and disposed of it in a black plastic bin on a pole. How demeaning. What about any on her anus? As a human, she'd have needed to wipe it. Why didn't she need to as a dog? Yet another mystery, but animals never seemed to have a need to wipe their bums. Why? She decided it was better not thought about.

He pulled a luminous green tennis ball from his pocket and held it in his hand in front of her. A strange immediate lust for something struck her, an instinct she'd be chasing this thing. Did her host still have enough control over her actions to make her chase it? There was an increase in her heart rate and a growing anticipation. Without conscious control, she found her tail swishing back and forth.

He bent and disconnected the lead from the choker collar. She was free. He threw the ball. She watched it but didn't move.

'Go on, fetch!' he shouted.

She faced this nice young man who had once been an old man. What she was about to do would break his heart. She reached up to his hand and licked it affectionately, several times.

'What's up, Bunty? Don't you want to play?'

She moved back a few feet, sat and shook her head slowly from side to side. He frowned, walked towards her, she backed off, he stood still. The two species eyed each other. He scowled, offered his hand towards her, but now knew something was wrong and there was no way she was going to let him get within grabbing distance of her choker collar. She walked towards the park exit.

'Bunty, come here!'

She faced him again, sat and shook her head several times, stood and continued to walk.

'Come here. You *bad* girl. *Come here*!' he shouted and chased her.

She broke into an easy stride and left him far behind.

Even when she reached the main road, she still heard his calls for her to return. He'd realise what had happened soon enough, but she hated the idea he'd lost his pet and his only company. Still, he was a young man now, perhaps he'd find love in his new guise. Heading away from Hitchin she ran southwards at a leisurely pace, taking extreme care when avoiding abandoned vehicles.

The roads made life difficult. Twice she had to reach up to press the "cross" button and worried it would draw attention to her. Most people didn't seem interested though. When she crossed roads alone, she took extra special care there was no traffic coming. People might not be as aware of a dog crossing as they would a person. There was also a lot of zigzagging going on as cars avoided the abandoned vehicles. Several were damaged, particularly at the back and front where they had run into each other.

It didn't take long to reach the A1(M) motorway by the Comet roundabout, so named because an ancient, red comet aeroplane statue still stood beside the art deco building which was now a chain hotel. At least, this was a landmark she recognised, but following roads offered too much danger with her poor eyesight. She ran southwards parallel to the road but outside its fence.

It wasn't as easy as she expected. Twice she hurt herself climbing gates, and she snagged her left hind leg on some barbed wire which now stung. She'd be better travelling inside the motorway fence. At least there'd be no obstructions, except crashed cars, until she got to London. She'd also expected it to get dark, but as the sun dipped towards the horizon, Betelgeuse climbed even higher and was almost as bright as full daylight. Yes, the road would be the safer option.

She encountered more seriously damaged vehicles here, pushed onto the hard shoulder. Some had run off the road and down the slopes to either side. She passed at least one burned out and others still smouldering. At one location, a squad of people was pushing vehicles off the carriageway and bulldozing wrecks with a mechanical digger. Traffic was flowing freely in the outer two lanes as these squads cleared the accidents. She saw people loading body bags into a transit van on the other side. She tried not to watch and continued at an easy pace.

The miles passed, it should have been dusk, but Betelgeuse was casting as much daylight as the sun. She'd have to sleep in daylight. She descended the embankment, curled up in a shaded spot beneath a hawthorn hedge and made herself comfortable. No sooner had she closed her eyes than sleep descended.

Her peaceful slumber didn't last. A few hours later, a threatening growl awoke her.

20 TEN DOWNING STREET
Geoff attends a COBRA meeting

During the morning, I carried out various housekeeping duties including shopping. Staff at the supermarket thought the supply chain would soon sort itself out, but shelves were poorly stocked and dairy products almost non-existent. Milk was restricted to a single litre per customer.

The news told us tests were available to check each farm animal for awareness, and those who passed were sent to secure areas in farms, having been told they would be the first to be repatriated to their bodies if a way to do so could be found. The dairy industry would adapt. Cows full of milk had to be milked eventually, and even those with human intelligence found it to be in their own interests to comply for the time being. Many found it a huge relief to have their overfull udders drained, but yes-no communication was a real problem when they tried to express themselves.

The biggest problem was dairy cattle occupied by other creatures' minds. They didn't know the routine and caused chaos. Predators in the minds of domesticated animals also attacked their neighbours and had to be put down. It was an awful mess.

In homes, some cats had a compelling need to escape, perhaps occupied by sheep or chickens unfamiliar with human company. Similar problems were occurring with dogs, and warnings of attacks were taken most seriously. The army was placed on standby to deal with vicious animals in whatever guise they took. Some horses refused to be mounted and other creatures containing domestic pets behaved strangely in the countryside.

Later, I met James for lunch at the Festival Hall restaurant. The city was busier and, having had Suzy's lessons, I watched people with amusement. It was pretty obvious who were male transferees by the poor way they dressed. Some older women dressed in jeans and sloppy pullovers without bras and there were many girls with twisted skirts and men with no socks.

On the basis that Suzy had told me I only needed confidence to wear a skirt, I bit the bullet and wore a pin-striped knee-length skirt suit with a cotton top. I checked everything several times before leaving the house. The skirt was straight and level, my underwear hidden by the slip, my bra wasn't visible through the top, my hair was neat and tidy. Suzy would have been proud of me. James was most impressed and called me "stylish". Compared with how I'd dressed the previous day, I was. No harassment today either, although I was aware of many appreciative glances on the train and the walk through to the Festival Hall. It amused me. If only they knew it was a man they were admiring.

I told James about my visit to Suzy's and we wondered how she had got on with Gerald after I left? At least, they hadn't changed sex, and were a similar age despite both losing a few years. We hoped they were able to comfort each other, and there would still be love for them.

James's wife being a man was obviously a problem for him and my own change of sex seriously worried me. James said Helen had moved into the spare room although they still conversed normally and ate together. He guessed his relationship was doomed in the long term.

Whichever gender Caroline turned out to be was going to be a problem for me. We could maybe have a loving same sex relationship if she was still female, but the thought of sex with a man was horrific to me. I certainly understood James' dilemma. There was little we could do to ease each other's minds and our lunchtime chat soon returned to the question of Mindslip.

Following lunch, a smart elderly gentleman was awaiting us. Only James and I were from our group, the remainder of whom were continuing to meet in other parts of the complex. The aide checked us all off on his clipboard, and we boarded a waiting coach for Number Ten.

Twenty minutes later, I was in Downing Street for the first time in my life, and an assistant ushered us into the Cabinet Office Briefing Room A, the famous COBRA. The name sounds so intriguing but it was just a boring acronym.

It wasn't particularly large as a room but housed a huge teak table with a central leather rectangle surrounded by inlaid walnut. About twenty black leather chairs ringed the table with a similar number against the walls. A classy place for a meeting.

The workshop heads occupied the main seats around the table. Four seats at the end of the table were empty. Along with other deputies and minute takers, I sat in one of the extra chairs, carefully, with my knees together or legs crossed. I was a quick learner. It was a strange novelty being able to cross my legs in either direction.

We'd been there for a few minutes, chatting amongst ourselves, when the door opened. Four people entered, including the new youthful Prime Minister. We all stood.

The four sat at the head of the table, and another man with a notepad sat behind them with four others.

'Ladies and gentlemen,' said Charles Browning, waving everyone to sit and catching sight of the child on his right, 'and children, I suppose. Instead, let me simply say, revered citizens, welcome to the Cabinet Office.

'I suppose you will all know me from the television bulletins. I am gradually becoming accustomed to my new, youthful existence. Those alongside me will not be familiar to you.

'On my right, here, is the Home Secretary, Pam Jury.' A young woman, perhaps eighteen or twenty with long blonde hair, but dressed more formally than would be normal for such a young individual, smiled.

'On my left, Ron Clayton, our Defence Minister. Unfortunately, we cannot trace General Sir William Austin so, in the interim, I have appointed his deputy, Mr Clayton.'

Mr Clayton appeared to be in his early forties. I didn't know what age the original had been, so had no way of judging whether his real self was older or younger.

'This young man,' the Prime Minister continued, directing our attention to a sixteen-year-old youth, 'is Marion Whitfield, who is Minister for Science and Technology. Behind us, is the Cabinet Secretary and the heads of the Royal Air Force, Army, Royal Navy and the Chief of Staff. Excuse their lack of uniforms. They are being made as I speak.

'Our appearances, as with yours, might seem incongruous, but I would remind everyone here we are all experts in our own fields. I caution everyone to give due respect to the views expressed, without being prejudiced by apparent ages. The event, which now goes by the name "Mindslip" is, I fear, going to create a whole new area of discrimination, although it will destroy the more traditional forms like gender and shade of skin.

'We face a serious crisis not of our own making. Some countries have been dealing with it better than others. The USA now has an eight-year old boy in the White House. The German Chancellor is in another young male child. Some of the African countries are in chaos, and a civil war is taking place in the Arabian Peninsula where female transferee leaders of Yemen and Saudi have ironically been refused access to the seats of power.

'Anyway, I shouldn't really make light of such an incongruous situation, but it relieves the tension, and we have incredibly difficult decisions to make because of this crisis. We might all appreciate the unexpected changes to other nations' cultures and customs which this will ignite. Everything said in this room is confidential, so we can relax a little.

'Down to business. Marion, you take the helm.'

The sixteen-year-old minister for science stood up and spoke confidently, telling us how the original workshops had been established and asking for a report from each head. It was extremely strange hearing confidence and authority from such a young individual.

After the reports, some general discussion followed.

The meeting told us little new. Mindslip was universal – as far as was known, no creature avoided the process. Mindslipping within individual species seemed to be the norm, but there were many instances of interspecies transfers. We had no way of telling if a human was occupied by the minds of insects or larger mammals, but tests were being designed for just such a purpose.

Mindslip was also irreversible, at least in any mass sense, but there was some hope of a reversal on a one-to-one basis, although it would be a long time coming. No one was sure how it could actually be achieved.

It was considered that the economies of most western countries, plus Russia, China, the Far East, India, and Pakistan would remain secure. Australia, New Zealand, Brazil, Argentina, and Chile were also recovering. The US and Canada were soon organised but Central America had mixed fortunes, similar to some South American regimes.

In Europe, the Pope, now being in a middle-aged woman's body, was causing uproar in Catholic circles, some wanting "him" replaced, others saying it was the work of the devil.

Africa and the Middle East were suffering most, although Israel had rapidly sorted itself out – as might be expected. Within Africa, South Africa was faring best, and in the Middle East it was, unexpectedly, Iran and Libya who were taking the lead.

We spent the next couple of hours discussing the findings, during which I presented what we knew about supernovae and the types of radiation we had encountered. Afterwards, Marion Whitfield summed up the results and swore us to secrecy.

Finally, the PM dismissed us. My time in the limelight at the United Kingdom seat of power was over. We drifted off through the backdoor of Number Ten into obscurity, a few of us invading a local hostelry for a drink or two.

At five o'clock, I boarded the train back to Guildford. The two suns were in the sky again playing havoc with the shadows. The next day, I'd be picking up Sandra from St Pancras. How was I going to tell a young child she was going to be in a woman's body from here on in? I was thankful the Damay girl was only twenty-two. Five year's intensive education might do the trick and get Sandra up to speed. She'd been a clever child and was a quick learner.

At home, there were no more answerphone messages. Still no word from Caroline or Wilson. I was beginning to think the worst.

I would have to deal with my sex change before I found myself face-to-face with Sandra at St Pancras station. I rang Jean Damay, and he let me speak to my daughter.

'How are you, darling?'

'Oo are you?'

'Has anyone explained what has happened, Limpet?'

'Only my daddy callz me Limpet.'

'Do you know about people slipping from one body to another, Sandra?'

'A bit.'

'Well it has happened to everyone. You've moved into the body of Mr Damay's daughter. Did you know everyone had changed bodies?'

'Zey said I had sifted.'

'Yes, well I've shifted, too. I'm your dad, but I'm in a lady's body, Limpet.'

Silence.

'I'm still Daddy, but I'm now a woman.'

'No.'

'Yes, Limpet. Just like you are now grown-up. It is still you inside. I'm inside this woman.'

Silence.

'I love you, Limpet. It is me. Remember the funfair at Southsea, and we went on the dodgems? It is still me even if I sound different. Ask me a question only your dad would be able to answer.'

The line remained quiet for a while longer. She said, 'Vot's my favourite toy?'

'Your toy kitchen,' I said, hoping it hadn't changed recently.

'Oh, Daddy. Vhy am I in Lafrans?'

'France, Limpet. It's called France. The people who live there call it La France. It is all part of it, Sandra. We moved as well as changed. You moved to France. You'll be home tomorrow. I'll be waiting at the train station.'

'Yes please, Daddy.'

'Limpet. You know you don't look the same as you did?'

'Yes.'

'Mr Damay has given me a picture of you via the Internet, so I will recognise you. You look lovely. The station will be very busy and I want you to find me easily.'

'Yes. I'll zee you.'

'No, darling. I've changed, too. I'm a young woman like you now. I will have your panda with me. You know your panda.'

'Oh, yes. I've missed 'im.'

'Well, I'll be holding him up beside my face so you know it is me. Do you understand?'

'Yes. By your face.'

'That's right, darling. Now you must promise me not to leave the station until I find you, and you find me. Do you understand?'

'Yes, Daddy.'

'Okay, Limpet. I'm sending Mr Damay a picture of me. He'll give it to you. Don't go off with anyone else except the woman in the picture. Remember only I will look like the picture and only I will have your panda. Are you sure you understand?'

'Yes Daddy.'

'I'll meet you tomorrow. Can you give the phone to Mr Damay now?'

'It's Missyer Damay.'

'Yes, I know, Sandra. I love you, Limpet. Give the phone to him.'

'Madame Arnold?' he asked.

'Well, in reality I am Monsieur Arnold in a woman's body, but let's not confuse things. What will Sandra be wearing?'

'Oui, I understand. She has a green coat in a light pastel. She'll also have a, how you say, red scar.'

'Scarf?'

'Oui, scarf.'

'Give me your email address and I'll send an image of my new face to give to Sandra.'

'Oui. Jean point Damay at telefrance point fr. Don't forget the point before Damay.'

'Thanks. Call me when the train departs, so I know for certain she is on it. I'll send the image in the next few minutes.'

'Oui, of course.'

'I'll be holding her toy panda near my face when the train arrives. You know a panda?'

'Yes. Black and white animal toy.'

'Please remind her. Thank you so much for being so kind to her. I hope everything works out for your families too.'

'Oui. It is not a good situation.'

'I'll let you know when I've got her.'

Suzy's emotions took me over. There were tears in my eyes for poor Sandra, but also for Wilson. Where was my son? And where was my wife? Why nothing at all from either of them? I resisted the impulse to run the back of my hand over my eyes, ran to the bedroom for a tissue to dab, and checked they were still okay in the dressing-table mirror.

If I was going to be doing a lot of this crying, mascara and eyeliner might not be ideal for me. Now I knew why women carried mirrors in their handbags. I'd have to borrow one of Caroline's.

After dinner and a couple of large glasses of chardonnay; shame I no longer liked whisky, I watched the news and decided to have an early night. I took the cordless phone up to the bedroom where I undressed, marvelling at the reflection of the most gorgeous, young woman performing a striptease in the mirror.

I looked at myself from various angles and felt strange sensations in my groin. It had to be a form of arousal. I was becoming aroused by looking at myself. Weird. It proved I was still Geoff inside. My skin was immaculate. Suzy wouldn't mind if I did some investigating. I lifted my breasts and enjoyed the feeling. Guilt overcame me anew, but I was resigned to being in my new body permanently and it was almost certain Suzy and Gerald, in their new bodies, had made love last night. Surely it wouldn't hurt for me to explore my sexuality in this new form.

I climbed into bed. Curiosity overtook my reticence; exploration morphed into desire; energy became determination; and in surprisingly short measure, my new body absolutely astonished and delighted me by generating the most thrilling and unique experience. It left me breathless, with my thighs trembling, but with an incredibly satisfying inner warmth radiating outwards, like the comforting heat of dying embers. Spectacular.

I lay still for ages, listening to my breathing returning to normal and my heart rate gradually subsiding after my exertions. Thirty minutes later, I still felt warm, relaxed, and simply marvellous. I curled up in the foetal position, pulled Caroline's pillow into my arms and enjoyed my unexpected and surprisingly enduring, post-orgasmic glow until I drifted into sleep. I'd had no idea Caroline experienced something like this during our lovemaking. I knew she enjoyed it, but this was sensational.

I was going to enjoy some aspects of being a woman after all!

21 DEADLY ASSAILANT

A growl has awoken the greyhound from her slumber

She was instantly alert. Another dog, bigger than her, a German Shepherd, was standing a few yards away in a threatening stance. Its hair bristled along its back, a low, rumbling growl was breaking the silence. This was serious. Her instinct told her she was in trouble. This was no human in a dog's body, this might not even be a dog in a dog's body. Its demeanour was of a wild animal. It saw her as prey.

She stood, cautiously, keeping her eyes on her adversary's, checking her orientation. She could run south away from it. She must get up the slope to the road before it closed the gap.

It growled and took a half step forward.

She barked loudly, causing it to step back in surprise, and she was off, running diagonally up the slope with the Alsatian in pursuit. Her tactic had given her a head start. Being a greyhound, she might be faster in a sprint, but she was aware age was against her. By the top of the slope, she had opened the gap and ran with long athletic strides. The traffic was much lighter, owing to the lateness of the hour. She guessed it must be the small hours as the supernova was high in the sky, creating its strange coloured daylight.

The pursuer fell back rapidly, but her breathing was not good. She couldn't maintain this pace for long. Passing under a motorway bridge, she stopped fifty yards beyond it. Where was her pursuer? It was still coming.

Continuing southwards at an easy pace, she hoped to out-distance her would-be assailant. Surely it would lose interest and go off in search of more available prey. There were sheep in the field on the right about a mile earlier, but the Alsatian hadn't seemed interested in them.

At a bridge a mile further on, she stopped. The dog was still coming and, worse, the gap was closing. She was tiring, running out of energy. She needed a different strategy. Hiding was out of the question. Its sense of smell would suss out wherever she was. Another idea came to mind. She would apply her intelligence against it. A dangerous strategy but rapidly becoming her only option. The hard shoulder was clear of wrecks on this stretch of road. She sat facing him and breathed deeply to recover, ready to put her hastily conceived plan into action.

As the panting German Shepherd approached, it slowed to a walk, wary of its prey's strange behaviour. She moved to the outside edge of the hard shoulder beside the grass and sat still. It continued its approach, hackles rising as it neared. When it was just ten feet away, she put her plan into action. She ran straight at her assailant as if attacking. This caused it to crouch. At the last second, she diverted around it. Too late, it tried to lunge towards her, but she'd been too quick. Once she was twenty to thirty feet beyond the dog, she stopped and faced it. Now she was also facing the traffic.

The Alsatian was puzzled by her tactics. Step by step, it approached again, slowly and deliberately as if it knew it had sapped its prey's strength but was wary of any further tricks. She eased her way leftwards, closer to the main carriageway as the gap narrowed.

A single lorry in the distance approached along the inside lane. There was no traffic in the middle or outside lanes. It was crucial it was a lone vehicle and she was in luck. The truck approached. The dog closed the gap. She kept her eyes on both, flitting between each of them. Two hundred yards, one hundred, fifty, twenty-five.

She sprang out into the road, accelerated across the tarmac surface, heard a dull thud and squeal of brakes behind her. She'd reached the central reservation and spun around quickly in case she needed to run again.

Her assailant was lying still at the outer edge of the inside lane. God, it had almost avoided the vehicle which was now stopping on the hard shoulder a couple of hundred yards further to the north. The Alsatian had been no more than a second short of escaping her trap. She hadn't expected it to be so fast. She'd been lucky. Incredibly lucky, but her luck appeared to have killed the dog outright.

Having once seen the film, *Halloween*, she wanted to be certain her stalker was dead.

She waited. A few cars flew by in the central and outside lane. One van swerved to avoid the obstruction. The road was clear now, a few lights way in the distance. She crossed the outer lanes, approached the German Shepherd and saw it was lying in a pool of blood, its stomach split open when four sets of wheels had hit it. It was most certainly dead.

The driver was walking back to find out what he'd hit, so she ambled southwards along the hard shoulder, her hip hurting more than ever and her heart still beating erratically. She'd survived, but only just. She needed rest, went down the slope a mile further on and curled up to sleep again, but with enough space to be able to run in any direction if another predator should arrive. She licked the sore on her leg to ensure it was clean. It hurt.

Thankfully her sleep was not disturbed. She awoke refreshed but aching all over.

Being built for racing, this endurance run was not at all easy. She left the motorway at Potters Bar, made her way past Borehamwood and on towards Harrow. Built-up areas had their drawbacks, but it was easier than trying to move cross country.

She drank from a river, but hunger was growing. In Harrow, she sauntered along the shopping street until she came to a butcher's. She sat outside, hoping to draw attention to herself.

'Look 'ere, Fred,' some woman inside said, 'there's a dog at the door.'

'Dog at everyone's door,' was the jovial reply.

'No. Serious, Fred. It's an ol' grey'ound,' the first speaker said.

Was she visually old? How did you tell when a greyhound was old?

'Oh, yeah. Give it this.'

There was the movement of something from one hand to another in a piece of greaseproof paper.

A large woman in white, the first voice, brought it out and emptied its contents on the path to the left of the door. Raw meat. Ugh! She liked rare steaks, but not blue and this was uncooked. Slowly and deliberately she shook her head from side to side with the most exaggerated movements she could muster. She looked pointedly back into the woman's eyes.

'Ha. You don' like raw meat?' she asked rhetorically and when the greyhound shook its head, the puzzled woman straightened up and put her hands on her hips.

'This dog 'as some'n inside it,' she said to her colleague. When her gaze returned to her, the dog nodded vigorously.

The woman reached for her collar. Oh, no. She wasn't having that. She took two steps back and sat again. The woman stood back upright and the dog moved forward again.

'You don't like raw meat?' The dog shook her head.

'Wot would yer like?' she said.

The dog had no way to answer her so simply raised her eyebrows quizzically.

'Silly me. You can' speak. Wanna pie, cooked pie?'

The dog nodded enthusiastically.

'Come on in,' and the woman moved aside to let her pass.

She shook her head. There was no way she wanted to risk capture.

'Okay. Wait 'ere.'

She went back into the shop and announced to her colleague, 'It's one o' them 'umans in a animal, Fred. I'm givin' it a steak pie.'

'What? Don't be daft, Pete.'

'Honest, it wants somefink to eat and I'm giving it a pie,' said Pete the woman. A sound of exasperation came from the man.

Gosh, the dog thought, some people are in different sexes! She waited patiently, starving, her stomach rumbling. She licked the sore on her leg. It tasted bad and might be infected.

Pete came out and put a plate on the floor with a steak pie on it, broken open by a fork. She approached it and sniffed. Lovely. Pete reached down, perhaps to pat her, but she jumped back, all too conscious of the fact anyone grabbing the collar would have her trapped again.

'Okay, okay, won' touch yer. You eat yer pie,' the woman said and stepped back into the shop to give her confidence.

Oh boy, what a lovely pie! She bolted it down. Wonderful. Hot meat, delicious gravy and tasty pastry too. Pete brought her some water in a bowl, took away the plate and brought it back with another pie. She was so grateful and made short work of the second pie too, lapped some more water and sat wagging her tail.

'Enjoy yer lunch?' female Pete asked, and the dog nodded.

She committed the shop name to memory, stood, wagged her tail, gave a small bark and moved on. If the opportunity arose in the future, she'd tell Pete, the woman, how grateful she'd been. She left the shopping street and followed south-westerly signs. How far had she come? Maybe twenty-five miles and a similar distance still to cover. Halfway home.

Her feet hurt, her hip hurt, and her sore irritated. She limped slowly along the road, entered a cemetery, curled up behind a large gravestone and yew tree and fell asleep.

She ached dreadfully when she awoke, relieved herself away from the graves and re-joined the road.

As she moved, the pain in her hip became less noticeable, but the pads of her feet were sore. She stopped and examined them. Her front feet were not too bad but both back feet were almost raw. Oh well, nothing for it but to walk on. Wherever possible she stuck to grass verges for a softer walk.

Unable to run, she was limping badly and needed some more food.

She passed a Spar supermarket and the doors opened. There was no one else around. They closed again. She walked the other way and they opened once more.

She peered into the shop and saw the bread was all on the left of the shop, inside the door. She walked past again, saw the doors open, sat and counted. One thousand and one, one thousand and two, one thousand and three, one thousand and four, one thousand and five, one thousand – and they shut. About five and a half seconds.

She stood up, the doors opened, she dashed into the supermarket, grabbed an unwrapped Hovis loaf and was back out again in less than two seconds. A boy in the shop shouted, 'Oi, there's a dog stealing a loaf,' but she was long gone and saw no sign of pursuit.

She walked along the street, checking from time to time for anyone following her and, when she was sure she'd got away with her heist, she took a side street and ate her loaf in the backyard of a haberdashery store.

About half an hour later, she returned to the supermarket and carried out the same smash and grab, but this time taking a pack of Crawfords shortbread. The second heist did result in a pursuit by two men, but even with sore feet she was more than a match for them. Once clear of the shopping area, she sat and ate her ill-gotten gains beside a boating pond, from which she also drank her fill. She wished her feet weren't so sore. If she'd known the motorway's hard shoulder would do such damage, she'd have taken more care to stay on grass, but there was no point in crying over spilt milk. She had to get on her way.

The second half of her journey took three days and, a mile from her destination, her energy had gone. Her feet hurt so badly she couldn't continue. Both rear feet were bleeding, as was her left front paw. To make matters worse, she seemed to have picked up an infestation of fleas which irritated continually.

She was determined to cover the last mile of her journey in the morning. She couldn't fail at the final hurdle, surely? Absolutely exhausted, she sought refuge under a garden hedge and fell asleep, whimpering from the throbbing pain of her feet.

22 FAMILY

Geoff meets the Eurostar

Saturday

Dressing today was with collecting Sandra in mind. I showered without wetting my hair to save time, pulled on ankle socks, a tight pair of maroon jeans and powder blue jumper.

Remembering Suzy's advice, I used the full-length mirror. Would my sexual desire for my new body eventually fade? As a man, I occasionally would use a mirror to check I was smart, but I never saw myself as a desirable man. What I saw now was incredibly desirable. Lust for oneself, what a strange sensation. I looked fabulous in this casual outfit. I saw how the coins, keys and hankie made the jeans a bit lumpy on the one side but decided to live with it. Women's failure to use pockets for their intended purpose always seemed odd to me. I resolved to buy a small wallet for my notes and bank cards today. I'd have to buy some clothes for Sandra, so shopping was inevitable. I carried my daughter's panda toy in a small bag.

The call arrived from Jean Damay, and I'd need to be at St Pancras for midday.

Two men catcalled me on the way to the train. It was so annoying. I was angry but resisted the impulse to respond.

Waterloo wasn't so busy today, and the tube to St Pancras wasn't full either. I arrived early. I spoke to officials, and they agreed to let me onto the platform, as Jean said Sandra was in a carriage towards the rear of the train.

I'd bought a magazine to read and sat on one of the platform benches. What on earth had made me choose

Hello? Suzy, I guess. I found I wasn't reading it. My mind was rehearsing different scenarios for meeting Sandra. What if she refused to believe it was me? What if she wasn't on the train or someone convinced her to change coats and I wouldn't recognise her? I kept taking the picture of her from my bag and studied the face. I mustn't get this meeting wrong.

Slightly behind schedule, the Eurostar approached the station, its sleek, futuristic lines a delight to watch. I held the panda at face height as the doors opened and the passengers disembarked. I was riddled with anxiety. Please let it be okay.

In seconds, the platform was a mass of people, all heading for the exit, many carrying cases, but an equal number with little or no luggage at all. I searched for the green coat both up and down the train.

Nearby, I saw a middle-aged lady step off the train with another woman in a green coat. Was it Sandra?

The lady saw me, pointed at me and kissed the woman in the green coat on both cheeks. She ran flat out towards me, but slowed to a halt as she got closer. She'd seen the panda but was now trying to comprehend the reality of me in Suzy's body. I waved the toy. She examined a piece of paper, probably the printout made by Jean from my webcam picture, looked back at me, ran over to me, and threw herself into my arms. We hugged tightly as other passengers treated us like a traffic island.

'Daddy, oh, Daddy. Ooo are my daddy?' she asked in her odd childish French accent.

'Yes, Limpet. It's me. How lovely you're back. I've so missed you. Here's Panda,' I said.

She took the well-worn toy and pressed it to her cheek.

My eight-year-old daughter was now taller than me, slim, with long mahogany-brown hair instead of her ebony locks, and attractive narrow face with dark eyes and long lashes. She was typically French in appearance. I hugged her again and we stood in our embrace for five or more minutes.

'Come on, Sandra. Some clothes shopping to do, and then we can go home.'

I took her hand. Some of Caroline's things might fit her, but I decided it would be a good idea to get her some casual clothes. It was bad enough dressing myself without having to worry about dressing my adult eight-year-old.

Emerging from the station, I telephoned Jean with the news Sandra had arrived safely.

We entered a large store and made a beeline for the women's section. We had to wait for an assistant. I needed help and explained Sandra was only eight, and I was her father so would be no help in the selection.

'Sorry, Madam, I need to ask if you have enough cash or a valid credit or debit card?'

'Oh, of course, yes. Credit card.'

'And you know the PIN?'

'Yes.'

'Sorry, I had to ask.'

'No, I understand. Collected my new cards yesterday.'

We purchased lots of easy-to-wear clothes and I had Sandra choose as many of them as possible. Laden with a dozen bags, we caught a cab to Waterloo and took the train back to Guildford.

Entering home, I had Sandra run all the bags up to Wilson's room and said we'd sort things out later. I checked the answerphone; still no message from Wilson or Caroline.

That was bad news indeed. My heart sank. There had been nothing from them for four days.

I joined my daughter upstairs, and we cleared out her drawers and wardrobe and hung up her new clothes, placing the old clothes in bin bags and storing them in Wilson's room.

Later, Sandra was sitting in her bed in pyjamas reading one of her books about the Gruffalo. A bit young for her, but one of her favourites, so I guessed she was reading it as a sort of security blanket. I mustn't forget she was a grown woman of twenty-two, but with the mind of a child. She'd need protection from sexual predators. I wondered what ideas there were about educating such people. There must be hundreds of thousands of children in adult bodies. The news said the information centres would attempt to be open every day, so I resolved to visit ours the next day.

«‹«o»›»

In the middle of the night there was a scream.

'Mummy, Mummy!'

I grabbed my dressing gown and dashed through to Sandra's room. She was sitting up in bed bawling her eyes out. I put my arm around her shoulder, picked panda off the floor and helped her cuddle it.

'It's all right, Limpet. Daddy's here. Was it a bad dream?' I sat on the bed beside her.

'Yes. I vas lost in Lafrans again.' She sat up and I put my arm around her shoulder. So strange. She was so much larger than me.

'Oh, Sandra, you're home now. You're safe now. Daddy's here. I'll keep you safe, Limpet.' She was shaking with the trauma of the dream.

She cried, deep sobbing tears, turned towards me and held me so tightly, unaware of her own strength, crushing me to her like her panda. Gradually the tears subsided, and the grip loosened.

'You get some sleep, Sandra, and tomorrow, we'll go through everything you've been doing. You can tell me all about your great adventure. You're okay now, aren't you?'

'Yes. Jes got frightened.'

'I know. Call me again if you need to. I'm right next door.'

I eased her back into the bed and sat on the side of it, squeezing her hands. I wiped her tears away with a tissue and sat with her for another five minutes.

'You can come in with me if you want, Limpet,' I said.

She shook her head and I set the main light glowing on the dimmer switch when I left, so that she wouldn't be in complete darkness. Some of the nova's light penetrated the curtains too. Would I ever get used to twenty-four-hour daylight?

In my room, after shedding my dressing gown, I put on a nightdress in case Sandra did decide to join me. Normally I wore nothing. I had a fretful night myself and lay awake, trying to figure out our personal future. I'd have to go to work, and I couldn't leave Sandra on her own. Could the information centre put me in touch with babysitters? What if the hospital wanted me to take Sandra's body home, too, with a baby or toddler in it? What a mess! It was a double loss. I'd never see my darling Limpet as she was again.

I fell into a fitful sleep.

«‹‹o››»

There were no more nightmares during the night. Neither were there any answerphone messages in the morning. I guessed our friends were too busy trying to pull their own lives back together in exactly the way I was. I hadn't even telephoned my aunt, or my own or Caroline's mother's care homes.

I had a nice thought. Our mothers, both in their late fifties, had early onset dementia. Perhaps they'd migrated to better bodies and would now enjoy a full life. I saw no point in telephoning. If my mum's mind had recovered, it would not take her long to find me. She knew our house. I feared the mind might take its dementia with it, perhaps freezing the horrible disease at the stage it was currently in for the transferee, but dooming the transferor's new resident to sudden confusion and despair. If my mother couldn't find me, there was no point whatsoever in visiting the husk of her body which might still reside in Dunholm Care Home.

The morning's news was depressing. The death toll was over two and a half million in the UK, and there were a further couple of million people with animal minds. There were easily millions of animals now occupied by human minds too. The mess was growing exponentially.

After the news, a debate programme discussed how we should deal with the situation. What should we do with animals within humans? Should they be culled? If so, what if a way were later found of reversing the process? If the original bodies were dead, there would be nowhere into which to repatriate the human minds. The cost of the situation was another problem entirely.

The news said special farms would care for humans in animals. There was a simpler solution for the animals which could no longer be farmed. These included predators lurking in domesticated animals, wild animals in family pets and so on. These animals would be put down. If they were suitable species, they would enter the food chain.

Government was recovering and so far, although there had been periods of chaos in public transport, spasmodic power cuts, hospitals struggling to cope, and social work problems, most services were gradually returning to normal. One of the biggest problems was personal grief. Where were our husbands, wives, children, and extended families? Were they alive, dead or suffering some worse fate? Where was my lovely wife? I couldn't believe she was gone. Where was Wilson? He was such an energetic and intelligent lad with the whole world before him. Where on earth could he be? I hated the thought he might've come to harm.

Sandra came downstairs; still a shock seeing her as this twenty-two-year-old woman. She entered the kitchen, wiping sleep from her eyes with one hand, grasping panda with the other, dressed in her new pyjamas. Both top and leggings were twisted, as would be normal for a waking child but was incongruous on this adult woman.

'Hello, Limpet. No more bad dreams?'

'No. Vhere's Mummy?'

'We don't know yet, darling, but I'm sure wherever she is, she'll be trying to get back home.'

'Vhere's Wils?'

'We haven't heard from Wilson. He might not have been as lucky as you. You had the wonderful Damay family to care for you. We must write them a lovely thankyou card. Will you help me choose one at the supermarket today?'

'Okay. Vhy am I big?'

'We don't know, darling. I don't know why I'm a woman, either. We're nearly the same age, Limpet.'

She was surprised at my comment. She looked downwards at her chest and feet, 'I'm really big. Bigger zan you.'

I laughed. 'Yes. Bigger than me. What would you like for breakfast? Some cereal? Toast? What would you like as your first breakfast back home?'

'Frosties… and some toast and honey and some milk.'

'And…' I said accusingly.

'Please,' she added quickly.

'Come and sit at the breakfast bar,' I said, patting the seat next to mine as I found the Frosties pack, took out a bowl, the sugar bowl, a milk container, and spoon. I put them down for her to help herself. I wanted to watch how she was doing with the motor functions of the Damay girl's body.

I put two slices of bread in the toaster and put the honey and marmalade onto the counter.

'One slice or two, Sands?'

'One, please, Daddy.'

Odd, hearing "Daddy" from this woman, but nice, too. I wanted to hang on to what we had here, thankful for her presence.

'Vhy am I big? Zhey'll laugh at school.'

'No, they won't darling, school is probably going to be a lot different. You have a lot of grown-up things to learn now. All your friends will have changed too.'

'Vot, even Angie?'

'Yes, even Angie.' One of her friends from school.

'Vill she be big like me?'

'Don't know, darling. We'll try to find out, later.'

She wouldn't be able to go through the usual ten-year process she'd have had if Mindslip hadn't occurred. She needed to learn how to become an adult quickly. There were dangers with her being so attractive but with the mind of a child. This was one of the reasons I wanted to keep her in simple clothes, nothing which would exhibit her sexuality to the world at large. I hoped she wouldn't be too appealing if someone had a mind. She needed my protection and the same from any educational authority.

I put a slice of toast on a side plate for her. Caroline always buttered and spread her toast.

'Now you're a big girl, Sandra. Why don't you spread your own toast?'

'Ooh. Can I?'

'Yes. Go on, but remember knives can be sharp so be careful,' I cautioned.

She had no trouble handling the knife or spreading the butter.

'Put the tops back on.'

'Now I'm going to go and get washed. When you've finished breakfast, will you go back to your room, make the bed and play or watch the television in the lounge?'

'Mummy usually makes ze bed.'

'Well, while Mummy's away, can you try to do it to help me?'

'Okay.'

I returned to my bedroom, checking her room and that her bed was okay on the way. We'd had some rare occasional bedwetting in the past, but it was fine today. I hoped Mademoiselle Damay's adult reflexes might prevent those problems now.

I showered, amazing myself once again by the beauty of my new body. I was more fortunate than many transferees. Poor Michael in his seventies. Thirty years of his life gone.

After drying and fixing my hair – better at it today, I donned blue jeans and sweatshirt. I wanted neither of us to stand out in the crowd. The thought of my daughter being harassed in the way I had been, really bothered me.

I found Sandra in her room, the bed perfectly made. I lifted back the quilt and found she'd even straightened the under sheet. Good.

'You made a great job of the bed-making, Limpet,' I said. 'Now, into the bathroom and use the toilet. Are you managing the toilet okay in your new body?'

'Sink so,' she said, jumping up and stripping off her pyjamas unselfconsciously.

This was why I was so worried about her innocence in this adult form. I was going to stop her – but no, I needed to treat her as the little girl she was for as long as possible.

'Tell me when you've done,' I called as the bathroom door closed. I wished Caroline was here. This was so awkward for me.

'Done,' she called, and I entered the bathroom, where she was brushing her teeth.

'My nice toosepaste tastes strange.'

'Yes, we might taste things differently now. It is part of what happened to us. I no longer like sugar in coffee.

'What do you do in the morning, Sands? Does Mummy bathe you, or do you use the shower?' I asked. We were in the family bathroom which had both.

'Usually a baf.'

'Well, now you're a big girl, would you like to try the shower?'

'What? For more than hair?'

'Yes.'

'Okay.'

In no time, she was showering. I brought a big towel over to her and put the bathmat down by the shower door.

'Done everything?'

'Sink so.'

'Rinse off.'

When she stepped out, I got her to make sure the shower was off and dry herself. I showed her how to hang the towel over the heated rail and put the bathmat over the bath. Her mind was going to have to grow up much more quickly, so routines would be important.

We headed back to her room. I made her wear a dressing gown and told her she ought to use one to go back and forth to the bathroom. I didn't want to destroy her innocence but was worried about any guest or babysitter we might have seeing her naked. It was disturbing enough for me. Even though it was my daughter, it was not her body – I was seeing a very attractive, naked French girl. It was going to take some getting used to.

The two of us managed to dry her hair and get it into a ponytail. We chose which jeans and top she wanted. I now had something more delicate to bring up and explained periods to her. Blind leading the blind.

I took my time, explaining the reproduction cycle and warning her about what would happen one day. I gave her two towels, one to keep in the bedside cabinet and the other to always keep with her. I made sure she knew making a mess would not be a problem, either. God, the period conversation was difficult and similar talks were, no doubt, taking place all over the world. I'd done my best.

'Right, now put on your socks, briefs, and jeans,' I picked up the bra, 'Do you know how to put this on?'

'Yes, Mad-ame Damhay showed me.'

'Okay, put it on and the sweatshirt and your trainers, then come down. Don't forget to put the emergency towel thing in one of your pockets. Maybe best in your left-hand jeans pocket which you won't use too much,' I said. I made a mental note to get her a bum-bag and to buy a selection of towels and tampons for both of us.

Twenty minutes later she looked very presentable. I'd have to get her hair cut. I couldn't manage this long style in anything but a ponytail. Tomorrow, maybe.

We set off with Sandra travelling in the front of the car for the first time.

Firstly, we visited the Royal Surrey Hospital to take in two bags of Sandra's old clothes. The place was mobbed with dozens of people coming and going. I'd been here before from time to time but had never seen it as crowded as this.

I had Sandra sit down in a row of seats with her panda and her Puffin Book of Stories, and she promised she'd stay there. I went to the main information desk and joined a queue under a sign marked 'NON-URGENT' in felt-tip pen.

Eventually, I asked what I was supposed to do about the original Sandra, and how she was being cared for.

The lady was most helpful and explained there'd been hundreds of similar cases and they were all being cared for as well as possible in various hastily prepared outbuildings and Portakabins. I asked what I should do, and whether I should make contact. She advised me not to, right now.

I left the labelled bags of clothes with her. She said a porter would collect them later.

I returned to my new Sandra and my blood boiled as I saw a man sitting beside her, talking to her, with his hand on her knee.

'Won't be a moment,' I said to Sandra, trying to hold my temper in front of her. I beckoned him to come with me.

We walked a few paces away, I stood face-to-face with him and asked, 'What do you think you are doing?'

'Trying to be friendly. What's it to you?'

'She,' I said nodding towards Sandra, 'is my eight-year-old daughter and I am her father. What part of being friendly is the need for you to have your hand on her knee?'

'Trying to befriend her. She was alone.'

'She clearly had a toy and child's book with her. She was not alone. She was waiting for me. I suggest you leave the hospital now unless you can prove you're a member of staff.'

'Go to hell!'

'Right. I'm getting security.' There was a woman in uniform by the doorway to my left. I shouted, 'Excuse me,' in a loud voice and she came over.

The man pushed me into the wall and ran off along the opposite corridor.

I got to my feet, my heart pounding, dusted myself off and explained what had happened to the security officer. She promised me they'd find him on CCTV and circulate his description. That I could be pushed over so easily was a real shock. I needed to remember how slight I was now. I'd checked this morning out of curiosity and was only one hundred and ten pounds on the digital scales. My old weight was one eighty.

Sandra was oblivious to all of this and was quite happy as we returned to our car. It took a while for me to recover my composure, though. Sandra knew not to talk to strangers, but I had to emphasise to her that "not talking" included not being touched by anyone except doctors and nurses. She said she understood. I kept my fingers crossed and resolved to continually hammer home the importance of being aware of the people around her, especially men. How awful to force worry and anxiety on our women and children. It made me see my old gender in a whole new light. The anxiety had given me a headache too.

In the city centre, we treated ourselves to a burger and fries for lunch and walked along to the historic Guildhall where information and help was promised.

It was surprising how many people were walking around. Outside the Guildhall, we joined another queue.

I was glad I'd brought two or three books for Sandra, as we were over an hour in the queue before we even entered the building. We'd left home shortly after ten, it was now three thirty, and all we'd done was the forty-minute visit to the Royal Surrey, a fast-food lunch and joined this queue. Many in the queue had simply walked away in frustration.

We both suffered from attempts to chat us up. Easy for me to brush off but not for Sandra. These men were maddening. It was giving me real concern.

One man came over to us in the queue and said to Sandra, 'Hi, lovely. When you've finished here, d'you want to come for a drink?'

I suppose it was a nice enough and polite request, but Sandra had no idea how to deal with it and looked to me.

'Tell him, "Thank you, but I'm not interested", Sandra.'

'Sank you, I'm not interested,' she said.

The man looked at me and said, 'What's it to you?'

I closed the gap between us and spoke quietly, directly into his face, 'I am her father, and she is only eight years old.'

'Right. Sorry. Didn't realise,' he said and walked away.

It was no problem with me being beside her, but what if I were not? She was so vulnerable. I didn't want to continually frighten her with stories of people wanting to hurt her, but I needed to impart ten years of learning about relationships into as short a time as possible. I also decided to try to get her to speak English more clearly. She knew the language well enough, but she sounded decidedly

French. All the "th", "w", and "s" sounds needed to be dealt with. While we waited, I began the task and she was a quick learner.

Eventually we reached a yellow, taped line on the floor. We were next in line. The person in front of us was searching for her husband and didn't occupy the desk too long. Presumably they would tell her to check the lists on the website. I knew the pain I had for Caroline and Wilson and guessed there were millions of people suffering the same sort of loss. There was a bank of computers on the right of the hall and she was sent to one of those. It wouldn't help, of course, there wasn't any point in examining the lists of dead as the bodies were no longer the missing people.

We moved forwards and both sat at the desk which had a pleasant, but overworked lady behind it. A mug of tea and some biscuits arrived for her. She smiled and asked, 'Don't mind if I drink and talk?'

I explained the reason for our visit was the mismatch between Sandra's mental age and physical appearance. Sandra sat with panda upside down under her arm while she read her book.

'You need to meet with one of our counsellors, Mrs …'

'Mr Arnold.'

'Oh, sorry, Mr Arnold – I expect your change is an additional complication for you, but you seem to have adapted fairly well.'

'I had the transferor's help.'

'Well done. The way some people are dressing usually makes it clear they are sex-change transferees. You fooled me.'

'I should say thanks for the compliment, I suppose.'

'Not at all. Now, who is going to be free first?' she said and peered at the laptop on her desk for several minutes.

'Right. Gren Pointer should be free relatively soon. Take this number and sit over there,' she said, indicating one side of the hall.

My goodness, no wonder they were so flustered and overworked. We were appointment 253. The lady at the desk put our manila folder into a tray labelled POINTER on the table behind her. What did "relatively soon" mean?

It was interesting that I had fooled her into thinking I was a woman. Suzy had been right. Her lessons were a good idea and I'd thank her for insisting when next I spoke to her.

Our wait seemed an age. Sandra was on the last of the books we had brought with us. We'd also been working on the, this, that, they, wish, what and why sounds to the point where she was becoming frustrated, so I stopped.

To make her books last longer, I had Sandra tell me about the content, making her conscious of always using the English sounds we'd been learning.

We were not waiting alone, there were several others sitting with us. The man in the seat beside me was chatty, and we discussed how we'd changed. He had been a pregnant woman of twenty-five and was now a middle-aged man and broke down at one point. I understood the distress. I'd had a good switch, if a comparison were possible. More worrying was his reason for being here. He was hoping to take the newborn child from his previous body. I made no comment. His original body was the one which would give birth and have all the attachments to the baby. How could he expect to sail in and take the child away? I was glad it wasn't my dilemma.

We'd have to live with the cards which Mindslip had dealt us. Sandra was twenty-two – she needed to become a twenty-two-year-old woman. I was a twenty-four-year-old woman and needed to live my life as her.

In my view, there would never be a return to my old body, wherever it was. I'd still heard nothing, and my mobile phone continued to ring unanswered. It must be on standby somewhere and the battery must be close to exhausted. I wondered if I could get the police to trace its location, but guessed they'd be too busy. My old self must have been sitting on the train which arrived at Waterloo during the fateful morning. I'd checked the train hadn't crashed. It arrived at Waterloo normally, if very late. Where the devil was my body? No one had used my credit and debit cards, and they'd been cancelled to let me use the new ones. Nothing had gone missing from my bank. I'd checked my mobile phone bill online, and nothing had been spent on it. In fact, because of the password, no one else could have been using it. A real mystery.

For the umpteenth time, I looked at Caroline's watch which I was borrowing. It gave me pangs of worry over the lack of communication from her. Where could she be? There was no way she wouldn't be making every effort to make contact or come home. She and Wilson must be dead. They wouldn't have failed to call home after all this time, surely?

It was now four fifteen. I'd sent Sandra off to use the loo and waited until she came back before paying my own visit. I didn't want to lose our place after all this waiting.

No sooner had I returned, than a good-looking, thirty-year-old man in a smart suit came over to us. There I was again, thinking about a man being good-looking! I silently scolded myself. It was becoming a habit, but, I had to admit this one was extremely fit in *that* sense.

He stood six feet tall, athletically built with rugged features, deep blue eyes, designer stubble and short, dark brown hair. Even my male component realised he was handsome. I'd particularly noticed his blue eyes, as mine had been a similar colour and were now brown. He looked fit in both senses of the word. What was happening to me? My cheeks were warm. I was flushing, for God's sake!

He examined his clipboard as he approached, 'One of you two ladies is Geoffrey Arnold?'

'Yes, me,' I said. 'This is my daughter, Sandra. She's eight.' Sandra looked up at him.

He leaned down to see what Sandra was reading, 'Hello, Sandra, that's a good story you have there. I'm Gren Pointer. We're going into my room to talk about you and your dad's…' he raised his eyes questioningly, and I nodded, 'you and your dad's situation. Would you like to come this way?'

We both rose and followed him as he talked to Sandra about her panda. He appeared to be genuinely interested in her and her toy.

We entered a large, sparsely furnished office with an old wooden table in the centre and half a dozen chairs scattered around. Gren pulled over an extra chair for Sandra and politely moved mine behind me to help me sit. Very thoughtful – thoughtful beyond his years – I wagered his transferor was no thirty-year-old. He sat on the other side of the table in a more comfortable, upholstered chair. The desk bore lever arch files on one side and a couple of dozen manila folders. He opened one of them and read the notes the assistant in the main hall had filled in on the form.

'Mr Arnold, why don't you tell me what you'd like us to try to resolve for you?'

I explained my concerns, mentioned the man in the hospital and the other in the queue. I told him I wanted to get her educated quickly to the point where she'd be able to care for herself with some elementary cooking, maybe a simple job, but also a crash course in self-defence and general studies to explain the world at large.

'She's clever, she'll be a quick learner, but I'm so concerned she could be guided off the straight and narrow. Also, I need to get back to work, not just for finances, but because I'm an astronomical physicist and might be of use in solving some of the problems we're facing.'

'And there's been no sign of your wife or son?'

'No, none at all. I fear the worst. While I'm sure you are very competent, I was hoping to speak to an experienced woman. A lot of the problems I'm having to deal with are because, inside, I'm a man, and I'm having my own share of problems adjusting to my body. Now, in addition I'm trying to help my daughter.'

'Well, Mr Arnold, I might be able to put your mind at rest a little. In my previous life, I was a sixty-year-old mother.'

'Oh. Sorry, I'd no idea. The name – Gren?'

'No problem. My name was Jen, Jennifer, and I chose Gren because it was close in sound to it.'

'Good idea. Maybe I should do the same?'

'Yes, perhaps. Geoffrey is not the most feminine of names, and it does save an awful lot of questions. You might feel more comfortable in yourself – although, to be honest, you seem to have carried off the transition better than most.'

'Thank you. The transferor helped. I'll give a new name some thought, but I'm already worried about this body influencing me more than I expected. I'm finding some men appeal to me, for instance, yet I've always been a red-blooded heterosexual,' I said and laughed.

'Yes. I know the problem with the transferor's feelings coming through. Let me admit, my host finds you very attractive,' and we both laughed nervously with Sandra watching us, wondering what was funny.

His admission about his attraction to me was interesting, but although I had an instant liking for him, the dread of being close with a man, in any sexual way, made me most uncomfortable. Was it my higher brain function overruling Suzy's sensibilities which rested a fraction below the conscious level?

'Anyway, Mr Arnold, we have many instances similar to Sandra's.' He smiled at her as he said her name, and she raised her eyes from her book to reflect it. 'We're arranging for education workshops from Wednesday. Sandra will be the twentieth adult-child I've seen today, and we are expecting it to run into hundreds. We plan to keep the classes to fewer than forty adult-children if possible, and it's intended the teachers will be experienced and taken from junior schools.'

'Sounds a good idea.'

'Once they're better able to take their places in society, we will also be offering adult education courses to help develop any potential they have, but that won't be an instant fix. You know – finance – budgets, et cetera.'

'Yes. The cost of this catastrophe will be substantial and ongoing, I fear.'

'Yes, I'm sure,' he smiled at me and I flushed again. 'Anyway, can I ask you to download the form on this web page?' He handed over a photocopied piece of paper. 'And dress Sandra accordingly. In fact, how you've done today. Casual and simple. Jeans and top, or tracksuit would be perfect. The teacher will let Sandra know when to bring any different clothes. Bring the form with you and come to the university main entrance reception with her at ten am the day after tomorrow.'

'Yes. It will be wonderful to get her the help she needs.'

'Please also read all of the guidance notes you'll find on the website. She'll need to bring a pen, notepad, comb, hairbrush, and other day-to-day items listed on the site, so it's important you check it. Mind you, I'm told the site will not be up until tomorrow lunchtime. We're under a lot of pressure here from all sorts of angles.'

'I can imagine,' I said.

'So, have you been involved in the talks in London?'

'I was at the South Bank conferences and the COBRA briefing. All extremely interesting and, I must say, most exciting too.'

'Is there any hope within this situation?'

'Well, I'm not allowed to reveal confidential discussions, but we did discover the chance of it happening again is negligible. It was a combination of the second supernova explosion in Orion and a coronal mass ejection from the sun. The combination is infinitesimally rare and could well be unique. Work is ongoing and will be part of my function at the Royal Institution. The International Space Station will be working with us when it is back in service.'

'What happened to it? I hadn't heard anything.'

'Well, apparently, it was suddenly manned by novices like us,' I said and laughed. 'We heard from NASA yesterday that it'll take a while to come back online.'

'I suppose so,' he said, taking in the possibility, 'they must have got a hell of a shock.'

'Yes, without a doubt. As for reversing the effect, it might become feasible in individual cases, but there could be years of medical work involved in devising a method. Any mass change-back is as good as impossible. The vast majority of us will live our entire lives in the bodies we now occupy.'

'Interesting about the cause. Most of us with any common sense were already ruling out a change-back.'

'Not impossible, but likely to be expensive and only on a one-to-one basis, so not for everyone.'

'Look, Mrs Arnold...'

Had he made the slip deliberately? I didn't correct him.

'...I'd love to talk more about this, but I still have a queue to deal with. You'll bring Sandra to the university yourself, yes?'

'Yes, for certain.'

'I'll see you then.'

He stood up, which was our cue to vacate the chairs. He walked around the desk and shook my hand. It was warm, strong, and held mine longer than was necessary. I tried not to like it but failed absolutely.

23 REUNITED

Geoff receives welcome news and a strange visitor

We got home. Sandra shot upstairs in a flash with her books and panda, left them in the safety of her room and came down again to watch television while I put away the shopping. I checked the fridge for something to make for dinner.

'Minced beef, Sands?' I shouted through to the lounge. I wanted to cook early in case of power cuts.

'Yes, Mummy,' she replied then quickly, 'Zorry, Daddy. I meant Daddy.'

'It's okay, Sandra.'

Where were Caroline and Wilson? It was the not knowing which was so hard.

As the onions sizzled, the news came on. It was worse than ever. The deaths for the United Kingdom alone were now close to five million. Many had taken their own lives, presumably finding themselves in bodies within which they were not prepared to learn to live. The number of animals corralled with human transferees was also more than two million, and there were television debates about it. Would it be possible to rehabilitate someone who was now a sheep, cow, fox, or dog? It seemed hopeless.

Trade and commerce showed signs of returning to normal and there was optimism that most industries would be virtually unaffected in the long run, although we were warned there could be lean times and shortages ahead. The Home Secretary had announced special classes for those who'd had sex change transfers to better understand their bodies, how to dress and care for themselves. It was not a secret this was primarily for the men who'd become women as most women had adapted to their new day-to-day behaviour more easily than men.

Sandra laid the table and we ate together. I always liked to have family evening meals at the table, and now it also gave me a chance to get my daughter to behave in a more adult manner. Elbows off the table; don't talk with your mouth full; don't bolt your food; mind you don't spill it; use your knife and your fork; mind you don't spill your drink; put your drink on the right, not the left; sit up straight; stop fidgeting. All the corrections seemed unimportant individually, but they made up part of being an adult. Gosh, this was going to be difficult!

The telephone rang.

'Can you stack the dishwasher, Sandra, please?' She nodded as I grabbed the handset.

'Arnold,' I said.

'Ah, is it Mrs Arnold of Walnut Tree Close?'

'Yes.' What was the point of telling him I was male?

'Good. Do you have a son called Wilson Arnold?'

'Yes, yes. Have you found him?' I asked excitedly.

'We have. He is in the embassy in Kigali, and we're arranging his return to the UK.'

'Kigali? Excuse my ignorance. I know the name, but remind me where is it?'

'Rwanda.'

'*Rwanda!* Is he okay?'

'Yes. It seems so.'

'He's nine. Is he the same age and sex?'

'Yes, well, almost. He's a boy, and he's about eleven as far as we know, but we can't be certain about his age.'

'Wonderful news. He was nine so not too bad from the age point of view. When will he be back?'

'With him being a minor, we needed to know he has a safe home to go to, hence the reason for my call. He could be back in the UK for Thursday. Rwanda has not fared particularly well as regards its infrastructure but is now recovering.'

'Is he well?'

'Yes, fine. He's black. Is that going to be a problem for you?'

'God, no. Not at all. Being alive is all that matters. You shouldn't need to ask.'

'Well, sad to say, there have been some unpleasant situations with some families when they've found their relatives are a different race.'

'Unbelievable.'

'Glad to hear you say that. Most have been fine, but we've been taking care to ask the question. There is nothing worse than someone getting home and finding they're not welcome.'

'No. I understand the reason for the question now.'

'He was living in a primitive outlying village, and it was some time before he was able to persuade his family of his origins.'

I imagined my young son, with no knowledge of anything but English, trying to persuade a tribal family that he belonged halfway around the world.

'Thank goodness he was able to convince them who he was. To whom am I speaking?'

'Edward Wright. I work for the newly created Repatriation Department. I'll call you again when we know for sure what flight he'll be on.'

'Is there anything to pay?'

'No. Not at all. We're only too glad to help.'

'Well, so many thanks, Edward. We're most grateful.'

I entered Mr Wright's number into my iPhone. How wonderful. Alive and still a child. I couldn't wait for him to be back with us.

I ran through to the kitchen where Sandra was finishing the stacking of the dishwasher.

'Good news, Limpet! We've found Wilson. He'll be back later in the week.'

'Not Mummy?'

'No. Not yet. Keep wishing.'

'Vhere is he?'

'In Africa.'

'Africa. Cool! Iz he all grown up too?'

'Watch those s sounds, Sands. No, only a bit. About eleven. He'll be black.'

'W-hat, Wils?' she said, putting great effort into her w.

'Yes, remember only the mind gets swapped. As he's a boy in Africa, he's black, but it is still Wilson inside, just like you are still inside this French woman.'

'French. Ooh. I'm French?'

'No, you are you. Your appearance isn't important. I'm not Japanese, am I?'

'No. S'pose not.'

All we needed now was to find Caroline and we'd be a family again. It gave me new hope.

«‹‹o››»

I was up early in the morning, showered and dressed before Sandra awoke. She managed to shower and dress herself without my help. Today was the twentieth. I didn't feel any different. No headache. No sickness, but I wore one of the towels to be sure. I was not looking forward to this female experience at all. I'd bought some of these things with flaps, but it still felt uncomfortable.

We both ate breakfast. Cereal and toast, with Sandra drinking orange juice and me coffee. Promptly at eight thirty, I rang Diane at the Royal Institution, gave her the news about Wilson, told her what was happening with Sandra tomorrow and that I hoped to be in to work by midday. She asked about Caroline, and I told her no news. I asked about Michael and learned he hadn't arrived yet, and my boss, Justin, was due back today. She told me he'd been delayed.

'Ask him to ring me when he gets back to the office, Diane. I spoke to him briefly the other day.'

'Will do. Downing Street wants to talk to him too. By the way, have you checked the deceased list recently?'

'No, why?'

'I'm not sure how to say this... but you're on it.'

'Really?'

'Yes. Your name and address. Sorry.'

'Well, it seals my fate. I am a woman for the rest of my life,' I said quietly.

'Think so. Sorry. Anyway, I hope it goes well for you both tomorrow.'

I hung up.

I was dead. No chance of a transfer back now. In that instant, the enormity of the mess the population of the world was in, struck home. Suzy could no longer have her body back without leaving me in some sort of limbo. It wasn't going to happen. No one would allow themselves to be disadvantaged by a transfer. I was even more certain we would forever be who we now were. I sat at the breakfast bar with my head in my hands.

I banged my fists on the countertop and became determined to pull myself together. I was alive, fit, healthy, younger. I should thank my lucky stars. Now if only we could find Caroline.

Online, I double-checked Diane had seen it correctly. Place of death was Waterloo Station, but no cause shown. I supposed it didn't matter in the great scheme of things. After all, it wasn't me any longer.

I sat back on the sofa, watching the TV. It was showing the American Secretary of State arriving at Number Ten. It made me wonder what Downing Street wanted with Justin. Were the corridors of power not finished with us yet?

I got stuck into some domestic chores, including the hoovering and some washing. I got Sandra to empty the dishwasher, put away the dishes, and load the washing machine with some coloureds. Afterwards, I left her to enjoy her books and doll in her room. She seemed to be happy to have chores to undertake, so I put her in charge of dishes and washing from this point onwards.

I finished cleaning, put away the Dyson, and was just about to sit down with a coffee, when I heard a strange scraping at the front door. At first, I ignored it, thinking it was the wind, but it persisted. The frosted glass revealed the shape of a dog pawing the glass.

I opened the door cautiously – the last thing I wanted was a dog bite. It was a greyhound. An old greyhound. It was sitting on the doorstep with its right paw in the air as if it was sore. It wagged its tail.

'Hello, doggie. You lost?'

What a surprise I got when it firmly shook its head.

'Can you understand me?'

The dog nodded vigorously and walked away towards the back gate which separated the front of the house from the rear garden. The dog was in a poorly state, and I saw some blood on the doorstep where it had been sitting.

Despite being in a fluffy pink pair of Suzy's slippers I followed it along the path. It seemed to want to show me something and was obviously intelligent. There must be a human in it.

The dog sat beside the rear gate where there is an area of gravel. It looked firstly up at me and then down at the gravel.

Good God! There were four letters clearly scraped into the loose stones in two lines.

CA
ME

'CAME'

What did it mean? The dog tapped its sore paw on the ME, its head on one side as if expecting me to react to what I was being shown.

Came. Why "CAME"? Why two lines, "came" could have been spelled on a single line? There was enough space.

The dog looked at me and back to the gravel. It tapped the "CA" then looked back up at me and tapped the "ME" three times. It sat still, tail wagging slightly.

This wasn't "came", it was "CA" is "ME"! CA – Caroline Arnold! It hit me like a grenade.

'Caroline?' I asked tentatively and knelt, bursting into tears at the realisation this poor old dog was my darling wife. The woman I loved.

The dog had a questioning expression.

'Cas. It's me, Geoff.'

She leapt at me. My gut reaction was to fend her off, but it was instantly clear this wasn't an attack. Her paws went either side of my face as her tongue licked me passionately, and she whined pitifully. Her back feet had left blood on the gravel. I picked her up and carried her into the house, quickly finding a blanket and laying her on it on the settee. Her front left and both rear paw pads were bleeding. There was an open wound on her front right leg and a scabbed wound on her rear thigh. I hugged her tightly.

'Oh, Cas, Cas. What have you done to yourself?'

She gazed at me and whined again.

'Do you want anything to eat?'

Nods.

'Drink?'

Nods.

I fetched another blanket and folded it twice before laying it on the kitchen floor.

Back in the lounge I used a damp flannel to wash her paws and a towel to dry them. They had open wounds. I didn't know if I should attempt to bandage them.

I lifted her and carried her through, laying her on the kitchen's warm, under-floor heated tiles. I kneeled beside her again, caressing her head and neck.

'Nods or shakes to answer, now. Water or tea?'

Shakes.

I jumped up, put extra water into the kettle, took a Pyrex bowl from the cupboard and placed a tea bag in it, adding another in a mug for me. My mind was racing, trying to come to terms with the situation. I needed to get her to the vet.

While the kettle sang, using nods and shakes, I figured out she'd like some cereal with milk and I prepared another bowl.

She'd almost finished the cereal and I sat on the floor beside her. The tears were rolling down her cheeks. I held her neck tightly. I'd no idea dogs could cry.

'I love you, Caroline. Don't worry. We'll sort things out.'

She appeared sad, finished off the cereal and lapped up the tea. While she was eating, I found our local veterinarian's number on the web and called, saying I needed an urgent appointment.

I brought Caroline up to date, telling her all about Sandra, Wilson, the conferences, the planned education for Sandra tomorrow and of my visit to Downing Street.

'I'm going upstairs to tell Sandra, darling. I'll brief her, so it is not too much of a shock. I'll put you on the sofa, first. We've got the vet at eleven.'

She nodded. I picked her up, carried her through to the lounge and headed upstairs to Sandra's room, knocked gently at the door and poked my head into the room. My adult daughter was sitting among a pile of Lego bricks, constructing some sort of building.

'Hi, Limpet. What're you doing?' I asked as I entered.

'Just playing wiv my Lego.'

'With, Sands, not wiv. I've got some more good news.'

She put down her Lego and regarded me. Strange seeing this grown woman sitting cross-legged amongst an eight-year-old's toys.

'You know some people have transferred into animals? It was on the news.'

'Yes. I th-ink so,' she said carefully, remembering to correctly pronounce the "th".

'It is the mind which gets transferred in the same way your mind went into Georgette Damay, and Wilson's will be in the African boy. It is you in her body. It is the same with me in this Japanese woman's body. In the same way, someone might be inside an animal like a dog, but it is still them. Do you understand that too?'

'Think so. Vhy? Sorry. W-why?'

'We have a dog downstairs with a person inside them.'

At the word "dog" she was on her feet in a flash, and I had to grab her arm. Wilson and Sandra had been angling for another dog since we lost our Jack Russell, Rosy.

'Wait. Sandra, *wait!*' I said firmly.

She stopped her dash for the door.

'Listen carefully. Sit down again. This is *not* a pet dog. It's a person inside a dog's body. It's *not* your pet.'

She understood this time.

'This person hurts badly. We're going to take her to the vet shortly. She has bleeding paws and is unwell. We can't play with her. We have to take care of her and make her well.'

'Okay, Daddy.' Again, she made for the door. I grabbed her arm.

'Sandra, wait! There's more. This might be a shock, Limpet. The brilliant news is, Mummy is back' – I saw her eyes light up – 'but the less good news is she's now in a dog, and it's up to us to care for her until she can be transferred back.' I added the last to give her hope, although I knew any chance of repatriation was negligible.

'Mummy's a dog?'

'Yes. Did you understand what I said? Some people have transferred into animals. Mummy has transferred into a dog and the dog isn't well. You do know she's not a pet, you cannot play with her, and she's unwell?'

'Yes. Ve can make her better, can't ve?'

'I hope so, Limpet. Can you help me make her better?'

'Yes. If I can.'

'Now, come down to Mummy, but remember she hurts. You must be gentle. She can't talk, of course, but she can nod or shake her head if you ask questions.' I held her hand tightly as we left the bedroom, and I led her downstairs.

Sandra walked slowly over to the settee and asked, 'Is it you, Mummy?'

Caroline nodded. Sandra kneeled, put her arms around her neck and cried. Tears ran from Caroline's eyes too. I stood back, fighting to stop my own tears and failing yet again.

Caroline's condition worried me on a deeper level. We could repair the paws, but it was clear she was an old dog. She looked fifteen or more. I didn't know much about dogs, but her age seriously worried me. We might not have her long. It was a tragedy.

Thirty minutes later, I carried my wife out to the car and laid her on the back seat. Sandra jumped into the front and we set off to the vet. I'd wondered whether a hospital might be better but decided against it. The vet would know the anatomy and the most suitable drugs and doses for a dog.

We arrived with a few minutes to spare. I carried Caroline in and sat her on the floor. Sandra sat beside her, stroking her head, cheek, and neck tenderly. I asked to speak to the vet before taking "the dog" in, and they said they'd tell him. The receptionist also asked me to put my dog on a lead and I whispered furiously, 'She's not a dog! She's my wife and does *not* need to be on a lead!'

I turned away but immediately returned to her. 'Sorry. Didn't mean to get ratty with you.'

The woman smiled and whispered pleasantly, 'Don't worry.' I guessed she'd had similar cases to deal with.

We waited. An Alsatian came in with another owner, and they sat a short way along the row of seats. Caroline cringed back between the two of us. It appeared to be a genuine fear. Something must have happened involving an Alsatian. If only she could talk. She raised her eyes to mine anxiously. To reassure her, I held my hand tight against her neck to provide security.

A couple of minutes later, I was called over, and a young vet in a white coat, far too large for him, ushered me into a treatment room. It was small with cupboards along one side and a treatment table.

'Mrs Arnold, how can I help?'

'I'll be brief – I want the time spent on the patient, but you need to know I am *Mr* Arnold, and my wife's the dog outside. She's taken four days to get home, and her paws are seriously damaged. But I'm also worried about a wound on her leg and her overall health. She seems unwell to me. Money is no object. I'm hoping you can do your best for her. You can ask her questions, and she can answer by nodding or shaking. Okay?'

'Yes, Mr Arnold. Bring her in and we'll examine her.'

I went back into the waiting room and wrote on the receptionist's notepad, 'The young woman is my eight-year-old daughter. Please don't let her leave.' I showed it to her, and she nodded. I didn't want Sandra to be with me in case we were given bad news.

'The room is very small, so you wait here, Sandra,' I said, lifting Caroline off the floor and carrying her in to the veterinarian.

I whispered to Caroline, 'Don't worry, darling, I'm with you. If I answer a question for you incorrectly, shake your head.'

She nodded.

I placed her on the table. A veterinary assistant stood against the wall.

'Hello, Mrs Arnold, you've been in the wars. Let's see what we can do for your wounds,' said the vet directly to Caroline.

It was a long session. The vet treated and bandaged the paws, the sore on her right leg, and the barbed wire cut on her left hind leg. He manipulated her limbs, feeling and listening to her joints. He injected a long-lasting antibiotic into the skin of her neck and gave her a steroid injection in her thigh to help the leg infection heal.

'I want to take your temperature, Mrs Arnold. Can you keep your mouth still? It is less intrusive than the alternative.'

Caroline nodded and the thermometer was put into the side of her mouth.

He used a stethoscope to listen to her heart and put a cuff on her tail for blood pressure.

'We don't have any records?' he asked.

Caroline shook her head.

He spent a lot of time listening to the heart and spoke to the elderly man who was acting as assistant, 'Tell reception we're going to be another fifteen minutes and bring in the ECG machine.'

'Sorry, Mrs Arnold, need to shave you in a few places for electrodes. Can you lie nice and still and relax, please?'

I liked the way he always spoke to Caroline.

The tests took about ten minutes, and he examined the paper trace. Finally, he took some blood from her left front leg.

'Okay. Mr and Mrs Arnold. I can tell you the wounds will all get better. I'm giving you more bandages and cream for the paws. They'll need changing every day for a week. When healed, you should be able to leave the bandages off. The right rear paw might need to be bandaged another day or two. Leave the front leg wound covered for three days. If it's healing, leave the dressings off. If it's not healing come back to the surgery.

'You can walk as soon as you're able, but no running and keep to soft surfaces if you can. I'm providing a jar of painkillers as your rear paws might throb. This last injection is for pain relief, and you'll be tired for the rest of the day. Okay?'

Caroline nodded and I said, 'Yes.'

'You have pain in your hip?'

Caroline nodded again.

'You have some arthritis in the joint, and I'm prescribing a drug to help all of your joints move a little more freely. The painkillers will help, too. You must have walked a long way. More than twenty miles?'

She nodded. My poor Caroline.

'Thirty?'

A nod.

'Forty?'

Another nod.

'More than fifty miles?'

Yet another nod.

'Sixty?'

She shook her head. My poor wife had walked more than fifty miles to get to Guildford.

'The arthritis might not be so bad when you have recovered from the distance you walked. I'm also prescribing a joint supplement to take with meals.

'Now. Your heart. I've been trying to work out your age and, although you appear older, I believe you're about ten years old. For most dogs, such an age is late middle age but, in a greyhound, it's old age owing to the type of life you'll have led when you were younger. I see signs that you were used for racing. I can hear murmurs in your heart and some atrial fibrillation. I'm prescribing a drug to steady the heart and another to lower blood pressure. Come back in a couple of weeks, please. Do you have any questions?'

Caroline's eyes met mine, and she shook her head.

'She will have,' I started, 'but we'll have to set up a communication method to work them out, and we'll ask them next time we come. Can we be certain it'll be you? I'd like the continuity.'

'Yes, of course. I'm Mrs Reid.'

He's a she! Another case of sex transfer.

'Now if you'd like to take your wife out to the waiting room, come back in, and we'll sort out the bill.' Odd. In the past, the consultation bill had been paid at reception.

The assistant opened the door for me, and I lifted Caroline and put her on the floor beside Sandra who was reading her book. She petted her head, and Caroline rested her chin on Sandra's leg. I returned to the treatment room. Mrs Reid closed the door.

'I wanted a quiet word with you,' she began. 'Mrs Arnold is not well. She is suffering from heart failure and general old age.'

My heart sank. 'What are you saying?'

'A year at most. More likely months and it could be any time. Sorry.'

'And there's nothing more we can do?'

'Not unless they find a way to transfer us back to our own bodies, no. The drugs might stabilise her heart, and if we can reduce the blood pressure it'll take stress off the heart, too. A year would still be a good result.'

'Surgery? Money's no object.'

'No, surgery would not change the prognosis by more than a few months, and those months would include pain and discomfort from the surgery itself.'

I went quiet, took a moment, and eventually said, 'Thank you. The bill?'

'There's one other thing. Your wife has a bad flea infestation.'

'Yes. I was going to buy a proprietary flea shampoo, some litter and bowls from the pet shop on the way home,' I said.

'I can supply a stronger shampoo. You'll need to put polythene bags on her feet to keep the dressings dry. Freezer bags will do. Give her a shower with this liquid.' He placed a bottle with the other medicines and a spray can on the table. 'It should clear them in a single application. She'll be a lot better in herself without the fleas. After the shower, paint the rest of her with a one in ten solution of the shampoo, leave it five minutes and wash it off without getting the dressings wet. Use the spray on anything she has been lying or sitting on before you brought her in. Reception has the bill. I'm so sorry for what's happened to your wife.'

'Yes. Thanks. You want us back in a couple of weeks?'

'No. Thinking about it, I've taken some blood and am going to check liver and kidney function, so bring her next week. Make an appointment as you leave.'

On the way home, I picked up a large cat litter tray, litter, and some bowls from the pet shop, cotton wool and dressings from the chemist, and a selection of pies and other meals Caroline might enjoy from the supermarket.

The afternoon went quickly with me lifting Caroline onto the settee, strapping the bags onto her paws and showering her in the bath. She stood still, her head and tail down, dejected, putting up with the humiliation of me washing her and rinsing her off. I used the hairdryer on her to make the whole event a little more civilised. There was a distinct sadness to her demeanour.

I carried her downstairs and put her onto one of the armchairs to watch the telly. I sprayed the settee, the blankets we'd used, and the kitchen floor, and headed out to the shed in the garden. An hour later, I returned with a leather mitten I'd made with a pen attached. She could slide it onto her front right paw to allow her to write. As I kneeled beside her, she licked my cheek. I embraced her tightly and told her how much I loved her. My darling wife was dying of old age and there was nothing I could do about it. My eyes were full of tears once more, Suzy's emotional nature overwhelming my usual stoical demeanour.

I cooked us all a family steak pie from one of the discount supermarkets and we sat around the coffee table in the lounge, eating. Sandra treated it like a picnic, and she and I talked and laughed about things we'd done in the past. Caroline's eyes flicking from Sandra to me as she listened and enjoyed the family meal. I'm sure, like me, she was wondering about our son.

When it was time for bed, I showed her where I'd put the litter tray in the utility room and left the kitchen door open for easy access. She got off the settee, slipped her paw into the glove and wrote a shaky 'SORY' onto the A3 pad I'd given her for messages. I caressed her neck and told her I loved her.

Upstairs, I felt a slight dull pain in the bottom of my abdomen. That night, I wore briefs and a towel. I was still dreading my initiation to "the curse".

I lay in bed trying to make sense of the day. My wife was a greyhound. Worse still, she was an old greyhound. Her body was failing, and she'd likely last less than a year. I had to make her life as good as possible.

Tomorrow I'd take her with me to the university for Sandra's first day at the new education classes. If she was up to it and wanted to come, I'd take her to work too. We still had Sandra's large pushchair in the shed, and it'd hold Caroline without any problem. I wouldn't want her to walk any distance on her bandaged feet for a few days, especially outside. With problems and solutions churning around my mind, I finally drifted into sleep.

In the middle of the night the bed moved. Caroline crept in beside me. I enveloped her in my arms, curling my legs up to press against her tail. I cuddled her tightly and whispered my love to her. She whimpered, and I squeezed her tighter. God, the flea shampoo smelled awful. I steeled myself to ignore it. Her body warmth was comforting and an improvement upon the pillow I'd been cuddling at night. Today had been long and stressful. We soon fell asleep in our loving, if not incongruous, embrace.

24 THE CURSE

Geoff thinks about a name change

I awoke with pains in my lower abdomen, below my stomach and above my private parts, but deep inside. I was overcoming my morning shock of being a woman more quickly, but this was an uncomfortable reminder. I supposed I'd gradually adjust. My breasts no longer belonged to someone else. I touched them. They were tender. Caroline used to have tender breasts when it was her time of the month. This must be it, I guessed. What Caroline had always called "the curse" was upon me.

The alarm clock on the other side of the bed said six in the morning. The light from Betelgeuse penetrated the curtains making the bedroom look less homely. Where was Caroline? She was no longer lying beside me. I stretched. Ooh, there was a real ache, as if I'd pulled a muscle where I supposed my womb was. I expected the pain to be lower, but it was several inches higher. I swung my legs over the bedside and sat up. My back ached too.

In the mirror, I saw my legs protruding from the short nightdress. I'd been looking at them in a sort of detached way, then suddenly realised that they were just my legs. They were no longer the legs of a beautiful girl. Yes, I could see that they were shapely, but they no longer pulled at the part of my brain which had previously seen them as silky, sexy, and desirable. It was rather sad, really, that I no longer wanted to run my hands up and down my thighs every time I saw them. They were no longer objects of carnal desire, at least not for me – they were just part of me. They meant no more than that. Femininity had become dominant within me. Geoffrey Arnold had retreated, allowing Suzy to rule my body and subconscious. My wonder at being Suzy was dying.

After a minute or two's contemplation, I stood. There was no sign of where Caroline had been lying. I was glad we'd used the flea shampoo. All I needed was 'the curse' *and* fleas. I pulled on Caroline's dressing gown and made my way quietly into the en suite. I confirmed I really had *started* and, after a degree of novice fumbling, prepared myself for the day.

Caroline was sitting on the lounge floor, her tail wagging.

'Hello, darling. When did you get up?'

She shook her head and walked into the kitchen where there were several A3 sheets on the floor. She'd managed to slide her own foot into the writing glove. She sat, switching her gaze from me to the sheets expectantly.

I wondered if she'd like some tea before I started reading the sheets. 'Tea first?' I asked.

She shook her head and walked to the utility room door. She obviously had something else in mind.

I followed. She sat at the door and I went in. There was a neat pile of dog poo in the litter tray. I ran back upstairs, grabbed one of her purple bags from the bathroom cabinet and dealt with the task, disposing of it in the outside bin.

'Tea now?' I asked as I washed my hands. Caroline nodded enthusiastically and wagged her tail. I bent and gave her a hug, kissing her on the head. She was warm. Her tongue flicked my cheek and I hugged her tighter. Too much tea wasn't very good for dogs, but any harm it might do was outweighed by the pleasure it seemed to give Caroline.

So, armed with a large mug of tea and with Caroline lapping hers from her bowl, I sat on the floor beside her and took the top sheet. Why had she brought the paper through to the kitchen?

'Why in the kitchen?' I asked.

She tapped the floor with her paw. Ah, the floor was hard so it would be easier to write no doubt. I must add more writing pads to the shopping list and a couple more bowls. I read the first sheet.

LUV U

HTE SMELL SHOWR

YOU PRETTY HA HA

LIKE STEK PY

RT PAW HRT

'Okay, darling. You can shower with me, and I'll get more steak pies,' I said and laughed. 'We'll examine your paw after breakfast. Do you want one of the painkillers now?'

She nodded and I gave her one of the tablets, rinsing her bowl out and putting down fresh water.

I put the first sheet to one side.

SAND SKOOL

ME OLD DYNG

LUV U XX

DON'T WORY

I couldn't help myself and burst into tears, hugging her tightly and feeling her tongue on my neck and cheek. Once more my emotions were overflowing. I was unable to move for a couple of minutes, but managed to speak through my tears. 'I love you, too. Yes, you're old and not well, but we can give you the best treatment in the world. If they find a way to transfer back, I'll pull strings to get you as an early case.'

She broke free of the hug, dragged over the pad and her glove. I helped her on with it and she scribbled, one letter at a time. The pad moved about as she wrote. She needed something to grip the pad or paper in position. There was a heavy slate tile in the shed. If I made something to allow it to hold the pad it might help. Her sheets all had tears in them too. I put my hand on the pad to anchor it for her.

CAN EXPRMNT WI ME

'Yes. I'll investigate the possibilities.'

She scribbled again.

B QWIK I THNK

'Yes. I'll find out today,' and cuddled her tightly, 'What do you want for breakfast?'

WBIX MLK N SGR

'N means no?' she nodded.

I added Weetabix to a bowl one at a time until she stopped me.

'Do you want me to break them with a spoon?'

She nodded.

'You asked about Sandra's education. This morning I'm taking her to the university where there are going to be special classes for younger children trapped in adult bodies. Seems a good idea.'

Caroline nodded and went to her pad. She made some sounds, 'Nah, neh.' She wanted a new sheet. Obviously tearing sheets off was difficult.

I GO WIT U

'Okay, you want to come. No problem. I'm worried about your feet, though. Is it okay if I use Sandra's pushchair?'

She took a moment before giving a sort of resigned nod.

'You said I was pretty.' I laughed again. 'Feels strange, darling, and, guess what…'

She looked up at me puzzled.

'The curse started today!' I laughed again.

'Hnh, hnh, hnh,' she said, and I embraced her neck. She was laughing at me.

I put the second sheet to one side and read the last of those she'd pre-prepared.

WILS?

MUM

LITR CURTN? PLS

LUV U

'Oh, I love you too, Caroline. You'd like a more private toilet area?'

Nods.

'Wilson is on his way back from Kigali in Rwanda. Be prepared for a shock. He'll be black, but he's a male of about the same age as he was, or maybe a year or two older.'

Caroline nodded.

'Heard nothing about your mum. She'll have moved into another body. I don't know if the dementia will have moved with her. Dementia is meant to be the brain shrinking so hopefully she'll have a better life. This house might still be a memory so there is some hope she'll find us if she is able. No point contacting the home. Anyone in your mum's body won't be her, you know. I'm guessing my mum is in the same situation.'

Caroline nodded slowly.

'Let's put the bags on your paws and we'll go to the shower and get rid of the flea treatment smell with some of your Chanel.'

I knocked gently on Sandra's door and we entered. She sat up in bed.

'Good morning, Limpet,' I said, and Caroline let out a bark.

Sandra jumped out of bed, gave me a kiss on the cheek and kneeled to hold Caroline in a lovely, long hug.

'Sands, can you get yourself up? I'm going to help Mum shower. Clean underwear and top after you've had a shower. Can you do it all yourself and make your bed?'

'Yes, Daddy.'

'I'll do the breakfast when we come down. Okay?'

Caroline was soon clean and smelling better. I removed the bags from her feet. After my shower, I applied the dryer to my hair as I combed and brushed it into the usual style. It was quicker today. I was getting better at it. Caroline sat and watched, occasionally making the 'Hnh, hnh, hnh,' sounds which I recognised as her laughter.

'Shut up, or I'll tell the vet to put the thermometer somewhere more embarrassing next visit.'

'Grrrrrr! Hnh, hnh, hnh.'

Eventually, I'd done my lips, the touch of mascara, eyeliner, and applied the hint of rouge Suzy had taught me to use, to Caroline's great amusement. I was done. It's funny, I hadn't planned to wear any make-up once I'd got away from Suzy's flat, but I found I was enjoying looking good, much more than I did as a man. Was this another girl thing that Suzy's resident subconscious was imposing upon me? Today I dressed in her dark blue trouser suit with a colourful, flowery blouse.

'Am I okay?' I asked as I did a twirl and checked everything in the mirror as Suzy had instructed. Caroline yapped approval, laughed, and we both headed downstairs. Stairs were difficult with her four feet. Rosy, our Jack Russell used to have the same problem. Perhaps it was something to do with the free-hanging steps we had.

After breakfast, I gave the old pushchair a thorough clean in the utility room and rigged up a strap on the slate tile to hold the writing pad steady. There was no easy way to keep Caroline's litter tray private, but I fitted a small ball-clasp-catch so she could open and close the door herself. A printed card with red and green sides now hung on a hook on the kitchen side of the door.

'There you go. Now if the red side is showing we'll know Mum wants privacy. Understand, Sandra?'

'Yez.'

'Sands…' I cautioned.

'Sorry. Yes.'

'Are you ready to go? We'll need to leave soon?'

'Yes, Daddy.'

'You've got some tissues, your towel thing, yes?'

She nodded.

'Get your briefcase. You've checked you've got everything you are meant to take? Your pens, notepad, sandwiches, bottle of drink?' I tucked the registration form in my jacket pocket.

'Yes. Th-ink so.'

'Not good enough, Limpet. Adults need to be sure. It's called responsibility. Check.'

She fiddled around in her case, 'Yes. Got it all.'

'Good girl. Right, let's go. Caroline, wait until I've opened the car. Don't want you walking on the gravel,' I said.

The entrance to the campus was attractive and we followed makeshift finger signs pointing to "Adult Children Education."

Once parked, I helped Caroline into the pushchair. Inside the Austin Pearce building were crowds of people and I was fortunate to spot Gren Pointer.

I left Sandra with Caroline and walked over to him. His eyes lit up when he saw me, and I couldn't help it pleasing me. I had to quell my strange interest in him. We shook hands. The warmth of his grip was not lost upon me, and he held my hand longer than was necessary, meaningfully, exactly as he had the previous time.

'Lovely to see you, Mr Arnold. Have you brought Sandra?'

'Yes, and my wife. She's turned up.'

'Oh.' Was that a hint of disappointment in his voice from which he rapidly recovered? 'Wonderful news,' he said hurriedly.

'Well, not as good as it might have been. Come. I'll introduce you. They're over here,' I said and, with a puzzled expression, he followed me through the growing throng of people queuing to hand in their registration documents.

He was plainly shocked when I introduced Caroline. I explained she'd hurt her feet, and he said hello and quickly sprang into his administration role turning to Sandra whose eyes were flitting in every direction in the busy hall.

'Ready for school, Sandra?' he asked. 'Do you have your form, please?'

I handed over the form to Sandra who passed it to Gren. He wrote something in the bottom right box, handed it back to Sandra and said, 'Right, Sandra, join the queue over to the right, the short one. When it's your turn hand the form to the man at the desk. Can you do that?'

'Yes, I sink so,' she said.

'Saandraa…' I said in my language tone of voice.

'Sorry. Th-ink so,' she said and ran over to the end of the queue in a childlike manner, demonstrating the mind inside the body was truly still eight years old. Gren looked at me, puzzled.

'Trying to get rid of the worst of her accent,' I explained.

'Yes. Good idea. At her mental age, it shouldn't take long. I've put Sandra into a small class of twenty. They are all girls in adult women of differing ages, so she'll have a lot in common with all her classmates. The teacher is Janice Howard, who was already a woman and is skilled at working with mentally challenged individuals. She should be ideal for Sandra and her classmates. If you want to observe the class in action, come back for Sandra at three fifteen and we'll watch the tail end of the final lesson of the day.'

Caroline gave a small yes bark and I told him we'd both be back. Why were we getting such special treatment in among this huge assembly of distressed people? Surely not simply the fact he "fancied" me?

'If you'd like to say goodbye to your daughter, I'll see you later. I'll keep an eye on her in the queue.'

'Kind of you,' I said and shook his hand again, 'Thanks.'

'My pleasure,' he said and eventually released it.

Awful mixed feelings ran through me: I was heterosexual; I didn't find him sexually attractive; my wife was back; I was a woman; he was a woman even if he looked male; I was a man in my head – my mind was in turmoil.

I pushed Caroline over to Sandra, said we were off to London, and she shouldn't go anywhere until we got back. She understood well enough, but would she remember? I kissed her; Caroline licked her hand and gave a tiny bark.

«««o»»»

We got some strange glances on the Waterloo train, especially when I spoke to her. She made noises occasionally. I knew her "yes", her laugh, her "no" and several other noises were becoming intelligible, but it was going to take a while before we'd be able to conduct a sensible conversation. Some people ignored us, and others watched our communication. How common was it? Of course, they might simply be trying to be polite – it was England, after all.

Meeting Gren had reminded me about the incongruity of being called Geoff in this young woman's body. Which name would be easiest to remember? Perhaps Caroline could help me choose. Which would be easiest for her to try to say?

'I'm going to change my name to something feminine. What do you think of Jess or Beth? Which do you prefer? Nod for Jess.'

She shook her head. 'You prefer Beth?' She nodded. 'Beth, it is then unless you have other suggestions.'

She said, 'Brech, Breft, Berf, Beff,' and looked at me for approval.

'The last one was pretty close.'

'Beff. Ochy,' she said and wagged her tail.

Her "okay" seemed good too.

At Waterloo, I managed to get a black cab, and we soon found our way through the still strangely quiet city streets to the Royal Institution. Diane was even smarter than before. She was standing at the reception desk talking to a tall, slim, black man.

'Ah, here he is, Dr Mayweather.'

So, this was my boss in his new guise. I shook Justin's hand and introduced him and Diane to Caroline. She responded with a pleasant bark.

'I couldn't leave Caroline behind so I've brought her with me. Hope you don't mind.'

'Not at all. How do I greet you, Mrs Arnold?' said Justin.

Caroline lifted her right paw and Justin shook it.

'We've been summoned to Number Ten, Geoff.'

'Me too?'

'Yes. Caroline, will you be all right with Diane for a while?'

'Href,' she barked.

'Caroline's word for yes,' I explained. 'Diane, she'll need fresh water, and she loves tea and biscuits. No sugar in the tea. If you can give her access to an A3 pad she can write. Her writing glove is in the pushchair bag.'

Diane laughed, 'No problem. We'll get on fine.'

'Is Michael in?' I asked Justin.

'He was, but I've sent him home to sort himself out. He's still living at the care home.'

'Right. You know, he might be better off there. He's an old man now and probably could do with some help.'

'Yes, hadn't thought of that. Okay, next time we're all together let's talk through the options with him.' It was fascinating listening to him speaking with such a distinct African accent.

I kissed Caroline on the head, caressing her cheek and enjoying the tender lick my hand received. Armed with my laptop and briefcase, we took a cab to the heart of government.

'What's going on, Justin?'

'We've been asked to act as part of a brainstorming group who'll be advising government on how to deal with the situation. I told them I'd attend the first few meetings, but my astronomy work would likely stop me from being too useful.'

'Ha-ha, so you've volunteered me!' I said.

'Yes. Should be interesting though.'

'But as astronomers and physicists we can have little relevance, surely?'

'They probably feel we might have some input as scientists. I do know they are seriously concerned there might be a repeat.'

'But that's daft. It was a billion to one coincidence if what we know so far is true. There's never going to be a repeat.'

'You might be right, but the government is still concerned about the possibility and our clear thinking could be of use. Don't you want to be part of this, Geoff?'

'Oh, yes, but I don't want us to be later criticised as an irrelevance.'

'No. Fair enough, but let's give it a try. Maybe we can be the wild cards in this setup.'

'I suppose it'd be good to have an input.'

We sat quietly in the cab for a minute, and I decided to broach the subject of Caroline's health.

'Justin. Caroline is old. She has less than a year to live owing to her heart and old age. I want to pull strings on the medical front if they start to get close to reversing the procedure. Her health is my incentive.'

'Okay, but would she be prepared to be experimented upon?'

'Yes. She's already told me she would if it weren't some hopeless shot in the dark.'

'Fine, Geoff. If an opportunity comes up, I'm with you on it.'

'Thanks, Justin. By the way, I've decided to be called Beth in future. Saves complications. What do you think?'

His expression told me he'd hardly noticed I was a woman.

'Sorry, Geoff, I hadn't appreciated how feminine you were. You're asking the wrong person. Beth seems fine to me. There must be a large number of sex-change victims so why not keep your own name. Names will probably become unisex. No reason Geoff, James or Mike shouldn't be feminine, and Linda, Carol and Averil male.'

'Yes, I see the point in the long term, but right now, if we are going to be in an intimate discussion group, I want a name which makes sense and will not make me stand out as a sex-change subject. Beth is closest in sound to Geoff.'

'Okay, Beth it is.'

I always liked the fact that I could argue with Justin and, once the point was resolved, he'd support it. I tried to do the same, not always successfully. I'd had my name all my life, and now I'd consigned it, with my body, to the past.

At Number Ten, we entered the cabinet briefing room. There were about a dozen others already seated and chatting. A tall, black gentleman came over to us and introduced himself as the Deputy Home Secretary, Mr Giles Burton. Justin introduced himself and me as Dr Beth Arnold. It surprised me when he said it as if I'd always been Beth.

'I have Dr Geoffrey Arnold on my list,' said Mr Burton.

'I've decided to adapt to my new situation, so it is now Beth. I'll make a legal change when the authorities are back to normal.'

'So, you've given up on being switched back?' he asked, marking the change on his document.

'My former self is dead. What will I be switched back into? I'd like to know if it is possible but there can never be enough time to sort out the increasingly convoluted mix and match we're encountering. My wife is a greyhound.'

Burton's eyebrows rose, 'Really?'

'Really, and it's a good reason for finding a way to do it on a piecemeal basis. She's an old greyhound with a short life expectancy. If there's any way to achieve repatriation it should probably be people like her who should be the first to benefit.'

'Yes, we must keep it in mind during our discussions. We're waiting for another four people to come. Help yourselves to tea or coffee from the flasks over there and introduce yourselves to the others.'

Him mentioning that Caroline should be kept in mind during discussions was heartening. I could use his support if opportunities arose. Justin and I took coffee and wandered around separately introducing ourselves. A few minutes later Giles Burton returned with four other individuals and sat at the head of the table.

'Well, let me say welcome to Number Ten. I'd like you to please introduce yourselves and your expertise to the other members of this brainstorm panel,' he said.

Each of us in turn explained who we were. There was Len White, a consultant neuropsychologist at Imperial College Trust; Dr Mark Weston, neurological surgeon also at Imperial; Margaret Mead, head of mathematics at Kings College; Greg Pastor, quantum physicist from CERN; Bill Wright, a neuropsychologist from Queen's College; Bishop David Moran, Church of England; Jonah Martyn, deputy CEO of Endron Media, a handsome, thirty-something Chinese man. I mentally slapped my wrist for noticing his appearance. Brigadier John Ellis, ex-army; Peter Stone, back from secondment with NASA and a ministry of defence consultant; and finally, Gillian Smart, senior financial advisor at Her Majesty's Treasury who would also be taking minutes.

Almost everyone's age or sex belied their official titles and occupations, but none more so than Bishop Moran who was now a young teenage girl.

'Thank you, people. Now let me tell you a little more about our proposed function,' began Giles Burton.

'Members of the cabinet are desperately worried about how to deal with the myriad unknowns in this situation. We've millions of humans inside animals of all shapes and sizes from as small as domestic cats to cattle, horses, and even an Indian elephant. They're being fed and watered and from what communication has been made between us, they're most unhappy with their lots. Know what I mean? They'll be a priority if we can transfer minds. What do we do about them short term and potentially long term? I should perhaps mention Dr Arnold's spouse is a greyhound which could be useful for us when discussing the problems animals are experiencing in their new existences.' Everyone looked at me. Yet another lever to help Caroline was in my armoury.

'Secondly, we've lost nearly ten per cent of our population. Accidents and suicides mainly. The army are already carrying out mass burials. The cabinet needs your ideas on this. Is it the best solution?

'Thirdly, we have farmers with extremely worrying situations. They have cattle, sheep, and pigs with other animals in their bodies and controlling them is difficult. Dairy farmers are trying to force cows to be milked. We're heading for a shortage of milk and other dairy products.

'Finances. Even sorting out payroll is a nightmare. Companies need rules to ensure money is passing to the right people. We don't want businesses to run themselves into cash flow problems because they've lost control of their salary ledgers. Banks tell us there are going to be millions of inactive accounts. After cash, we need to be examining assets. Who owns what? How do they prove it? Know what I mean?

'What about couples? Homes with same sex parents who no longer want to live together with children in adult bodies. How do we educate young children in adult bodies? What do we do about babies in adult bodies? We don't even know who their parents are. We think there've been cases where foetuses have been transferred into adult bodies prior even to their births. They can't move, eat or drink, they're incontinent and their minds are not capable of conscious thought. The reverse is almost too nightmarish to contemplate, but *we* must. There have been instances of infants speaking when being born. What age of a foetus could someone be transferred into and still retain their memories? When they're finally born, will they try to reclaim their property? How do we deal with any and all of this? What other bizarre situations haven't we even had the wit to yet imagine?

'Currently, physical repatriation of people who ended up overseas is going well. We've been bringing UK citizens back from all over the world and, of course, we've people here who need to get back to their own countries. We suspect many of them won't want to leave and will keep quiet. You know what I mean. They, however, have no access to work or places to live unless they've stayed in the homes where they were during Mindslip. Because Mindslip occurred during rush hour, large numbers of transferees will have little idea where their body resided or worked. Another problem for you to resolve.

'Some will want to immigrate and there's surely going to be a labour shortage as things get back to normal. Can they help? Should we relax immigration rules if they wish to stay and have useful expertise?

'I could go on.' He walked to the end of the room and pulled down a white board with three columns of lists.

'Your task, people, is to strike off each of these problems. We need you to come up with solutions. I'm here to provide resources from anywhere within government. Gillian will be watching the financial implications and can call on further treasury support. The brigadier is tasked with military and defence implications and will keep the Minister for Defence in the picture. Among you, we've included medical, psychiatric, astronomical, and other scientific *boffins*, if you'll excuse the term, tasked with examining your suggestions laterally and assessing the practicalities of the various ideas and solutions. Jonah, from Endron Media is the wild card. He will act as devil's advocate and if he asks a question, we'd *all* better be able to explain our answers. Other experts will be called upon as and when required or at your suggestion. Don't be afraid to ask if you need further expertise. You're not the only group, but most of the others have specialist project lists with which to deal. They're listed on the noticeboard beside the door.' We swung around in our seats to see a large bulletin board covered with lists.

'As a group, you have much more freedom of thought and action than the others. You're the government's prime Catastrophe Committee. This afternoon, I'd like you to chew over the problems, sleep on it and be here tomorrow, early.

'Finally, I need to make you aware that everything we discuss is subject to the Official Secrets Act.'

Structured discussions began.

Owing to my commitments I left early, picked up Caroline from Diane and we returned to Guildford. I'd need to sort out my priorities if I were to be of any real use to this Catastrophe Committee.

We made it back to the university on time and found the entrance area of the building almost deserted.

Caroline barked, 'Hrop,' so we stopped and she eased herself out of the pushchair.

'You okay with your feet?'

'Href.'

Did she want to show Gren she was not an invalid? Pride, perhaps. Had she sensed his interest in me? I wished we could talk to each other. I resolved to work on better communication with her tonight.

Inside the building, Caroline walked gingerly on her sore paws. There was a small group of people standing by the central desk and one of them was Gren Pointer.

As we approached, he came over and shook my hand but as he squeezed I yanked it free. I didn't want to give him any encouragement, but he was nice. I needed to stop myself from seeing him as attractive. It was wrong the way he was flirting with me, particularly while Caroline was at my side.

'Come, I'll take you to the class. Can you manage a few stairs, Mrs Arnold?'

'Href,' she said. I translated, 'Yes, thanks.'

'You're building a language?'

'I suppose we are,' I responded as we went up a flight of stairs and stood outside a lecture room.

'Be quiet, please, as we enter? People entering a lecture theatre can be very distracting.'

We both nodded. Gren eased the door open. Twenty or thirty young women sat in the front couple of rows and Janice Howard, was talking to them. She had a domestic cooker to one side with pots and pans upon it and an electric kettle on a table. Behind her was a large projected image of a pan of boiling water.

Gren whispered, 'Today has focused on domestic dangers. Tomorrow will cover telephones, communications, bank accounts and so on, but there is light relief during each day. They were playing a boardgame during lunch. Tomorrow, it's making cakes.'

As we listened, I stroked Caroline's head and ears, her favourite caress. The teacher was asking questions of each of the women, and all the questions were about electricity, cookers, and hot water. After about ten minutes talking about electric shock dangers, the class was ending and she recapped some of the subjects the girls had been learning.

'Some questions, class. Think clearly before answering. Remember back to when we were discussing these matters in class. Ready? Lucy. What must we do if we are using a pan on the stove?'

A middle-aged blonde woman answered, 'Make sure the handles are not sticking out.'

The teacher illustrated this by moving a saucepan on the dummy cooker, 'Correct. And after cooking, what do we do, Sandra?'

'Check everysing's off and move pans off hot rings.'

'Correct again, Sandra, but it is everything, not everysing. Now if you are burned by water or touching something hot. What do you do first, Jean?'

I was pleased that the teacher was also helping with her accent.

'Put some cream on it,' said a white brunette lady beside Sandra.

'No, it wouldn't be the first thing. What is the very *first* thing? You've been burned by something hot; it is hurting. What is the first thing to do? Anyone else who knows put your hands up,' and most of the hands went up, but there was no shouting out.

'Oh yes,' said Jean, remembering from some earlier part of the day, 'water.'

'Yes, but what do you do with the water?'

Jean tried again, 'Put my hand in it.'

'Hot water or cold water, everyone?'

'Cold,' a jumbled chorus from most of the women.

'Yes, plunge your hand into it quickly or run the cold tap over it. And next, Sally?'

'Turn things off and get help,' came from a stout black woman.

'Yes, very good. All of you are very good. Now, personal safety. What do you do if a strange man starts talking to you? Rebecca.'

'Tell him not to talk to me, because I'm a child,' said a young oriental woman.

'And then? Margaret.'

'Get home quickly or tell someone nearby that I'm a child and need help,' said a slim mousey-haired woman.

Gren whispered, 'We have a judo teacher who will spend an hour with each class every week on basic self-defence too. He starts with this class tomorrow.'

The teacher continued, 'Class will end now, but tonight I want you to remember today's lessons, and what you need to do in each of the situations we talked about. Can you promise me you'll spend twenty minutes on it? Maybe when you're lying in bed before going to sleep?'

There were many mumbles of general agreement.

'We'll all be here again tomorrow. We're going to learn about credit cards and banks, but I also want each of you to bring an apron so you won't get your clothes messy as we're going to make cakes in the afternoon. Do you want to make cakes?'

There was a chorus of "yes" and "yes, please" from the assembly. Gren guided us out before any of the students saw us, and we stood in the corridor.

'We're privileged to have been able to watch this. Thank you,' I said and Caroline let out a muted 'href'.

Gren's eyes told me there was more to this than him being kind to one of many parents. 'I'm glad you found it interesting. Now I must go to a meeting. Make your way to the lobby. Good to see you both again. I hope you can work things out. If you ever want to talk to me about Sandra, please call me. This is my card.' He handed over a newly printed business card, shook my hand – again trying to hold on to it too long – and walked away along the corridor. The card proclaimed he was *Head of Adult-Children Education, University of Surrey*. We had the boss attending to us.

Caroline licked my hand, and we went down the stairs, where we saw a growing number of people gathering to meet their daughters and sons from their various classes.

Shortly, Sandra's group came to the top of the stairs and ran down, Janice Howard's voice bellowing after them, 'No running, girls! Walk as you've been learning! Running is for parks and playing fields.'

They all stopped and walked more sedately down the stairs. It was sad they were losing this aspect to their childhood. Sandra waved at us and came over as soon as she could. Three other women came with her and Sandra said, 'See. Told you my mum's a dog.'

'How do we know it's your mum?' asked one of the women.

I said, 'This *is* Sandra's mum. You can stroke her back gently if she'll let you. She'll bark twice if it is okay.'

'Href, href.'

Each of the young women came over and stroked her, but Sandra sat beside her mum and cuddled up tightly to her. I didn't know what to do or say. I saw tears in Caroline's eyes. She licked Sandra's cheek. Damn it, my own tears welled up again. I must find a way to better control my emotions. It was becoming annoying for me.

'Enough for now. Better get back to your own parents,' I said, dabbing my eyes.

One woman ran over to a teenage boy and I heard her say, 'You see the dog, Dad. It's Sandra's mum. She's a dog, Dad.'

The teenage father said, 'That's nice,' and took his, much taller, adult daughter's hand as they left the building. It was all so outlandish.

'Come on,' I said, and we headed off to the car.

»«o»«

Back at home, Sandra helped me change Caroline's dressings by fetching and carrying water and healing cream. I let her apply cream to the least bad rear paw. Her left front paw was now almost healed, but we decided to leave it dressed for one more day. Sandra brought the tablets through to the lounge with a small amount of water in one of the new bowls, and they were quickly downed.

Caroline went to her pad and spent a while writing. After a while she called, 'Beff. Grmm hrrr,' which I translated as "Beth. Come here."

I sat on the floor, and Caroline cuddled into me. I put an arm around her and picked up the first sheet. The writing was better and there was more on the page.

THX TDAY
LUV U
GRN LKS U LTS
DNT MND

TL ME TDAY STF

I worked through it.

'Gren likes me and you don't mind, but I love you.'

'Href.'

'Don't worry. I'm not running off, but it feels peculiar. It's being in this body. I pick up things from her. He's handsome, I don't know why, and it makes me feel uncomfortable.'

She tapped the DNT MND note.

'You might not mind, but I do.'

She went to the pad and wrote, 'IM DOG NW.'

'You're still Caroline to me even if you are a dog now. I still love you.'

Tears rolled down her cheeks again. Her doggy tears still surprised me, but they do have tear ducts. I embraced her tightly for a couple of minutes. I put her bowl of tea on the floor and took my mug to the sofa.

When she'd finished, she trotted into the lounge, jumped onto the sofa and cuddled up onto me with her forequarters on my lap.

'Trk,' she said. Her word for "talk".

She wrinkled her nose and poked it into the junction of my thighs.

'Nh,' she said and moved off me, 'Nh, nh.'

Oh, my God, I had forgotten my period. I'd changed when I arrived in Downing Street and again at lunchtime but forgot later. I pressed my fingers against my crotch. Damp! I'd made a mess of my underwear and the trousers.

I jumped up. None on the sofa, thank God. I rushed upstairs to wash and change. I vowed I'd *never* forget again. I'd learned an important lesson, and I'd soon have to deal with my daughter having similar accidents.

I came back downstairs and sat at the other end of the sofa, Caroline curled up beside me, taking great pleasure in making her laugh sounds on and off for several minutes while I recounted my exciting day in Downing Street.

She wasn't going to let me live this down.

25 HUMANIMAL FARM

The committee takes a road trip

The alarm went at six.

I drifted into consciousness. The warmth of Caroline lying beside me, curled up tightly against my breasts and tummy was comforting. My arm had fallen asleep underneath her and I quickly reached over to stop the annoying digital beep from the bedside clock and to shake off the pins and needles.

I needed to be in Downing Street by nine and the trains were still unreliable.

I hugged my wife. Her tail moved against me indicating her enjoyment. Her long tongue passed across my face. I'd always hated it when people's animals licked me or jumped up at me, but this was different. It was such an affectionate caress and I squeezed her tightly.

'I need to get up and get ready to go,' I said, heaving myself out of bed and heading to the shower.

When I returned to dress, Caroline had gone. My confidence was improving, and today I chose one of Suzy's ultra-chic suits in light blue. The skirt was short, about six inches above my knees. Was that too daring? I decided to brazen it out. As Suzy said, it was just that I still thought of myself as a man which held me back. No other attractive woman would have the slightest hesitation in wearing this outfit. With it, I chose a pure white blouse and shoes to match the suit colour. They only had two-inch heels, so I'd manage fine.

I'd spent quite a deal of time choosing what to wear with the suit. As Geoff, I used to put on the first shirt in the drawer, first tie which came to hand. Was this more influence by Suzy over my subconscious? A small wallet

I'd bought to hold my credit cards and notes fitted nicely into the inside jacket pocket. I didn't need a handbag as I had my laptop case with me and put my necessities in there. I set alarms on my new iWatch to prevent yesterday's "bloody accident" recurring.

I checked myself in the mirror. Skirt straight and level, blouse buttons straight, all colour coordinated. I hurried downstairs as my newfound fashion consciousness was in danger of making me late. I was annoyed at my wasting time on my appearance but was seemingly unable to prevent myself. Extremely strange and confusing.

Caroline only had bandages on her rear feet now, and I left her with Sandra who'd, again, managed to shower and dress herself without any problem. I'd written a taxi number for her on a notepad. The plan was for the taxi to take Sandra to class for nine. She had enough to pay for it. In the afternoon, Caroline would be picked up by a cab to go and meet Sandra. I'd written notelets for Caroline to show to the taxi driver as required. I'd also bought Caroline a purse and I'd attached a stiff loop so she could get it on without help. I was planning a new collar with other accessories and simple pannier-bags for visits to shops.

Communication was still the most difficult issue, but I'd an old Hudl tablet which might be adaptable for her to use when we had time to experiment. She could select messages from a menu. Time was the problem. While it was exciting to be part of this Catastrophe Committee, I was letting my family down. I'd require time off to collect Wilson at some point too. They'd said tomorrow, so I expected a call today.

At COBRA, there were two absentees for personal reasons. We all knew there would be these intrusions into our work. It was part of the problem we were commissioned to resolve.

We decided to spend the morning working out what to do about the individuals who'd been transferred into animals. It seemed the most pressing need, but by lunch we weren't making much progress. We called the cabinet secretary and asked for a minibus to take us to one of the holding farms at two o'clock. Caroline would have been useful here today, but I could hardly expect her to be allowed to listen-in to everything.

We ate lunch in COBRA. An unexpectedly good spread arrived. Sandwiches of smoked salmon, ham, chicken, roasted peppers plus quartered pork pies, halved Scotch eggs and innovative salads, fresh orange juice, coffee, tea, milk, and coke or lemonade. No expense had been spared providing for us. A veritable banquet of a picnic.

At two, we boarded not a minibus but a luxury twenty-six seat coach and set off north into Middlesex. En route to the farm, we passed through Harrow, which Caroline had spelled out as where she'd been helped by a butcher. I resolved to get their name and take her with me to thank them sometime.

Around two forty-five we pulled into Colne Park Farm through an impressive entrance with automatic barriers. In adjacent fields were the most extraordinary collection of animals. Creatures you would never normally find in the same location. Many of them ambled over to the fence nearest us.

We piled off the coach and a sturdily-built lady in a gentleman's suit came out of the house to greet us.

Giles Burton walked up to her and they shook hands. He introduced us as members of an emergency committee. The lady was Brian Isherwood, the farmer. He was obviously not going to compromise by dressing in any female clothes and had squeezed himself into one of his old tweed suits.

The trouser legs were rolled up as they were too long and the same with his sleeves. It would be comic if it weren't so sad.

'How can we help?' he asked in a voice far higher pitched than I'd expected with his gruff and businesslike appearance.

We explained we wanted input from the humanimals and were led over to the gate where, by now, there was a crowd gathering including dogs, cats, sheep, pigs, cattle, horses, Shetland ponies, two badgers, a number of foxes, a lioness, an orangutan, a camel, and several varieties of deer. It was most bizarre seeing the lioness standing beside a sheep.

'Good afternoon, everyone. My name is Giles Burton. I'm from the Prime Minister's office, and these people are members of one of our emergency committees. They wanted to meet some of you in person. Know what I mean? Can we ask you some questions?'

There was a chorus of barks, bellows, growls, and other farmyard noises from the assembly. More humanimals were approaching from a further field.

I asked Brian, 'What arrangements are there at night?'

'Well, it doesn't really matter with twenty-four-hour daylight, but we've four huge barns. A surprising number prefer to sleep outside. The supernova has probably helped the nocturnal species adapt to being awake during normal day hours,' he said.

Mark, the neurological surgeon, made his way to the front and spoke to the herd, 'I'm a neurosurgeon. There's a whole medical department investigating the possibility of a reversal process. I'd like to know about the effects of this transfer within your individual minds. Can I ask you all to move back from the fence about six feet?'

There was a general shuffling and noises from the throng of beasts as they retreated a short distance, no doubt wondering what he had in mind.

'Thanks. What I'd like to know first is this. Any of you who are finding your thought processes impaired, please step forward to the fence. For instance, if you are having trouble adding one hundred and twenty-six to one hundred and thirty-two mentally or reciting the Lord's prayer in your mind as well as you would normally do.'

There were more strange noises. How do a variety of animals look and sound when they're testing their knowledge of the Lord's prayer or mental arithmetic?

Smaller animals came forward. Several cats and smaller breeds of dogs, one of the badgers, a couple of foxes. Most of the others didn't budge.

'Thank you. Interesting. It was what we expected. I'd like you to come to one side with me please for further questioning.' The group of creatures followed him and Len along the fence to the left. I tagged along as a greyhound also has a small skull. The rest of the committee questioned the larger group of humanimals.

Mark sat on a stone trough and asked more questions, making notes of the answers on his tablet. He was trying to ascertain the extent of lost intellect. Would they recover it if they did return to human form? I decided to find out from Caroline later if her cognisance was impaired.

Using various methods, we managed to ask some questions of the animals, but it was a most unsatisfactory experience.

Back near the larger group, Jonah, the rather handsome Chinese thirty-year-old, was standing to one side on an in-depth phone call. He had a self-satisfied expression when he'd finished the call. He'd sat beside me on the coach and we'd been talking together. Suzy's subconscious was exceedingly positive about him. It was disturbing to be drawn to someone but wanting to keep your distance. I didn't know if I'd ever get used to it. Did all women feel like this when dealing with good-looking men?

'You look like the cat that got the cream?' I said.

'Breakthrough. We need a communicator. I've got the R and D team working on something which can be used by anything from a cat's toe to a cow's nose.'

'Brilliant, it'll be most useful. We need to know what is going on in the minds of these creatures.' I felt it would be too selfish to ask for one for Caroline. Maybe later.

He was on the phone for another five or six minutes and returned to the group. He told Giles what he was organising and, by consensus, we decided to finish for the day when Mark had got everything he needed from his smaller humanimals. He was becoming frustrated with the limitations of yes and no answers.

Giles walked over to the fence and spoke, 'Can I get your attention for a moment, please?'

Eyes of all sizes and shapes turned to look at him. 'Communication is stifling progress here. One of our team has got an electronics group working on an interpretation device so when we return, we should be able to communicate better. Mr Isherwood has a whiteboard set up in shelter two. Between now and our next visit, it would be useful if you compiled a list of questions or suggestions.

'I must tell you not to hold out hope for a quick solution to this problem. It's likely to be months before we'll see progress in any repatriation of minds from one person to another and it could be even longer. It might not even be possible. Know what I mean? As a group, you're our number one priority, so you can be sure no effort is being spared, but there's unlikely to be a quick fix.

'We all wish you well, as do the Cabinet and Prime Minister. We'll send any extra information to Mr Isherwood by memory stick which you can view on your large screen TV in the shelter. Thank you so much for your help.'

There was much murmuring among the throng. We waved as we boarded the coach for the trip back to London. En route, Jonah's eyes spent more time on my knees than on the scenery. He made me uncomfortable and I resolved to sit next to Justin or on my own on our next excursion.

Back in COBRA we jotted down our findings. Mark announced he was returning to Imperial College to see what progress was being made there. I needed a few minutes with him and Len before they left.

'Mark, did you find much in the way of memory loss or drop in cognisance with those smaller humanimals? One was a dog about the same size as Caroline.'

'Yes, Beth. The smaller animals were having problems. We gave them other tasks to check out for themselves. One of the cats was having trouble adding up single digit numbers like six plus seven, so there is a problem there for sure. A rabbit was having difficulty remembering where it was from and it was gradually getting worse. I would imagine memories will eventually be permanently lost, but we're hoping intelligence will be retained which will be most important if we can find a way to repatriate their minds.'

'Surely any cognisance which overflowed the new brain during Mindslip will have vanished?' I suggested.

'Beth, I fear you might be right. Get Caroline to perform some rudimentary tests and see how she gets on. Nevertheless, repatriation into a larger mind might allow a rapid return to near normal mental ability even if specific memories have been lost.'

'What's the smallest animal we know of which contains a human? Any data on that?' I asked.

'Yes,' Len said. 'The smallest we know of is a mouse, which certainly was trying to communicate on day one, but by day three had stopped.'

'So, smaller animals lose their cognisance?' Mark asked.

'It would appear so,' said Len. 'I'll try to find out about other cases and report back.'

I said, 'I'm influenced strongly by my transferor. You know, how I stand and move, but also in my view of men, dare I say? The influence is disturbing, yet my transferor was human. I can only imagine the effect on humanimals.'

'Interesting, Beth,' said Len. 'I know exactly what you mean. I used to love strong curries but now hate the smell and taste. It must be owing to the new body influencing me. Strangely, I also had to binge clean my house at the weekend. My transferor does not want to live in the organised chaos of my untidy bachelor pad.'

The three of us laughed. More seriously, I agreed to report back on my interrogation of Caroline.

It was a little over a mile from Downing Street to Waterloo, so I decided to walk, but the wolf whistles and catcalls at the roadworks in Whitehall was enough for me. I couldn't believe it. Must be the short skirt. I managed to hail a cab and got it to drop me at the station. I stepped straight onto an express to Guildford and was home in fewer than forty minutes.

What a wonderful surprise when I walked into the house. Sandra was in the kitchen with her apron on, slicing up boiled potatoes, with Caroline watching from an old bar stool which had been in a downstairs cupboard. The potatoes were being put into a deep baking tray. I gave Caroline and Sandra hugs.

'Looks good, Limpet. Did you learn this at school?'

'Some, but Mum has been showing me sings using the notes.'

'Href.'

'What are we having? And it is things, not sings, Sands.'

'Sorry. Steaks and spicy tatties.'

'Sounds delicious. I'll go and change.'

I helped a little to get the steaks right and Sandra was a quick learner. She'd managed almost all of it herself, and I was so proud of her. It would've been impossible before the change when she wasn't allowed near knives or the cooker. The teaching had been brilliant. The meal was good.

Later, when I was tidying up, I found lots of A3 sheets Caroline had written for Sandra's cooking, including one which said two sharp barks meant "stop". I was glad she'd managed to make herself so helpful.

In the evening, a call arrived from Ted Wright at the Repatriation Department. I marvelled at government working at nine in the evening. Wilson would be on a morning flight from Rwanda and should arrive at two o'clock at Birmingham International Airport. We discussed it, and Caroline decided to come with me. The University of Surrey school had told us there would be after-school clubs if required. Perhaps Sandra could attend one of those, otherwise they would have to put her in a taxi home. I didn't want Sandra walking the streets until she was a little more worldly-wise.

We all curled up on the sofa to watch a football match. The government was encouraging anything which would be conducive to life returning to normal. It was a hopeless game with players, despite their skills, being tactically naïve. Others knew what they should be doing but lacked the skill to do it. Freakish and almost comical. I guessed the league system would be meaningless until the people who'd inherited the skill replaced the registered footballers who'd lost it. Must be alarming to find you were no good at something you'd previously excelled in. Supporting your usual club was something which did transcend Mindslip.

    Caroline and I sat up late, with me telling her about the day's events. I helped her shower with a more fragrant pet shampoo and dried her thoroughly before we went to bed and she curled up tightly beside me. I stroked her gently until her breathing changed and I knew she was asleep. I soon followed her into dreamland where lions and tigers were talking to each other and great apes were talking to us. It slipped into more of a Monkey Planet nightmare as the night progressed.

26 REPATRIATION ARRIVALS

Beth reunites the family

I dressed in jeans and a sloppy sweater for comfort and drove Sandra, who had chosen jeans and a cotton top, to the university and arranged for her to stay late in one of the clubs or be sent home by taxi if we were still not back from Birmingham to pick her up.

As I left, a voice called from behind me, 'Mr Arnold?'

It was Gren Pointer. He greeted me with a handshake, holding on the usual fraction longer than he should, exactly as he always did. Why did I like it? I pulled my hand free.

'It's Beth Arnold now,' I said. 'I've adopted my new situation.'

'Good move,' he replied, 'It'll make you feel better in yourself. How's Sandra getting on?'

'Brilliantly. We're amazed at what has been achieved in a couple of days.'

'And your wife?'

'Not well. Age related problems, but we're doing our best. I have an excellent vet treating her.'

'Oh, yes. I suppose a vet would be best. Good luck.'

I explained about our trip to Birmingham and we discussed Wilson for a few minutes including his actual and post-mindslip age.

'So glad for you. Speak to me if the difference is any greater and we'll get him into a class similar to Sandra's but for men. Anyway, I'm due to be here until about six so if you haven't arrived, I could take Sandra to your home. Can she get in?'

'Oh, yes. We've got her a key. A taxi would do.'

'Okay. Fine. I'll make sure she's in a taxi before I leave tonight.'

'That would be brilliant. Are you sure you don't mind?'

'No, not at all,' he said and smiled.

'She's got her purse attached to her belt, there's enough money for the cab in there and it also contains her key. Please make sure she has it before you let her go.'

'No problem at all. Any more news about what's happening?'

'Do you have an office or something rather than talk here?' I said, looking around the still busy reception area.

'No, but there's a students' coffee bar in the next building,' and he smiled disarmingly at me. Suzy's part of me could not suppress her appreciation.

'Fine, it would be nice. I've got fifteen minutes.' I found Sandra and told her what was happening after school. The adult-children were in an agitated conversation about hair. I guessed hair was also on the agenda today.

Gren walked close to me. Too close. Suzy's component of me was undoubtedly smitten. He was handsome. I knew men like Daniel Craig or Hugh Grant were handsome, but this was different. I felt it inside. I stole a glance at his face as we walked. Damn it. The idea of him, say, holding my hand, was no longer anathema. The possibility I was changing in and of myself concerned me. I liked who I'd been. I didn't get harassed. I didn't have to worry about my clothes or my appearance. I was spending less time on my make-up and hair but only because I was improving my dexterity. I no longer looked lustfully at my own nakedness. My thighs and mons looked sexy but seeing them didn't give me the same thrill they had only a few days ago. My naked body would soon mean no more to me than my male torso had done before Mindslip. Were Suzy's hormones working themselves into my very being? How did the mind and hormones interact? They must have an effect.

Gren pushed open the tall glass doors to the building with the coffee shop. It was a bit stark and functional, but the view over the grass area of the campus was pleasant enough. We both ordered latté and a pastry and sat beside the full height windows.

'So?' he asked, 'How are Caroline's wounds?'

'Her injuries are healing and we have a rudimentary communication system.'

'And the meetings, any progress?'

'I'm now part of what is called the Catastrophe Committee and we're using COBRA. Our current priority is the number of people who've mindslipped into animals. Yesterday afternoon we visited a farm where there were more than a thousand, and it is one of hundreds.'

'Is mindslipping the term being used to describe what has happened?'

'Yes, it is. I actually coined the term. If I go down in history for it, I wonder if it will be as Geoff or Beth,' I said and laughed.

While we talked, we drank our coffee and ate the pastries.

Gren asked, 'What was the farm like?'

'Those poor people, Gren. The inability to communicate is the worst aspect. One or two could draw on boards and there was an orangutan who said a few words but very guttural. Their voice boxes aren't designed to talk. Even worse, the people in smaller animals are losing huge chunks of their cognisant capabilities. The size of the brain is obviously an important factor.'

'Is Caroline finding she's lost faculties?'

'Not so far, we did some tests last night. Caroline's problem is having less than a year to live. Greyhounds have relatively low life expectancy, and she has heart failure. The vet has put her on several drugs but told me in confidence she hasn't much time. A little over a year if we are lucky. It's quite devastating.'

'Can't your group help?'

'There are some pretty proficient medical people working on it, and Caroline has offered to be a guinea pig, but I've not pushed for it yet. I don't want to lose what time I have with her until there is at least a chance of success. What I'm telling you is in the domain of any intelligent person's speculation of what we might be doing but keep the detail to yourself.'

'No problem, Beth. Safe with me,' he reached across the table and put his hand on mine. I snatched it away.

He took a sharp intake of breath, 'Sorry. So, sorry, Beth. It was a natural gesture. I do apologise,' he said earnestly.

'Wrong on so many levels, Gren. I'm married, and I'm also a man. The fact my brain and body are having trouble making sense of their new interrelationship makes it even more complicated.'

'Don't worry. I promise it won't happen again.'

'I'd be grateful if you can ensure it won't.'

We sat in silence for a minute. I decided to come clean. 'Gren, I've an odd attraction to you, which I'm having trouble controlling. If we can't keep this relationship platonic, it'd be better not meeting again. It scares me.'

'Sorry. It's the same within me, Beth. I enjoy your company and I don't know how much of it is your personality or your physical appearance. When we first met, it was all about you as a person. I certainly can't stop your appearance affecting me because you are extremely attractive, but I promise I won't make any further slips. It must be my own transferor affecting my mind too. Remember that he's a thirty-year-old man, of course, not the fifty-plus-year-old woman I was before Mindslip. I was a lonely divorcee, so my outlook would be very much different to yours and this man's mind is affecting the way I treat people so please, again, excuse my indiscretion.' His face took on a pained and contrite expression.

I'd hurt him and hadn't intended to. I was drawn to him, and it worried me, but I needed to hang on to my sanity during this experience, 'Okay, let's forget it,' I said.

'Thank you. Do tell me we can continue to be friends.'

I didn't want to stop having anything to do with him. I liked his views on things. I liked the attention he'd lavished on the situation in which Sandra and I had found ourselves. God, I liked him as a person too, and there was that growing attraction I couldn't seem to resist. I guessed he was finding it the same.

'No, don't worry. We'll still chat. Okay?'

'Thanks. No harm done then?'

'No harm done,' I echoed, 'But I must be on my way. You'll ensure Sandra is safe this evening?'

'Of course.'

'I'd better go,' I said and we both stood. He offered his hand. I shook it. This time there was no attempt to hold on longer than necessary. I was disappointed.

Back at home, I told Caroline what I'd agreed with Gren. I told her about his hand, too and she gave her laugh noises and said, 'Hrold hru.'

'Yes, you did tell me,' I confirmed and explained how we'd left it.

'Szz ukay, Beff. Drong rerry.'

'No, it's not okay, darling, and I do worry.'

'Hnh, hnh, hnh!'

We set off for the big smoke of Birmingham.

There were still dozens of abandoned vehicles along the roads but at least they no longer caused delays. I drove particularly carefully whenever we encountered recovery squads.

At about one, we pulled into a service station and went to the shop. As we entered, I noticed the *No Dogs Except Guide Dogs* sign now had *& Humanimals* added in felt tip. I bought us some wraps. Chicken fajita for me and a ham wrap for Caroline which I cut into sections. We ate side by side at a picnic table. We both drank water and for dessert I ate another Danish pastry while she enjoyed a pack of sherbet lemons. A strange choice, but she'd particularly chosen them as I touched each of the bags on the selection roundel. A little of what you fancy can do you good. I felt a little nagging doubt about my fitness. Suzy had told me to exercise and there I was scoffing Danish pastries. I resolved to set up a proper fitness regime.

When we'd finished our lunch, I gave Caroline a huge hug. 'We're doing all right, darling, aren't we?'

'Href. Hol rrigh. Hruf hru, Beff,' she agreed.

'Love you, too,' I said and hugged her again.

We continued our journey, arriving at the airport about forty minutes early. The airport façade was modular, like enormous sections of a honeycomb. Through it we accessed the main vestibule where I got Caroline to jump onto a bench to let me remove the bags from her feet. There was another person in the queue with an Afghan hound, also off the lead. It noticed Caroline but there was no move from either of them to approach the other, so I assumed the Afghan was also a person.

At repatriation arrivals, I spoke to a person on duty in an ill-fitting uniform who gave me a small blackboard.

'Write your surname in large caps. When the arrival appears on the board, wait by the arrivals channel over there.'

'Thank you,' I said, taking some chalk from him and writing "ARNOLD" in large letters. I sat beside Caroline where I could watch the arrivals list.

After a while, I noticed she wasn't looking at the monitor.

'Can't you read the monitor?' I asked.

'Nh.'

'It says the plane is due in at two ten pm,' I told her.

I put my arm tightly around her, pulling her against my side securely.

'You bored?'

'Href.'

There was no television or anything similar for her to watch here. I already knew her vision was too poor for reading print, but it was surprising she couldn't make out the white on black letters of the arrivals monitor.

'You go and have a wander.'

'Href, Beff,' she said, jumped down and walked off towards the shops.

After the flight had arrived, I held up the board each time a black person came through the double doors. I felt something warm pressing against my leg. Caroline had returned and was sitting alongside me.

We waited another ten minutes and a middle-aged white woman came through and approached me.

'Hello. Are you Mr Arnold? I'm Maureen Russell,' she said quietly, examining me carefully. She'd obviously been briefed by Edward Wright.

'Yes,' I said.

'I'll let you introduce yourselves to Wilson. We have a room available.'

She passed back through the doors and re-emerged with a smart black lad who was not quite a teenager. He was wearing some blue jeans and a colourful shirt hanging outside his trousers plus a warm padded anorak. I wanted to rush up to him and embrace him but resisted the impulse. He didn't know who I was.

'Come with me,' said Maureen and we all followed her through to a room with two windows overlooking the apron. Wilson couldn't take his eyes off Caroline.

Inside, I asked, 'Are you Wilson Arnold?'

'Yes, who are you?' he asked with wide eyes and a distinct African lilt.

'Right, if you'd all like to take seats, I'll stay to help with the explanation if it is necessary,' and she indicated the seats around a table.

This was so difficult. I said, 'Hi, Wilson. Do you know why you were in Rwanda?'

'No. Who are you? Is it your dog?' he asked reaching over to stroke Caroline's neck as she sat upright on the chair.

'I'll explain who I am shortly – and the dog – but we need to know what you understand has happened to people first.'

Caroline was leaning into Wilson's caresses. He was a nice-looking lad. Slim, perhaps even underweight. His skin shone with the glossy-black characteristic of some sub-Saharan tribes and he'd a lovely smile, behind which were some startlingly white teeth. His eyes were dark brown and his hair a short, but tangled mop. He studied my face.

I explained. 'The Earth has gone through a change which has affected every living creature, including you and us.

Your mind slipped from your own head into the head of the body you live in today. It's still you though, isn't it?'

'Yes. It's me in here,' and he tapped his head as he spoke, 'Why'd it happen?'

'You remember the supernova? Betelgeuse's second explosion and the sun's radiation met and caused the Mindslip to happen. Did you know some people have mindslipped into animals?'

'Someone said animals had slipped too.'

'But you haven't experienced it yourself?'

'No. Is there someone in the dog?' Suspiciously he snatched his hand away from Caroline and sat back.

'Yes, but it's okay. The dog likes your strokes and will bark twice to prove it.'

'Href, href.'

Wilson stared at Caroline in amazement and gently stroked her again.

'You can ask questions. You'll get answers as nods or shakes so you have to ask a yes or no type question. Why don't you ask something?'

'Are you a person?' he almost whispered the question. Caroline nodded.

'Do you know my mum and dad?' He always was bright. She nodded again.

I said, 'Your mum and dad have had their minds move, too. Come up with a question you could ask your dad which no one, but he could answer.'

He turned towards Caroline and it was obvious he was pondering questions. His fingers were wringing as an aid to cognition. I didn't interrupt his train of thought. My son was a clever boy. He'd come up with something without prompting.

A minute or more passed before he spoke to Caroline, 'Who signed my shirt last year? Was it Harry Kane?'

'Erik Lamela,' I replied promptly.

'I thought you were going to be the dog,' he said.

'No, she's your mother and can't speak, Wilson.'

'Mum?'

She nodded, he bent and gave her a proper hug.

'We're still a family, Wilson,' I said, desperately hoping he'd come and hug me too.

Caroline licked his face. He was crying. I went over and kneeled by Caroline's chair with Wilson so the three of us could have a family hug. Tears fell from Caroline's eyes too. They were soon joined by my own. My stoicism broke down completely. Hormones again?

Maureen stood up, 'I'll leave you to your reunion. Leave the door open when you've finished, so we know it's free.'

In a tiny voice, I said, 'Thanks.'

Caroline made a small whine, and Maureen left the room, telling us to take as long as we needed as she closed the door.

'Want to come home, Wilson?'

'Are you really my dad?'

'You know I am, who else was there when Erik Lamela signed your shirt after we beat Bournemouth five-one?'

'No one. But you're a woman.'

'And your mum is a dog. We've all changed. Sandra's all grown up.'

'What, older than me?'

'Much older. She's going to a special school because she's twenty-two years old now but still eight-years-old inside.'

'Is she still a girl?'

'Yes, a young woman.'

'My friends will laugh because I'm black,' he said, his eyes full of tears.

'They won't because everyone has changed in some way or another. I'm Japanese. It doesn't matter. Many people have changed colour, sex, and age. So, don't worry about it and, anyway, you're still you and we love you.' I stood up, and Caroline jumped onto the floor. 'Are you coming? Let's go home.'

Wilson took my hand and we left the meeting room and headed for the exit. He helped me put the protective bags on Caroline's rear feet and we set off for the car park.

As I drove, I looked in the rear mirror. Wilson was hugging Caroline. I was so glad he was sufficiently well balanced to cope with what had occurred and understood our situation.

We pulled into the university on time. Gren was standing inside with Sandra and another man and woman. He waved, and Sandra came out of the building. I met her on the pathway, reminding her Wilson was with us just as he jumped out of the back door.

'Gosh, is it really you, Sands? You're humungous!'

'Wils?' she asked with a shocked expression, and suddenly they were both hugging.

Sandra jumped in the front. I gave Gren another wave and we headed home. A strange family indeed.

27 CLIVE THE PIG

On the premise that the more professional I looked, the less harassment I would attract, I dressed in a chic pin-striped skirt suit today. I looked and felt good. The skirt on this one wasn't so short. The powder blue suit was six inches above my knee, this one only three. The combination of Suzy's subconscious giving me pride in her appearance and my own willingness to bend to it was working well.

We were now confident enough in Sandra to allow her to take cabs to and from the university, but I cautioned her about being wary of anyone trying to talk to her on the way. I felt Wilson wouldn't have a problem going to school and I had promised to call his teacher to explain his anxiety over his colour. Caroline intended some shopping using pannier bags I'd made for her over the previous couple of evenings. She had notes I'd written, which she could show to the shopkeepers, although her own writing was becoming smaller, neater and quicker.

I took the early train to London and arrived in persistent rain, the brightness from our two stars giving a false impression of the lightness of the cloud cover. Once I was outside the Royal Institution, I sheltered under a small pop-up umbrella watching the assortment of pedestrians passing by and called Wilson's school to give his form-teacher the heads-up on his anxieties about his colour. He sounded sympathetic and told me not to worry, but no doubt I would.

'Hi Geoff,' Diane called as she approached the building from behind me. She'd always been cheerful as the older woman and was even more so as this middle-aged man.

'I'm going by the handle Beth now, Diane,' I said as she gave me a peck on the cheek. How odd. I supposed it was natural with our roles reversed.

'Ah, going native?' she said in her gruff male voice, 'I suppose I should do the same.'

She opened her arms to give a mock display of her biceps, 'What do you think? Jock or Bill or Frank?'

'Well, I chose Beth because it is like Geoff. Maybe Brian?' I laughed.

'Hey, not bad. Brian, it is.'

I took the stairs to the office, booted up the desktop we used for inter-department communication and opened the latest findings by the Observatory. Betelgeuse was maintaining its luminosity and was still far brighter than a full moon. It was clearly visible in daylight, but no longer casting such disturbing shadows when the sun was visible. Hubble photographs showed it had pumped out two enormous clouds of material illuminated from within. The resultant object resembled an eye with the collapsed star as the pupil.

I analysed the data from summaries received from the observations of satellites and radio telescopes across the world. The electromagnetic blast from the supernova should not be damaging by itself, so my attention turned to the data which had been obtained from the coinciding coronal mass ejection and the second explosion.

It must have been an exceptional blast for the radiation to penetrate the atmosphere and cause Mindslip. There was no precedent for a supernova putting out two explosions only a few hours apart. In fact, science said it could not happen. There was now talk about there having been two stars and the one triggered the other, but I'd done quite a lot of work on Betelgeuse before the nova event and had seen no sign of a second star. We'd probably get to the bottom of the mystery eventually. A small black hole perhaps?

We were all even more perplexed about why computers and their memory chips remained unaffected, yet organic brains had been altered so dramatically. The science currently answered none of our questions.

When Mike and Justin arrived, we discussed it further, but it didn't improve our understanding. The closest we had to an answer was that the coronal mass ejection disturbed the protective magnetosphere and allowed harmful radiation through, causing Mindslip. It would have to do for now, but it was a most unsatisfactory situation as far as I was concerned as I was the acknowledged expert on supernovae, the "Not So Big Bangs", as my own book's title proclaimed.

The lack of a simple answer was becoming a problem. Religions were being born, claiming it was an act of God on the scale of the biblical flood. It was the ultimate Creator demonstrating to mankind the futility of racial and cultural hatred, since so many of the transfers were from white to black, brown to yellow and other combinations. Scientists like us needed to demonstrate a rational explanation before fanatics could hijack Mindslip for their own ends.

Even Christians were talking about it being prophesied in Revelations as being the first sign of Armageddon which, itself, was predicted to occur three score years and ten after the foundation of Israel. If I'd been a religious person, even I might've been swayed to believe the world was being punished during a tantrum by its magical alien deity.

Justin asked a tired-looking Mike to write with more specific questions to our colleagues, and coordinate with all the departments, observatories, and universities with which we were in contact. He was so frail. I hoped he'd be up to it.

Justin and I lunched with Greg, the quantum physicist, and Bill, one of the neuropsychologists. It was fascinating to listen to their take on the phenomenon, but nothing truly new or positive came out of our meeting. No data came close to supporting any one hypothesis for Mindslip's cause. We were all flummoxed. Justin decided to go on to Imperial College for more cross-discipline meetings rather than come to Downing Street with me.

We spent a wet afternoon in COBRA getting nowhere on the causes of Mindslip, but Endron's tech approach to communicating with the humanimals was a high point.

After lunch, Jonah surprised us by entering the room accompanied by an absolutely enormous, immaculately clean, pink pig and a large computer monitor on a wheeled tripod. An assistant put a flat device, about half a metre square, onto the floor in the corner of the room. It looked quilt-like with about sixty slightly raised pads, roughly six by ten. Some of the pads were in different colours, but the main colour was tan.

The pig put its front right hoof into the centre of it. I'd never been this close to a large boar and had no idea they grew to such huge proportions. Jonah stood beside the mobile monitor which showed a pure white screen. The assistant left.

'Good afternoon, people. This is Clive. He was a computer systems analyst with Endron in his previous existence. We've spent the last couple of days coming up with this provisional communication device which is a touchpad and monitor.'

As Jonah spoke, we saw large letters appearing on the screen, slower than typing but fast enough to hold the attention.

'HI EVERYONE.'

We all said "hello", "hi" or "good afternoon".

'The pad works on pressure variations. Clive has learned the position of the word components and, by using a harder pressure the device suggests words. This is more sophisticated than the usual text suggestions on a mobile phone, but is based upon a more comprehensive, touch-sensitive system we've been building for tablets for over a year. All we needed to do was scale it up for Clive.

Watch the screen. Clive is going to tell you he's enjoying being out of the farm. Notice how the words develop from the first letters.'

ITS GR – IT'S GREAT 2 B – TO BE – HEL – HELPING – U – YOU.

'It's intuitive, and notice how it converted text speak for two and *B* into *to be*. Of course, occasionally it'll still go off at a tangent but we've been programming it specifically for Clive. *I T S* coupled with *G R* was quickly converted to *it's great*. To demonstrate this, we've been using a delayed print function. Clive has now switched that off and will type the same message to show the actual communication speed.'

The screen wiped clear. The words IT'S GREAT came up followed instantly by TO BE then HELPING and YOU.

'It won't always be as fast. It all depends upon the context. I'll let Clive say a few more words.'

I KNOW YOU ARE ALL WORKING HARD TO RESOLVE THIS, BUT ALL OF THE HUMANIMALS BIG YOU TO COME UP WITH A SOLUTION AS SOON AS YOU POSSIBLY CAN – BEG

It was almost perfect English, only "big" in error for "beg". We all praised Endron's tech team.

We spent the next thirty minutes quizzing Clive and learning how his host's hormones and instincts were affecting his ability to think and work in the way he had before Mindslip. It was a fascinating session. He explained how the boar's mind influenced his actions and that wanting to mount every sow he saw was one of the most difficult impulses to control. We thought he said that tongue-in-cheek but could not be sure. Knowing how Suzy influenced my thoughts meant there was probably some truth to it.

BY FOR NOW, I'M OFF BACK TO COLNE PARK. JUST HOPING ROAST PARK ISN'T ON THE MENU TODAY! Again, just the E of bye and PARK for pork being incorrect.

We all laughed, but in a subdued manner. There was a serious undercurrent to his concern, born from the knowledge humanimals had been slaughtered by mistake.

'Extremely impressive, Jonah,' said Giles, once Clive had left.

We turned our seats back towards the table. Jonah made a point of sitting beside me and had smiled broadly at me several times during the demonstration. It made me uncomfortable. It was a strange sensation. I tried to analyse my thoughts and feelings about it.

Initially I'd found him attractive and enjoyed talking to him, but gradually I was coming to dislike him. Any attraction I'd had for him vanished. It was like a tipping point. He'd turned me on initially, but now distinctly turned me off. I assumed it was another 'girl' thing. I remembered, as a teen, how girls would be fine with you for a date or two and would then not want to know you at all, as if a switch had been flipped. As a man, any girl I found attractive never lost her attractiveness, however annoying she was. Obviously, it didn't work like that for girls. I shrugged my mental shoulders. I was one now! Jonah was no longer of the slightest interest to me as a man.

I stood to give my report and apologised to the committee for our failure to find anything other than a circumstantial link between the sun, the supernova, and the Mindslip, but said work was ongoing.

Len White, another sex change victim, now to be known as Jen, stood. She was the consultant neuropsychologist who worked with Mark.

She spoke slowly and clearly. 'Mark and I spent the morning going through our results in detail. We've made some progress. We have eighteen university medical departments working on this problem.

'However, the breakthrough may have occurred accidentally at St Andrews, where they've been working with rats on another project.

'They have two groups of rats. Originally, they had forty, but they've filtered them down to twenty-six genuine rats. I mean the rats are pure rats, not containing the minds of other animals. One group has been trained to perform a particular function at the end of a maze, but before they can enter the maze they have to press a button high on one side to open the entrance to it. The other group are being kept separate from the first group.

'Last night they used a modified type of MRI scanner to lift the memories of one trained rat and apparently transfer them into the mind of an untrained rat, which, when put into the maze, pressed the button and ran unerringly to the reward at the end, which required the manipulation of two levers simultaneously.

'I should add that this was part of ongoing experiments they've been conducting for some weeks prior to Mindslip.

'We're somewhat concerned about how sure they were there had been no mix-up between the control group and the trained group. Had some of their control animals slipped into the minds of the first group, passing on their knowledge?

'They assured us they'd checked for that and that none of the control group could complete the puzzle prior to the experiment with the scanner. We've a colleague from Imperial on her way to St Andrews to double-check their processes.' She sat and Mark, the neurological surgeon stood.

'I must say we're optimistic after our observations over the camera link. If there are no serious mistakes in their procedures, this is better progress than we could have dreamt of.

'Of course, the transfer of some memories, while astounding, might not mean the whole of the knowledge and memories of the first animal had been moved. A further concern is the original rat retaining the ability to carry out the task, so, *if* – and it is a big if – the experiment worked, the personality has been duplicated, not exchanged. There are some horrible implications.'

'What do you mean by "horrible implications", Mark?' asked Giles.

'Suppose we are able to transfer Clive's mind to one of the humans with animal minds. We will be left with two Clives. One of them in the human, hopefully, but another remaining in the pig,' explained Mark.

'But what's the problem?' Giles asked. 'We don't care about the pig if the person has been transferred.'

I spoke up, 'No, Giles, you are missing Mark's point. Clive is still in the pig. The copy which stayed behind is still a human being in a pig. Put yourself in the position of the copy. You are stuck in the pig forever. In the case of my wife, for instance, while it would be wonderful if she could inhabit a female body again, she would still also be in the dying greyhound.'

The ramifications were quickly obvious to the remaining members of the committee.

Giles asked, 'So what do we do with the copy still in the animal?'

'Put it to sleep,' chipped in Gillian from the treasury.

'You *can't* do that!' exclaimed the bishop forcefully, despite the weak voice of the young teen girl. 'It is the soul you're talking about. It would be murder!'

'Well, is it?' asked Mark. 'Can the soul be split in two?'

'Shades of Voldemort,' said Gillian, and laughed.

I spoke up once more, 'I don't know how I would feel about allowing my wife, the greyhound, to be put to sleep even if I already have her as a woman. It wouldn't be right.'

'Beth is absolutely right,' agreed the bishop.

'Okay, people,' began Giles, 'let's not jump the gun here. First, we need to know if it works. Next, we need to ask for a volunteer humanimal. That should be okay even if it is a copy being produced. If it all works and the human is fully regenerated within the new human body, we can resolve the question of what we do with the humanimals. Know what I mean?'

Bishop David stood and coughed for attention. All eyes were on the teenage girl who was carrying the authority of the Church of England. 'I cannot allow a situation to arise where souls are being destroyed. This will need a lot of consideration.'

The brigadier said, 'This is indeed an intolerable scenario. We cannot allow anyone to be killed or "put to sleep" for any reason. We need a proper exchange. A copying system is not sufficient.'

'Wait a minute,' said Mark, 'I can't believe what I'm hearing! You're all getting ahead of our abilities. First, we need know if we're copying the entire mind or fragments of it. Once we have established the scope of the process, we can discuss ethics.'

'It is not acceptable,' said the bishop.

'Stop. All of you,' commanded Giles. 'Mark is right. We must discover whether the process works. We'll worry about how we resolve it later. This is nothing more nor less than a scientific experiment. Bishop, you can monitor what is happening, but we must progress with the experiment. Mark, Jen, go ahead and find out whether the whole mind can be transferred. I'd also like to remind all of you about confidentiality on this matter.'

Jen said, 'I need to point out what happened was rat to rat. There will need to be many experiments between different animals before we try pig to human.'

The bishop protested, 'I object. This is wrong. We must not copy minds. It is against all the church's principles. As you said, it is splitting souls. It cannot be God's will.'

'Hold on,' I said, breaking into the row, 'so far we only know a rat's conditioning has been transferred from one rat to another. We have no idea if its mind has been transferred. Even if we were sure, the next stage would be to try a transfer between two different types of animal – a challenge all of its own. Only when inter-animal transfers are proven to be successful can we experiment with one of the humanimals. Moral implications can be considered at the humanimal stage.'

'Beth, you've summed it up perfectly. Mark. Jen. Report back on Monday,' said Giles with real authority, and the bishop grumbled into silence.

Mark said, 'We've borrowed the latest scanner from GeoScanCorp and our guys are working with GeoScanCorp's technicians to adapt it. I also have people sourcing a sufficiently powerful processor to carry the data. What we're attempting is at the fringe of our technological ability.'

'How much data is involved? What were St Andrews using?' I asked.

'St Andrews were working with minimal data needs, if we are looking to transfer an entire human mind, we'll need equipment capable of the transfer. The data is too large to be stored. We'll have to stream it,' said Mark.

'We assume financial resources will not be a problem,' said Jen.

'What sort of cost?' asked Gillian.

'We're commissioning new technology. We can't put a figure on it yet, but it won't be cheap. We could stop dead now and produce a report, but it won't reduce the cost,' said Mark.

'Go ahead,' said Giles. 'Just keep me advised of costs as they're incurred.'

Mark and Jen left the room, and the rest of us went on to talk about some practicalities of the payment of salaries and benefits. More general discussion took place about food supplies, and what should be done for people who could no longer carry out their duties owing to the physical nature of the changes. Examples were heavy goods vehicle drivers who were no longer able to reach their pedals; surgeons whose hands were too clumsy; manual workers who were no longer strong enough to continue with their work. All these people would need retraining and support during their transition. Giles promised to contact survey groups to discover the numbers involved.

We called a halt at five. Giles didn't want our minds to be dulled by working too long without proper rest and relaxation.

'Drink, anyone?' asked Giles. There was some general agreement and we all headed off to the Red Lion in Derby Gate.

Jonah was attentive and touchy-feely, taking my elbow to help me in through the door and his hand pressed upon my back as we moved towards the bar. It wasn't obvious and might have been done with gentlemanly intentions, but I no longer liked it. We moved to sit at a long table beside the window and I sensed his hand on my waist.

'Jonah,' I whispered, 'I want you to stop touching me, please. It's not welcome. We're colleagues and nothing more.'

He took a step back, apologised, and I hoped it would be the end of the matter.

After a few drinks and some less controversial conversation than we'd had in our COBRA meeting, we all dispersed and headed home.

Back in Guildford, Sandra shared her day with me as had become the habit. She'd been learning more about her body and gaining a far better understanding of her reproductive organs than my clumsy efforts had provided. She also brought home a form to complete for a bank account and debit card, all with safeguards, of course.

Caroline's day had been less good. She'd gone to the local shop with her pannier bags, some money in a purse and written notes for what she wanted but hadn't appreciated the weight of items she was carrying. It had exhausted her. There was nothing too heavy, probably about twenty pounds in total, but when she arrived home she couldn't get the new entry system I'd installed to work.

She'd continually pressed the wrong numbers as she couldn't see the pad because of her snout.

She became too exhausted to continue trying and sat outside with her shopping for ages until our neighbour arrived home. Caroline scraped the four-digit code into the gravel by the back gate and the neighbour pressed the correct sequence for her. I resolved to get a bigger number pad. This DIY version had not been designed for a dog's paw. I should have checked she could manage it. I was annoyed at myself, but it was difficult to think of everything.

When I arrived home, she was lying on the sofa still exhausted. I didn't like the nature of her breathing. Long deep breaths as if recovering from a run or struggling to obtain sufficient oxygen. I rang the vet and got an appointment for the next morning.

Sandra helped me with the meal and Caroline enjoyed her steak pie which she preferred to meals like mince or pasta dishes.

During the evening, we watched the television. Caroline curled up beside me, her forequarters on my lap.

The main news continued to be awful. The death toll had escalated to more than fifteen million. Samaritans were calling upon people to volunteer to help those who were suicidal. There had been a spate of rapes and murders throughout the world and our now fresh-faced Prime Minister and Home Secretary announced powers akin to martial law to try to control the crime wave sweeping Great Britain.

None of the COBRA news was mentioned, of course. I broke the confidentiality to tell Caroline what they'd done. It brightened her a little and gave hope. I also told her about Jonah's flirting and unwelcome attentions.

'Hnh, hnh, hnh, hnh, hnh.'

I slapped her gently on the rump, eliciting a 'hrgh' her sound for 'hurt' which I knew was for fun as she licked my hand. My new over-emotional reactions saw me join her tears. She licked them away, which did nothing for my make-up!

That night she curled up in my arms in bed and was quickly asleep. I listened with anxiety to the sound of fluid in her bronchia. It didn't bode well.

28 TIME TO TAKE STOCK

It was good to dress down in jeans and a sloppy sweater for the weekend. I even looked good in that and was more comfortable each day with my new persona.

Breakfast was good with the whole family, although Caroline was not as bright today. Her tail was hanging down, giving away her discomfort. Sandra's education was helping her develop exponentially. This morning, with little help, we were graced with eggs, bacon, sausages, and toast. A couple of the egg yolks broke, the rest was swimming in a little too much oil, but otherwise it was almost perfect.

Wilson kept examining his hands.

'You won't ever need a suntan,' I teased.

'No, and – guess what?'

'What?' Sandra and I asked in unison.

'I'm a brilliant footballer!' he announced.

'Vow, Wils, cool! How'd you find out?' Sandra asked. I ignored the accent slip.

'We had sports on Friday, and we played football. I was amazing at it. I could run like the ball was stuck to my feet. Cool.'

'Incredible because you were fairly useless before. I used to say you would only ever play right back behind goal!' I said and laughed.

'Yes, I know. Sands couldn't cook either,' he said wistfully.

'But I've been learning to cook! I couldn't suddenly cook, you know.'

'And you're extremely good at it, Sandra,' I encouraged, 'but there might be other things you're now good at too. Next time you're talking to Monsieur Damay, ask him what talents his daughter had. You might be a great tennis player or something.'

'You're ever so big, Sands,' Wilson said.

'I know. I'm a w-oman now. Not a little girl,' she said taking extra care over the "w" sound.

'So's Dad,' he added.

'Yes. Feels odd for me,' I said. It was good to see them coming to terms with their situations.

I saw Caroline had fallen asleep on the sofa. I was worrying about her overall health.

'Are you two okay while I take Mum to the doctor's?'

'No prob,' said Wilson and Sandra nodded.

'Not the vet this time?' she asked.

'You took Mum to the *vet*?' said Wilson with a horrified expression on his face.

'Quiet, she's sleeping,' I said, pointing through to the lounge, 'and, yes, Mum's doctor's a vet because he knows much more about dog anatomy.'

'What's natomy?' asked Sandra.

'*An*-atomy. It's her body and insides. A dog's tummy and muscles and things are different to a person, and the vet knows much, much more about keeping a dog healthy than a doctor would.'

'Will he stick a thermometer up her bum like they did with Rosy?' Wilson asked with devilment.

'No. They only do that with animals because they might bite the thermometer and break it. Mum won't bite it so she has it in her mouth the same as us.'

'Hope they wash it first!'

'Course they do. It's sterilised,' I said. He still had his old schoolboy sense of humour.

Wilson screwed up his face as he considered the implications.

We finished our breakfast and Sandra loaded the dishwasher. Wilson tried to help but she scolded him for putting crockery into the wrong slots, or at least the slots new-adult-Sandra considered to be wrong.

In the utility room, I changed Caroline's litter tray. Wilson followed me. There was obviously something preying on his mind.

'You're not going to have Mum *put down*?' he asked in a hushed voice, saying the last two words as a sort of whispered secret question.

'Good grief, Wils! No! She's not well, but we're going to fight to make her better. Notice how her paws have healed. No bandages needed today,' I tried to reassure.

'But isn't putting down what they do to sick animals like Rosy was?'

'Yes, but it's different. Animals can't understand suffering, so if the pain becomes bad and makes their lives unbearable, it's usually best to put them to sleep if there's no chance of improving their quality of life. We don't put them through the pain of an operation if it's only going to give them an extra couple of months. It's not fair on them so best to let them die in peace. We never put people down.'

'But what if Mum can't get better?'

I decided truth was the best policy, 'Well, we're a long way from Mum dying, I hope, although we can never be certain. The vet is going to give her a thorough check over and we'll get new pills which will help her. Also, at work we're hoping to come up with a way to move people's minds back from animals to humans.'

'That's daft. Granger says it's pie in the sky,' Wilson proclaimed. Granger was obviously some kid at school.

'Well, tell Granger it's not pie in the sky. There are scientists trying to find out how to do it right now, and there's always hope.' I wished I could tell him about the progress which had been made.

'Hrk,' sounded from behind me and I saw Caroline standing there. How much had she heard?

'Get your mum a fresh drink, Wilson,' and he ran back into the kitchen. I called after him, 'Aren't going to ask her what she'd like?'

He came back in, 'What would you like to drink, Mum?'

'Hre,' she said and licked his hand.

Wilson went through and put the kettle on.

'I'll have one, too,' I shouted after him.

Caroline laughed. I lifted her onto the bar stool and she soon had a ceramic bowl of warm milky tea to lap with some custard cream biscuits. She was becoming an expert at drinking at the table.

Once we'd had tea and tidied up the kitchen, I let Caroline out for a pee. She didn't use the litter tray for peeing any more as the new gadget I'd rigged for the front door meant she could get in and out on her own if she wished.

We set off to the vet with Caroline's list of drugs, after cautioning the kids to be careful and not cook anything while we were both out. Raising children had to change. We needed to trust them more, and I knew school classes were now building in much more awareness about household dangers.

As we drove, the streets were much quieter than they had been before Mindslip, and there were strange combinations of people on the pavements. Couples who didn't look like couples; families who didn't match each other in size or skin colour. This would become the new normal on post-Mindslip Earth.

Families and relationships would never be the same again. Even in Buckingham Palace the royal family had catastrophically changed. Our nonagenarian queen, who had recently taken the record for the longest serving monarch in the world, was now a ten-year-old boy and would get a second lifetime. The heir to the throne had vanished, William had lost two decades and Kate was a frumpy sixty-year-old Asian-Indian lady. It was time for Britain to become a republic because, genetically, none of these people were even remotely related, and neither was any other family. We had to do no more than look at ourselves. Ancestry and genealogy had become irrelevant for everyone.

At the veterinary clinic, we sat beside a woman with a yellow Labrador. I introduced us, and the woman explained the dog was her husband, so we were in similar situations. He had several large sticking plasters holding a dressing onto his right ear.

'What happened to his ear?' I asked.

'You'd never believe it.'

'Go on, try me.'

'He burned himself while trying to light a pipe!' She laughed, and it brought a threatening growl from her husband.

'Surely his tobacco addiction didn't transfer?' I asked.

'No, but he said if he couldn't read, write, or play bridge he might as well smoke again. Stupid old fool.' She laughed, and he barked loudly at her. 'Wonderful, he can't answer me back any more.' She affectionately rubbed his neck and his tail wagged.

Mrs Reid now had a nice, new white coat which fitted him. He examined each of Caroline's paws and the sore on her leg and made positive sounds. His stethoscope was applied to her heart and breathing. The electrocardiograph was standing nearby. Caroline lay on her side, and the assistant shaved the same areas as before for the sensors and attached the blood pressure monitor to her tail.

'You've been taking the medicines as directed?'

'Href,' she said, and I confirmed none had been missed. He connected the machine, asking Caroline to relax and keep still.

We all stood in silence for two or three minutes to allow the printout to complete. Mrs Reid studied it with concern.

'Caroline and I have discussed her situation in depth. You can speak frankly.'

'Okay,' he said to Caroline, 'I was hoping the tablets would make a difference, but they haven't. You might already have been under a similar treatment but we've no way of knowing.

'Your heart is weak. I'm going to increase the tablet for the irregular heartbeat. Blood pressure is okay. The blood tests came back not too bad, but kidney function is a little impaired although not enough to worry us. It's the heart which is giving me cause for concern.'

He left the room for a minute and I heard him on the telephone. He returned, wrote on piece of paper, and said, 'I've set up with the hospital for you to have an MRI scan at one o'clock. Take this letter with you. It explains what I want to know, and that Caroline is a humanimal and can follow instructions. Depending upon what the MRI shows, we might need a small operation for a pacemaker.'

Caroline looked at me anxiously.

I asked, 'You've no reason to change your opinion of her life expectancy?'

'No,' again speaking to her. 'A year if things go well, a little longer with the pacemaker if the MRI shows it'll be of use. But frankly, your heart could fail at any time.'

I put my arm around Caroline and squeezed her. I asked about what to do if she had heart failure, and Mrs Reid showed me how to give a dog CPR. He also provided some tablets to be put under her tongue if she suffered actual chest pain.

I thanked him, paid the bill and we set off for the Royal Surrey where we found a restaurant. I had fish and chips while Caroline demolished a bowl of minced beef with potatoes. We must have looked an odd couple.

As we still had some time to kill, we went to reception and asked to see our original daughter. Caroline and I had discussed this the previous day and we both wanted to be sure she was being well cared for.

We were sent to another building where the ward manager met us.

'I would like you not to single her out for any attention, please, we've found it to be disruptive. It might be very hard for you, but I'm sure you won't want to cause her any upset. We call her Sandra and, as far as we can ascertain, she has a ten-month-old mind. Come with me,' he said, and we followed him through to a large open ward with beds along one side occupied by people of all ages.

Some were sleeping, some making various baby noises but often with adult voices. There was Sandra, sitting on the floor. We both had to resist the impulse to run to her and give her a hug having understood what the ward manager had meant by not singling her out for attention. Nevertheless, it was hard to resist. She shuffled along in a sitting position towards Caroline. A dog would not normally visit this ward, so she was naturally curious.

It was an incongruous scene. A baby in an eight-year-old's body, wearing a nappy and sitting facing her thirty-five-year-old greyhound mother.

Sandra let out a series of unintelligible grunts and reached up to touch Caroline's snout. Her mother flicked her tongue along the girl's wrist as she was stroked. Sandra had a plastic spade in her other hand and she offered it to Caroline who took it and placed it carefully on the floor. Sandra lifted it again with a puzzled expression, let out a 'Nurrringggaharrr' sound and bum-shuffled herself back to where she'd been playing with a plastic bucket.

I stroked Caroline's head, noticing tears running down her cheeks. I managed to hold mine on this occasion.

In the scanner waiting room, we sat cuddling and I told her I didn't ever want to return.

'Nh,' Caroline agreed.

At home, our new Sandra was eager to prepare the evening meal, and Wilson was watching live football in his room. I joined him. The commentators told us people in their new bodies acquired much of the skill from the original person. They interviewed a white Tottenham player who had morphed into a twenty-something black man. He explained how he had all the knowledge he needed, but his control of the ball was poor. His original body, however, had the ball skills but none of the tactical or positional knowledge. It was a fascinating programme but the match which followed was pathetic, with managers and trainers screaming insults at their players as they got out of position, didn't stay in formation or were too hesitant to carry out tackles or make strikes at goal. It would take a long time for the Premier League to reclaim its place as the best in the world.

The news told us the economy was struggling along. Many people had returned to work, so factories and service industries were recovering. There were no real problems in the retail environment apart from staff shortages which people accepted with resignation.

The working population had fallen by thirty percent. Twenty percent of the population were incapable of going back to work owing to age (too old or too young), sex change or body musculature. Nevertheless, things were gradually recovering.

The Department of Agriculture had come under fire for allowing humanimals to be slaughtered for meat, although it couldn't be proven. Nevertheless, intelligence detector devices were now at all locations in Britain.

Several cold store warehouses had been hastily prepared outside bigger conurbations to store the large number of carcasses of animals which had been slaughtered because they were unable to live in their new hosts. Animals like seals in cattle, fish or reptiles in sheep, and chickens behaving in an extraordinary manner, failing to be able to stand or eat etc. There was no other sensible answer than to process for food. It was bad enough having herds of cattle and flocks of sheep acting strangely because other species now inhabited them, but if they walked roughly normally and ate without a problem they, at least, could be kept alive. The whole animal world was a horror. Pets had eaten their owners and each other, vicious dogs were still running wild, perhaps occupied by rats, stoats, or badgers.

There was a lot of international news. A nuclear power station explosion in North Korea had caused fallout which was spreading with the prevailing wind into China. Little news was emerging from some Middle Eastern countries, with the people revolting against both dictatorships and religious dogma. The Daesh terrorist group had recovered ground in Syria, Iraq, northern Iran and the 'stan' countries. They'd built Mindslip into their perverted ideology as being punishment by Allah for lack of devotion. Most of Africa was experiencing organisational chaos, but India and southern Pakistan were recovering well, as were most of the Latin American countries.

The news ended with yet another string of amazing situations where people had snatched life from the jaws of death. Inexperienced crews on fishing vessels, pilots having had to learn to fly instantly, children finding themselves in unexpected situations. Those who had not been killed because of Mindslip were now talking about their miraculous survival stories.

At about five o'clock in the afternoon, Mrs Reid rang with an update on the results of the MRI scan. I put the call on speakerphone.

'Well, mainly good news. There appears to be nothing wrong with the heart itself – no valve faults or problems with the major arteries or veins. A pacemaker would be a good move, and I'll order one on Monday. I'll let you know about timing.'

'Thank you,' I said.

'The congestion in the lungs is not caused by cancer or any benign growth, you'll be pleased to hear, but is mainly owing to the high blood pressure causing fluid build-up. If you can get to the surgery in the next twenty minutes, I've some tablets which will provide some relief. I'd like Mrs Arnold back on Wednesday for another blood pressure, blood and urine test. Please collect the urine on Wednesday morning before taking any food.'

'So, it's better than we might have expected?' I did a thumbs-up to Caroline.

'Yes, Mr Arnold. The pacemaker and the water tablets should improve things. Can you get here straight away?'

'Yes. Thanks. I'm on the way.'

29 COBRA FIELD TRIP

On Monday, I resigned myself to Suzy's influence and took pride in wearing a short, pencil-slim, green skirt suit for work today. Each day, how I dressed was becoming a mini adventure. I caught sight of myself in a plate glass window at Waterloo and I looked fabulous, even if I did say so myself. The Geoff component of my identity approved of my appearance, if not of the time it took to achieve it.

I'd just finished sorting through all the emails by the time Justin arrived. Still no sign of Mike this morning.

'We're no further forward on the actual cause of the effect,' I said. 'We know the coronal mass ejection and second supernova combination caused it to happen from backtracking on the actual times, but we don't have a clue what the mechanism was. Pascal at Observatoire de Paris-Meudon has come up with an interesting theory about the second explosion. Betelgeuse was extremely massive yet has always had a wobble. It was thought that might have been an orbiting progenitor star, but Pascal and his team think it might have been a neutron star or black hole in a very close orbit. Too small to have an effect on the light emitted by Betelgeuse, but with an enormous mass. When Betelgeuse exploded, the neutron star would have merged with the resulting object and could've caused the second explosion.'

'Interesting. So, two neutron stars spiral inwards and combine causing the second event,' said Justin.

'Possibly. I'd like to spend some time looking at their observations and calculations, though. Not totally happy with it.'

'Yes. You ready to go? We're going straight to Colne Park Farm today.'

'I feel a fraud attending this Catastrophe Committee.'

'Interesting you should say that as I was talking about our involvement with Giles, and while he does want to retain you on board, he's letting me go shortly so I can set up some international cooperation on monitoring Betelgeuse. So, enjoy being "in the know", your input must be appreciated. We'd better get off.'

'Okay, let's leave. You'll keep me in the picture on anything new on Betelgeuse? I've a new edition of my book in mind.'

'Of course.'

For a Monday, the streets exhibited nothing like the usual London congestion. Most of the abandoned vehicles littering the roadsides had been collected by their owners or towed away by squads of authorised volunteers and we arrived early.

Only a handful of humanimals were in the main paddock, so we made our way over to the farm buildings. Brian Isherwood met us there and we had time to enjoy a coffee before most of the rest of the committee arrived.

Jonah was next to appear, carrying several of the computer touchpads.

'Ready to give these a go?' he asked, and we entered the main barn.

A couple of hundred assorted humanimals eagerly awaited developments. I hoped whatever Jonah had produced would live up to their hopes and expectations.

He spent a few minutes wiring a hub into the main giant television, switched on each of the units and passed them to a selection of creatures.

They seemed to be having difficulty. 'I don't think they can see the screen and use the touchpads at the same time,' I said.

'You're right. We've some monitors in the van,' Jonah said and dashed out with his two assistants.

They returned with two extension leads and half a dozen smaller monitor screens which solved the problem.

As we walked among them, it seemed unnatural to not be separated by fences. I felt something warm against my hip and looked down in wonder as the lioness pushed against me as she watched a goat using one of the keypads. I wanted to stroke it, but realised it was not appropriate. This was not an animal, it was a humanimal and petting it would probably be unwelcome. Inside it might be male or female, of course. I controlled the urge, but it was difficult. I then had another, less pleasant, thought. It might be pressing itself against me for reasons of its own!

Normally you would expect to be separated from animals, but it was unnecessary here. The humanimals would not be likely to wander off or run away. A strange situation. Even the way one humanimal would avoid treading on a touchpad being used by another. Brute animals would soon have trampled anything being used on the floor.

'Notice how there's no muck or excrement on the floor in here,' I said to Justin.

'They must be leaving the barn. Interesting.'

'Expected, I suppose.'

The systems were a huge success, and there were soon real conversations being carried on between the participants.

'Beth,' Jonah said, 'there's a spare one in the van for your wife. The Bluetooth's not working so it must be plugged directly into the monitor, or you'll need a dongle. Will that do?'

'Will a standard Wi-Fi dongle work? I have one at home.'

'Yes, there's a USB port.'

'Magnificent. Thank you.'

'My pleasure. Remind me later.'

Once Giles arrived, we held a full question and answer session with the humanimals. There was obviously a lot of impatience about their situation, and we reassured as best we could.

'Giles, I need to select a couple of mid-sized humanimal volunteers to travel with me and Jen to Oxford to test out the *special equipment*,' said Mark.

'Our neuroscientists need volunteers for some experiments,' Giles shouted out.

There was an immediate gaggle of sounds. There were many volunteers. We guessed anything was better for them than being confined to the farm.

I overheard Mark and Jen discussing which would be best, and they selected a golden retriever and a goat. I found out later they needed species which they could match in size and stature with almost identical non-humanimals.

When we'd achieved all we could at the farm, I hitched a lift back to Guildford with Jonah who lived in nearby Godalming. Justin was returning to London and the lift would save me a trip into and out of the city. All but one of the touchpads were left at the farm; Mark took one to Oxford and Jonah had the faulty one on the back seat for me.

We stopped for lunch en route and he insisted upon paying. I turned down the offer of wine. I needed a clear head to write a report on the Betelgeuse nebula later. Several times he tried to hold my gaze and there was a deliberate 'accidental' touching of my leg at the table as he reached for his tablet. That forced me to say something yet again.

'Jonah. Please. You know I'm not available and I find your attentions disturbing. Don't forget there is a man inside me, not a woman.'

'Yes, I know, but I find you absolutely captivating. I don't think you realise how beautiful you are. When you begged the lift with me, I thought maybe you felt the same. There was plenty of room on the coach.'

'Both the coach and Justin were going back to London, and I'd have had to get the train from Waterloo. When you told me you lived in Godalming, I knew you'd have to pass by Guildford on the way. I wasn't intending to give you the wrong idea. You were being kind over the touchpad for Caroline. I didn't mean to lead you on.'

'I still want to spend time with you. I can't help it. You mesmerise me. Why not go for a meal with me? You can find a reason to be late, can't you?'

'*No*. There's no future in it, Jonah. Any closeness with another man is abhorrent to me.'

'But you're not a man any longer, and your wife's a dog,' he said as if he was selling me something.

How dare he? I sat bolt upright in my chair and took a firm line, 'Jonah. As far as I'm concerned, I'm a heterosexual man and I'm not interested in you or any other men. And Caroline is still my wife, even if she is a dog. So please let this be an end to it.'

'Sorry. You can't blame me for trying.'

'Yes, I can, Jonah. I've asked you several times, and I want it to stop *right now*. It's an unwelcome distraction in this situation. We must work together. Keep your feelings to yourself, or I'll get a cab home from here right now.'

'Oh, no. No! Don't do that! I'm sorry and, yes, I promise.'

'I'm most grateful for the touchpad, but it's not buying you a relationship with me.'

'I do understand. Sorry. I never meant it in that way.'

'If you're giving me the touchpad because you've an interest in me, then reluctantly I cannot accept it.' I so hoped he wouldn't withdraw the offer, but I'd had enough of his advances. Again, I wondered at how my feelings towards him had rapidly changed from positive to a real dislike.

'No. I want you to have the touchpad. All I want in return is some feedback on how useful it is.'

'Thank you. I'll make sure we give you a quality assessment.'

He dropped me outside our house. I would normally have invited him in, but the dislike had grown too intense. I took the touchpad, my case and my laptop, thanked him for the lift and waved goodbye. That was the last lift I'd accept from him.

Inside, Caroline bounded along, jumping up so her paws were on my chest and her tail was wagging furiously. I stroked and cuddled her head and neck.

'Hello, darling. Got a present for you.'

'Href,' she said and happily followed me through to the lounge, where I put down the case and touchpad. She seemed so much better today.

'Going to change first,' I said, and she followed me up the stairs.

'Trk.'

'Well. We had a good day,' I said and filled her in on the developments with the humanimals as well as my having to fight off Jonah's advances.

Back in the kitchen in a pair of skin-tight, blue jeans, I made some tea and took the cup and bowl through to the lounge. Caroline no longer splashed when she drank.

I connected the touchpad to the old Tesco Hudl and showed Caroline the procedure for using it. The biggest problem was the size of the Hudl screen, but I knew I could rig it up with a bigger, smart monitor later and attach a spare Wi-Fi dongle I had for my laptop.

Once she understood the rudiments of its system, I said, 'I'll go get Sandra and leave you playing space invaders.'

Caroline jumped up and ran through to the kitchen, 'Hrrr,' she said, calling me to one of her notes.

WILS AT FB

'Football?'

'Href.'

'Do I need to collect him?'

'Nh.'

'Right. I'll go get Sandra.'

'Href. Hruf hru.'

At the university, I knew Sandra was in the after-class study room learning more about relationships. Through the pane in the door I saw Gren teaching the class. I retreated and sat in the reception area to wait. When the class ended, she was full of all the new things she was learning. I was so pleased it had now become just a fun adventure for her.

Back at home, I learned Wilson had scored two goals in the school game and was full of excitement at his newfound football prowess. Lovely for him – it was making up for the disadvantages he might now discover in his new skin. I was grateful for Britain's improved race relations in recent years. With any luck, his skin colour would not disadvantage him at all in the future. Attitudes were bound to have changed after the effects of Mindslip. Perhaps racial discrimination would finally disappear forever? I knew from personal experience, that sexual harassment was not going to disappear with it.

Dinner was good fun, with all of us taking part in the conversation. I'd rigged the dongle to put Caroline's touchpad words through to a monitor by the dining table. What a strange family group we were. A greyhound sitting on a raised chair with a lipped bowl of steak pie, a Pyrex bowl of water on one side and the pad on the other. Some of her words came out as garbage, but the device was learning her most common phrases and would improve over time. Ingenious.

30 INEXPLICABLE SUCCESS

The next week flew by.

Sandra was making phenomenal progress, and Wilson had become his school's star football player. Wednesday saw Caroline's pacemaker fitted, and the whole family breathed more easily.

Justin and I joined some of the others from the committee at the Oxford laboratory where the mind experiments were being conducted.

The humanimal goat was standing at one side of the lab. Three more goats of similar variety, size and colouration were in a small plastic-sided pen with a sawdust floor at the other end of the room. A full-size MRI scanner sat on the right of the room with a young man in a white coat at the controls. Massive cables ran from one end of the scanner to a computer with an equal number coming back to its other end. We'd all had to leave anything metallic in the anteroom.

'Come in. Come in,' said Mark as the last of the group entered. The bishop's absence was a little unexpected given his vocal opposition to the experiments.

'We're using the same procedure here as St Andrews used with the rats but will be scanning at a vastly greater resolution. Gordon, here,' he indicated the goat, 'has agreed to participate. We're going to be trying to transfer Gordon into one of these other goats.'

'Why not directly to a human body?' asked Giles.

'We did consider it but need to get a goat to goat transfer working first. Similar skull and brain sizes. We don't have the luxury of a control group of trained goats with which we can experiment, as St Andrews had with their rats, so we need to work with Gordon to judge success. Can you prepare the specimen?'

A lab technician went to the cage of goats and extracted one while another assistant held the door. He injected something into the goat's back and, in a matter of seconds it was unconscious.

'It's not necessary for the object to be unconscious, but we need its head to be still. Gordon has no problem keeping still, but the pure animals can't.'

'You're sure these are goats in goats?' Giles asked.

'As sure as we can be. They came from a larger herd and any which were being unsociable were not included in our selection,' said Jen.

'So, there's no chance one could be a sheep in a goat?' I asked.

'The farmer is pretty sure a sheep or donkey in a goat's body, for instance, would have an obviously different behaviour when in the herd,' said Jen.

The assistant lifted the goat onto a trolley with its head closest to the centre of the scanner.

'Okay, Gordon. If you will.'

Gordon trotted to the other end of the scanner. The assistant helped him onto the second trolley to lay opposite the object goat.

Mark, Jen, and two lab technicians spent some twenty minutes fixing strong ceramic struts to the two creatures' heads, holding them firmly in the same positions each side of the scanner's centre point.

'The way this works, is we scan the brain of the subject, pass it through a computer processor and transmit it into the brain of the object animal,' continued Mark.

'Can you store the scan digitally?' I asked.

'Well, there's no reason we couldn't store it, but we don't have sufficient storage. I doubt anyone has. If we tried to store it, we would need a physical memory size of many thousands of cubic metres using, say hundred and twenty-eight gigabyte microSDXC cards. It is all we can do to handle it as a continuous data stream.'

I nodded. The possibility of holding our memories, in fact our entire minds in storage offered incredible potential. I tucked away the information. I knew work was ongoing using DNA in fluid to store data, building on Aldeman's work from the nineties. It offered vastly expanded memory storage within a relatively small space. Molecular and even quantum computers were also on the horizon.

Mark continued. 'This scanner has been enhanced to ensure we're picking up the radio waves from every atom in the brain. We've set this scanner up so we can manipulate the resultant information and then project it back into the object as we scan the subject. To be honest, we're not sure why this should work, but the theory is the electrical activity in the brain of the subject is implanted into the brain of the object by the transmitted radiation via that computer.' He indicated a desktop computer near the goat cage.

'I thought MRIs didn't use radiation,' I said.

'I use the term loosely. It's radio waves, but all part of the electromagnetic spectrum.'

Jen said, 'We're using the fastest development computer available in the UK for this. It's borrowed from London University. The green cables each contain two hundred and fifty-six high-grade USB cables to reduce the transfer time. Even then, and at huge data transfer speeds, it'll take close to half an hour. The computer processor is being cooled by liquid nitrogen, such is the heat it generates.'

Mark said, 'Now don't raise your hopes too high for this experiment. I would consider it a success if anything at all transferred. Remember the rats at St Andrews only obtained the information to travel through a maze. Transferring a whole mind is a somewhat grander objective.'

'Okay to go, Doctor,' said one of the technicians, ducking out of the scanner's tunnel.

'Ready, Gordon. I'll tell you when to hold as still as you can. Breathe normally,' said Mark.

Gordon made a braying sound.

'The object is still unconscious?' asked Mark.

'Yep.'

'And it'll stay under for more than thirty minutes?'

'Yes. No problem.'

Mark peered into the scanner and satisfied himself the experiment was ready. He said, 'Okay, Bruce, go for it,' and another white-coated technician switched on the scanner.

For two or three minutes, we saw nothing other than a beam of light running around each end of the scanner. Gordon's end was slightly in advance of the animal's end, presumably the data-processing time differential in the computer.

'Warming up,' explained the technician.

'The magnetic field is aligning the atoms in the subject and objects during this phase,' said Mark.

'Ready,' said another technician.

'Right,' agreed Mark, 'Hold still, Gordon.'

The sound from the machine increased in pitch. The light whizzed rapidly around within the scanner moving from the outer part towards the centre where the heads were two inches apart.

'The light's a guide to progress,' said Jen. 'The actual radio waves are, of course, invisible and will pass through the ceramic fixings, which is why they're not metal.'

The process took twenty-eight minutes and the machine noise rapidly dropped to zero.

The technicians undid the clamps at Gordon's end first and he was lifted onto the floor.

'Any ill effects, Gordon?' Hugh asked.

The goat shook its head.

At the other end, the object goat was disconnected and lifted down onto a blanket in a third pen with an open top. A technician injected it and said, 'It should come around in less than a minute.'

Eventually, there were some movements in the goat's legs, its head lifted a couple of times and shook, before it scrambled to its feet and surveyed its surroundings.

'Can you understand me?' asked Jen, standing in front of the goat. It made a braying sound. The transfer had failed.

'Nod, if you can understand,' said Jen.

The goat looked blankly at the speaker, surveyed the room, shook itself and then, miraculously, nodded.

'Shake your head.'

It shook from side to side.

'Is your name Duncan?'

The goat shook its head.

'Gordon?'

It nodded.

'Well, people, we have a measure of success here,' said Giles.

'We still have a lot of problems to overcome,' said Mark. 'Firstly, we're dealing with two similar brains here in similarly shaped and sized skulls. We now need to check, through extensive questioning, how much has been lost in the transfer. It'll take us at least a couple of days.

'After that we've an even bigger problem. If we put Gordon in one end of the machine and a human head in the other, we could have a catastrophe. How do we know the correct brainwaves will end up in the right part of the host's brain? We believe inter-species transfers to be the most difficult obstacle we will have to overcome if everything does work well with similar brains.'

'What Mark is saying is, we should not expect instant results,' said Jen, trying to dampen the obviously rising expectations we were all beginning to experience.

'Yes. We're still a long way off. Particularly between species. The major problem is not knowing the mechanics of why this works. There is no way to move forward without a lot of additional experimentation, and each experiment producing another humanimal? Also, we now have two Gordons. It isn't the best of outcomes, but we always knew we'd have to pass through this stage,' said Mark.

'You've done wonderfully. It might be best if we now get out of your hair. I have to report this to the PM,' said Giles.

'Come with me, first,' said Mark, 'Coffee before you leave. We want to know what has been happening elsewhere within our committee's domain.'

Jen took the two Gordons out of the laboratory for further examination and the rest of us made our way to a canteen-like coffee area. We sat around the table discussing the events of the day and what others had been working upon.

When we broke up, I walked over to Mark, 'A quiet word, if I may?'

'Yes?' he replied.

'My wife is in an old greyhound with a lot of health problems. She had a pacemaker fitted this week, but the prognosis is not good. Less than a year.'

'Yes. I knew about your wife, but not about the life expectancy problem.'

'If we could find a similar, younger greyhound and transfer her into it, would that be an interim option?'

'Let me know if she deteriorates. I'd prefer to transfer straight into a human if possible. Do bear in mind we must check Gordon "two" thoroughly to find out if we lost anything before we can take this to the next stage. Wish I knew more about why the transfer works. St Andrews say they're working on the metaphysical aspects and are leaving the practical side to us as they're so far away and don't have enough processing power to handle what we're attempting.'

'You're hopeful, though?'

'Yes. Hopeful would be an adequate word. We're full of hope, but no more. What we do with the original humanimals if transfers to humans are successful is preying upon my mind. We now have two Gordons. In effect, we're going to end up with two beings with identical people inside if we can perfect the process. What will the bishop have to say about that?'

I laughed and said, 'I guess we'll find out soon enough.'

'Frankly, I'd like to do a lot of trials, for instance transferring someone into a large and small mammal to check what happens and how much loss occurs, but don't suppose I'd be allowed, ethically.'

'No. You're in a difficult situation as your hands are tied in the most bizarre manner. Experimentation is important, but each experiment adds to the moral issues. You need to make a good case. The bishop is likely to be a serious obstacle.'

'Yes. I'll keep a greyhound experiment in mind if we find the results satisfactory. It would give you a safety net for your wife.'

'She's offered to be experimented upon, by the way.'

'Okay, good. We had to get Gordon and Richard to sign releases.'

'Richard?'

'The retriever. We plan a second test with him when we know Gordon "two" is okay.'

We shook hands and I hurried to catch up with Justin for the return journey to the Royal Institution.

'What's most worrying is them not having any real idea why the treatment works. It'd be like us not knowing why the sun shines, only seeing its light,' Justin said as we crossed the M25 on the road back to central London.

'St Andrews must have some idea, otherwise they'd never have come up with an experiment with rats to try it.'

'Maybe we ought to get one of them down for the next meeting. What were you discussing with Mark at the end?'

'Caroline. After watching the experiment, the possibility of moving Caroline into a younger greyhound struck me. It would buy her time.'

'Yes, it would. Did you say a pacemaker's been fitted?'

'Yes, but she sleeps with me and her lungs rattle badly when she's asleep. The vet says it's fluid build-up. He's hoping it might improve with the steadier heartbeat, although he's also got her on a diuretic to reduce fluid. Caroline hates it because after she takes the tablet in the morning, she has to make three or four visits to the garden within an hour.'

'I understand the problem. I'd keep the discussion about it strictly between you and Mark, if I were you. We're working for the government on this and we'll need to be careful we're not accused of taking advantage.'

'Yes, I will. There's another implication from today's experiment which no one voiced, Justin.'

'Which in particular? I'm full of questions anyway.'

'They've demonstrated a human mind can be transferred into another human body – both the same species and skull dimensions.'

'Yes. So...?'

'Immortality!'

'My God! I hadn't thought of that, Geoff. Sorry, Beth.'

'The implications are considerable. The rich are going to want to transfer to younger bodies, and we know there's currently a large supply of humans with animals within them which could be used.'

'Yes. And who is going to make the allocation? How about Mike, who has lost all his useful life? I bet he'd jump at the chance.'

'Money talks,' I said.

'You could go back into a male body and your daughter back into her original body, perhaps? Is it a blessing or a curse we've been observing?'

We travelled in silence for a mile or two. The ramifications were considerable. I resolved to speak to Mark about it again in confidence. To hell with abuse of privilege, this was my wife we were talking about, and I'd like the safety net of a younger dog. Surely there would be no harm if it were part of ongoing experiments?

During the afternoon at the Royal Institution, I pulled in radiation data from a number of sources, trying to ascertain whether or not it supported Pascal's theory for the second explosion. Observations of Betelgeuse had been ongoing, and it was now a pulsar with a period of one point five three seconds. Through a reasonable telescope, a growing halo was visible. It was expected to become visible to the naked eye in the night sky in a year or so. In a century, it will have grown to become a beautiful, colourful nebula like the Crab but ten times the diameter of the visible moon.

On the way home, I churned over the possibilities for transferring Caroline into a younger dog as part of Mark's experiments. Not a transfer, of course, only a copy. I'd then have two Carolines, and one of them would still be her and still going to die soon. Had I the right to get a copy made? If they succeeded in transferring from animal to human before Caroline died there would be two. How could we deal with such a circumstance? One was still Caroline and would still die. If they were both transferred into humans, which would be Caroline? They couldn't both be her... or could they?

The more I contemplated the combination of scenarios the more complex it became. Would Caroline the greyhound permit euthanasia if the transfer was a success? Possibly a solution. It would still be an assisted suicide, though. The original mind would know it was going to die.

What if I transferred into a man to continue my relationship with the human Caroline? I would still exist in Suzy's body. Would *that* me be prepared to give up its existence to let Suzy recover her own body? Then there would be two Suzys. It was a nightmare whichever way you saw it. Who on earth would be responsible for sorting it out?

A black-market involving body snatchers could easily develop. The ageing millionaire kidnaps a virile and handsome young man and copies himself into the young body. The temptations would be enormous for rich, vain individuals who believed themselves above the law. Was my idea for duplicating Caroline a step along a slippery slope? Would there be a blanket ban on the practice? Should I try to get it done before such a plan came into place?

What if Caroline were transferred into a man to save me having to change? No. I wasn't sure which would be most awful, making love with her as a man or as a greyhound. I smiled at the bizarre thought. Neither appealed.

Of course, this led me into the religious aspects, or at least how religious authorities might view such events. A sensible law might be to euthanise the subject once the mind had been transferred into the object. How would religious bodies view euthanasia in those circumstances? Was it still murder? Could a compromise be reached owing to the extraordinary circumstances which had been forced upon us? Did the end justify the means? There might well be more humans in animals than there were animals in humans to become objects. As humans were returned to their correct sex and age groups, should their previous body become the object for another humanimal?

What about the underlying effect? Suzy's influence on me was changing my life. If someone moved into a body occupied by an animal, what effect would that have upon them?

No doubt there would soon be legislation on the matter. I needed to find a young greyhound soon and be ready to act.

My mind was so full of these convoluted arguments, I almost missed getting off the train at Guildford. I walked home, not knowing how to discuss this with my wife. I tried to switch my thought processes into contemplating something more pleasant.

What dinner would Sandra have prepared?

31 PHILOSOPHY OF CATASTROPHE

The Prime Minister sat, and we followed suit. The full complement of the Catastrophe Committee was in attendance.

'Good day, citizens. I've already been fully briefed, but Giles tells me you have some important views and opinions to express about last week's experiment.'

'Yes, sir,' the Deputy Home Secretary cleared his throat, 'We've witnessed an interesting experiment which permitted a humanimal's mind to be copied to a similar animal.'

The bishop jumped in, 'I'm most unhappy with the outcome. This shouldn't have been allowed. It's immoral. We now have two poor souls in two humanimals. These scientists are playing God!'

The Prime Minister spoke sharply, 'We're not going to get anywhere if this committee cannot make points without interruption. You can have your say later, Bishop. We need to understand what has happened and its results before we can move on to the philosophical aspects involved in resolving this catastrophe. Giles... continue...'

'Sorry, Prime Minister,' the bishop said, sounding more like the young girl he now inhabited.

'Thank you, Prime Minister. I'd like Dr Mark Weston to give the detailed explanation.'

Mark stood, 'Sir, fellow committee members. As Giles said, we transferred the mind of a volunteer humanimal goat into a similar, ordinary goat. This was a necessary step because, unless we can do that successfully, we wouldn't ever be able to go to the next step and try goat to human.

'The procedure, which we still don't fully comprehend, copied the mind, leaving the original mind intact. Jen White did a thorough study of both humanimals. Superficially the transfer was good, but when Jen started detailed questioning there appeared to be a number of problems, which I'll let her outline.' He sat and Jen rose to speak.

'Not everything was transferred. Many memories were lost, particularly of childhood, but also more recent – memories of the last few days.

'Motor functions were fairly accurate, but the object animal retained more goat-like characteristics than the original humanimal. Reasoning tests were similar, but an IQ test showed a serious drop of twenty points between the two from one twenty-eight to one hundred eight. We tested IQ and more memories two days later and discovered a further drop to one hundred and two with more difficulty with later memories from the time immediately prior to the transfer.

'Dexterity on the touchpad was not as good in the object animal as it was in the humanimal. This leads us to believe the original Mindslip replaced virtually all of the mind in the subject, whereas our own experiments are overlaying the subject mind onto the object.'

'Can you explain what you mean?' asked the PM.

'As an analogy, sir, we have two buckets. One contains blue water, the original Gordon's mind, and the other is clear water, the goat's mind. We are emptying the bucket of blue water into the clear water bucket and the capacity is not sufficient to hold both, so some overflows. We end up with a diluted mind in the object animal, but we also noted it was able to learn quickly when taught anything new. No lack of ability. A second transfer between the same two humanimals could resolve the situation. Using the same analogy, the amount of blue water in the second bucket would be much stronger. There might not be a limit to the number of times we could carry out the transfer and, until we examine the results from doing repeated transfers, we must assume an almost perfect transfer will become possible.

'When we fully comprehend what is going on during the transfer, it is likely we can solve the loss of IQ and most of the memory loss, so there's still much work to undertake.'

Jen sat and Mark stood again. 'I suppose we should have guessed this would happen, as it's not a mind swap in the way the original Mindslip was. We're trying to force a whole mind into another mind without making room for it.' He gave everyone time to let that point sink in. 'There are also the philosophical aspects to the experiment.

'We now have two humanimal goats who appear to be identical although, as we've said, one is an imperfect copy of the other but is nevertheless a human trapped in an animal's mind. Some of the other aspects are frightening.

'Do both of the goat humanimals warrant the procedure, if we can perfect it, to place them back into human bodies? Which of them will own their assets? We still have two humanimals so there would be four people, all of the opinion they're the original Gordon and all having the same claim on his money, job, family, and friends. However, those complications are only part of it.

'What we have done is proven a mind, or at least most of it, can be moved from one creature to a similar one. A human mind could be moved into another human mind. We know, beyond doubt we can do exactly as we did with the goats. Imperfect but achievable, with perfection probably following with more experimentation. This might mean we're on the track of putting people back into their own bodies, where we have all the components, but it also means we're opening the door to mercenary transfers – the rich old person wanting to move into a chosen healthy, young body

– for money, even. The legal implications would be… problematical.'

Mark sat and Jen stood up again. 'We think we can solve the problems, but are we creating the twenty-first century equivalent of a Frankenstein's monster? If we continue along this path, we're opening the door to many nightmare scenarios. We're seeking the advice of this learned committee on how, or whether to proceed. There are no laws to govern what we're trying to do. The fact we *can* do it cannot be unlearned, and that knowledge is likely to be abused, if not by us, then by others.'

Jen sat. My own heart sank. They were right. The whole thing would be classified as immoral. I was an atheist, but this was not a religious morality. It was the morality of us as living, thinking people. I saw the bishop's hand go up, as if in a school lesson. Giles acknowledged it and the bishop stood, speaking with more confidence than would ever come from the mouth of a young teenage girl.

'We must ban the whole practice. Stop the experiments. No good can come of any of it. I knew it was wrong before you embarked on this mad plan. Please, sir, this must be stopped immediately. Mindslip was an act of God, and we should not be attempting to reverse something God might have intended for his people.'

The Prime Minister waved the bishop back to his seat, and there was a lengthy whispered discussion between the PM and Home Secretary.

The Prime Minister was clearly rattled, but also determined, 'My goodness. This truly is a steaming mass of controversy!

'I'm slapping top secret all over it right now and, Dr Weston, I want you to get on to the other university, St Andrews, wasn't it, and stop them too. Tell them they must not talk about the work they have done and arrange for them, *all* of them, every one of them who knows of their experiment, to come down here to meet Giles so he can ensure they sign the Official Secrets Act and understand the penalties and implications for talking about their work. No one leaves this room without a formal signing either.'

'I'll need to tell the archbishop, sir.'

'*NO!*' he shouted, '*For God's sake*, Bishop Moran, didn't you listen to a word I said? This entire matter is now an Official Secret of the British Government. You won't talk about it to *anyone* and, if you do, you'll most certainly be prosecuted and imprisoned. *Do… you… understand me?*'

'Yes.' Almost a whimper of a response.

'Doctors Weston and White. The implications of what you have done – and I imply no criticism of your excellent work – are enormous. Dr Weston, you and your laboratory can continue to explore the possibilities, but Giles, you go back with them, and I want everyone working in the laboratory put under a security clampdown, and the staff must *all* sign the Act. Your experiments will be transferred to a new top-secret establishment and reported upon only to the Home Secretary via Giles. We should have foreseen the implications before starting this project. I suppose there was an imperative to resolve Mindslip, but we shouldn't have followed this path until we'd first fully comprehended the potential consequences.'

Pam Jury, the Home Secretary, left the room, I put up my hand and Giles waved me up.

'Sir, other countries will also be researching. What was discovered in a Scottish university is likely to be duplicated elsewhere. How can a lid ever be put on this technology? The benefits for sick and old people are obvious. Taking over another mind is better than nothing for them. Might it be better to licence its use on medical grounds rather than banning it?'

'Miss... er,' began the Prime Minister.

'Doctor Beth Arnold, Prime Minister.'

'Doctor Arnold, you miss the point. We need to make it top secret now to prevent exactly what you're suggesting. I understand the benefits, but the drawbacks and opportunities for abuse would be awful. Making the process secret is the answer, and you can be sure the Home and Foreign Secretaries will have GCHQ and the secret service keeping an ear to the ground. If we can, we'll stifle it elsewhere. If not, well... who knows, but we need to try.'

I was sure the secret could never be suppressed but decided there was no point in arguing here and now. Mr Browning was adamant. My heart was in my stomach. I knew this was the end of any chance of saving Caroline.

The Home Secretary returned with booklets detailing the Official Secrets Acts and told each of us to read them if we wished, but we couldn't leave the room until we'd signed an acknowledgement sheet.

She confirmed, 'Once you've signed, in fact, even being part of this committee, means you are bound to secrecy anyway, breaking the secrecy is a criminal offence, and you'd be tried in closed court. Prison terms are extensive and can be up to life imprisonment, possibly in isolation. You've heard how seriously the Prime Minister is taking this particular secret. You cannot speak to anyone or, and this is crucial, *each other*, about what has taken place in this room or anything described for your ears or shown to your eyes in COBRA. I must emphasise this applies to husbands, wives, and even your lawyers. *No one* can be told anything you've learned as a result of being on this committee.

'I should add for the purpose of clarification, you *may* talk to each other about any matter *not* related to the recent humanimal experiment or any future humanimal experiments, or even their possibility. It's the experiment and its results which can no longer be discussed amongst you.'

The Prime Minister had been walking around the table pondering the situation. 'Yes. This doesn't affect the other work which this committee is conducting. Continue to carry out all your discussions on matters other than the transfer of minds. We still have economic and domestic problems to resolve, and you were hand-picked to help with this. We don't want to lose your valuable contribution, but you must adhere to the secrecy here. Only our most senior ministers and the Privy Council[4] will be told.

'As far as any of us are concerned, we cannot find a way to transfer or copy people's minds or those of humanimals. There will be an official statement at some point, and you'll be expected to toe that line. We do need ideas about what we're to do with the humanimals as it is still very much the concern of you all.

'Bishop and Pam. Both of you please come through to my office when the bishop has signed the act.'

I guessed the PM wanted to emphasise the secrecy to the bishop who'd indicated the need to speak to higher authorities.

I'd already broken the act, of course. Even the little I'd said to Gren and the more extensive information I'd told Caroline were infringements. I'd need to ensure I kept to the rules from now on. I didn't want my career to be damaged.

---

[4] The Privy Council is a body of members of parliament, usually including the opposition leaders, who are kept appraised of government matters which would normally be regarded as secret.

Eventually, the signatures were obtained and the meeting broke up. I called a cab to take me to Waterloo and sat on the train, totally despondent. My signature meant I'd signed Caroline's death warrant. All the raised hopes the experiment had produced were dashed in a single statement from the Prime Minister. I was devastated. I couldn't even repeat my request for Mark to consider Caroline for transfer to a younger greyhound. All I could do would be to hope he remembered her plight as more experiments were conducted, as I was sure they would be.

With tears welling up, I stared out of the window as the train rumbled westwards. What was I going to say to Cas? How could I tell her it wasn't going to happen? There was to be no chance of a transfer. How could I explain?

By the time I got off at Guildford, I knew I'd no choice but to keep her hopes as high as they were. It was less cruel than the lie it couldn't be done. I'd have to tell her they could still find a solution at any time, the experiments had come to nothing, but they weren't giving up. Would such a statement be breaking the act? Surely not. The trouble was that I shouldn't have told her anything in the first place. By doing so, I'd already broken the law and raised her expectations in the process. Now I was going to have to hide the fact that we could help her. It was an awful situation.

I walked home from the station with a heavy heart indeed.

«««o»»»

At a later meeting, I asked Mark if I could see the release document they had used for Gordon. He looked at me strangely, but the next day I was given a sealed brown envelope which contained a copy.

That night I made a faithful copy of the agreement and got Caroline to sign it in front of two of our neighbours as witnesses. Although they witnessed Caroline's signature, I didn't let them see the nature of the document, nor that I'd dated it the previous week. I shredded Gordon's version.

Then, the next time I saw Mark, I gave him the document and simply said, 'You told me you might require this.' I think he guessed its nature as he didn't open it and slid it into his jacket pocket.

Now I needed to keep my fingers crossed.

32 NIGHT CALL

Some weeks later, Caroline and I were on the sofa watching television. Wilson was in his room and Sandra in the kitchen preparing minced beef with boiled potatoes and dumplings. She no longer needed supervision and both of us, while inwardly lamenting the loss of her childhood and teenage years, were overflowing with pride for her newfound abilities.

Wilson's achievements were equally fabulous. We'd both always been great Tottenham Hotspur fans, and his new footballing prowess saw him selected for the Guildford Schoolboys. The coach was optimistic he might make it into the game professionally. He so loved his football and his newfound ability was as if made in heaven.

The nine o'clock news started and the statement about humanimals, which I knew would come, had finally been released. It was the main headline news. I had to admit that a very clever line had been taken to explain it to the public:

'The Home Secretary has announced the failure of the attempt to repatriate people's minds. This is what she had to say,' the announcer said, and the scene cut to show Pam Jury standing behind a dais in the Home Office press centre.

'I am sorry to report that experiments to transfer people back into their own bodies have failed. There was some degree of success initially, but the new minds gradually lost their ability to function, leaving the object people with a form of dementia which took only days to develop and caused death within a week. Our scientists tell us the problem came from the object mind not being empty. The phenomenon known as Mindslip was a universal swap. Trying to transfer people back is not.'

Journalists tried to question her and she selected one.

'Reg Carbis, Sky News. Does this mean you're cancelling the project?'

'No, but we must fully comprehend the workings of the mind before any further experiments can be conducted. The almost instant onset of dementia is painful to see in an otherwise healthy individual.'

It was a clever explanation for why experiments were stopped so quickly. Well thought through. I was still sure the truth would get out one day and real human-to-human transfers would end up being conducted in secret.

'Jillian Welch, Daily Mail. What about the humanimals? What's their future now?'

'They'll be well cared for and now have communication devices which are improving their lives. Wearable audio devices are being developed to further improve their lots. There's no possibility of any transfers at this time nor in the foreseeable future.'

'Richard Chapman, BBC. Is it true the humans who are hosts for animal minds are to be put down?' he asked.

'No. No such plan is in place. Next.'

'Jane Ellis, The Sun. Are humanimals being allowed back to their homes?'

'Where practicable, yes. We're actively encouraging it and hoping family units can continue to function with state aid and grants to help adapt housing in some circumstances.'

'Brian Williams, The Independent. Has any more been decided about life insurance companies treating Mindslip accidents and deaths as uninsurable?'

'Sorry, Brian. I don't have that information. Now, one more question. Linda.'

'Linda Delve, The Observer. The Auckland University of Technology is claiming they've managed to transfer the mind of a dog into another dog and it was successful. What's the story there?'

'Yes. Their work must be acclaimed as excellent, but unfortunately, they've hit the same problem as us and hadn't noticed the dementia was occurring when they published their first announcement. You'll find a new statement being made by AUT shortly to that effect. Now I'm ending this press conference, but my office has put a full statement on the website. Thank you all for coming and I'm sorry I had to provide bad news which will be devastating for the humanimals in particular. Good afternoon.'

There was an immediate clamour for more questions, but the Home Secretary exited through a door to the rear. The scene returned to the news desk. I was impressed by the manner in which the Home Secretary had dealt with the AUT situation and guessed there would already have been frantic international calls to convince the New Zealand government to play ball.

'We'll be able to speak to our science correspondent shortly, but in the studio, we have the Shadow Home Secretary, Mr David Didsbury. Mr Didsbury, thank you for coming in today. How do you respond to this failure by government scientists?'

As he spoke, I reduced the volume and pulled Caroline closer to me, 'It's as I said, but you can be sure they'll keep trying, darling.'

'Href,' she said with little confidence. It so hurt me to know that saving her was still a possibility but was being denied to us.

A call from the kitchen, 'Dinner everyone. Can someone shout Wils?'

We rose, Caroline went through to the dining area and jumped onto her specially raised chair. I walked into the hall and bellowed for Wilson, who was down the stairs almost before I'd got to the table myself.

'What you done today, Sands?'

'What *have* you done?' I corrected him.

'Mince and tatties wiz dumplings,' she said proudly.

'Watch those "th" sounds Limpet,' I said quietly.

It was rare for her to make accent mistakes these days and happened most when she was excited or distracted. I cut up Caroline's potatoes and dumplings and stirred them around in the way she liked. We all tucked into a wonderful meal. I was so proud of my daughter and the French accent was beginning to be less noticeable.

'Terrific meal, Sandra,' Caroline's metallic voice came from a Bluetooth speaker on the table. She lapped some meat and pressed a few more keys, 'and tastes lovely.'

The sound module for the touchpad made a world of difference to Caroline, giving her the opportunity to interact with the rest of us. I was so grateful to Jonah and Endron. He'd given me the updated version personally without a sign of any ulterior motive. I was learning that being firm on all matters was an important part of being female.

«‹‹o››»

On Saturday morning, we all went to the football pitches on the park, where Wilson was playing for the senior school's side. He was a tiny figure amongst the older players who were mainly in their mid-teens, but his talent was immediately obvious. Although he only scored one goal, a lovely move which saw him beat three players before side-footing it into the net, he was instrumental in another three in the six-one victory. He reminded me of his hero Lamela, or Eriksen in his anticipation. I was amazed at the way he could run at speed with the football seemingly attached to his feet by elastic.

We all had a great time cheering and barking him on. The family was as one for the first time since Mindslip.

The evening was entirely the opposite. Caroline had finished her dinner, her favourite steak pie with gravy. We were watching the late Saturday soccer match. Suddenly she whined, got off the sofa, walked with a staggering gait into the kitchen and collapsed. She brought up her meal and, at the same time, left a puddle on the kitchen floor.

Sandra was upstairs, but Wilson and I were instantly by her side. She was breathing erratically. We quickly cleaned her up, I carried her back into the lounge and laid her on the sofa. Wilson cleaned the floor while I rang the veterinary surgery. Of course, being the weekend, there was no one there, but an emergency number was provided. After what seemed an age, but was probably only a few minutes, I got Mrs Reid.

'Caroline has collapsed, brought up all of her food and also weed on the floor.'

'I'll be straight there. Keep her warm and comfortable. Don't try to give her anything to drink. Put a nitro tablet in her mouth.'

I laid down the receiver, grabbed the bottle of white tablets from the bookcase, sat beside her, and pushed a tablet under her tongue. I lifted her head onto my lap and stroked her neck.

'You hurting?'

'Nh,' her word for no.

She was breathing irregularly and her tongue had gone a strange colour. I kept caressing her neck and ears, which I knew she liked, and telling her not to worry. I told Wilson to be ready to open the door for Mrs Reid.

'Hruf hru,' she said.

'Love you, too.'

Her eyes were trying to roll, 'Stay awake, darling. Mrs Reid will be here soon.'

'Href,' she said, and her tongue licked my hand as Sandra sat the other side of her and stroked her flank. Wilson was watching for the vet's car.

'She'll soon have you on your feet.' I saw tears in her eyes.

'Href,' she said, took a deep breath, then a shallower one, closed her eyes and slipped away.

I tried the CPR which Mrs Reid had shown me but to no avail and Caroline's body was already cooling by the time the vet arrived.

'Sorry,' she said after a short examination, 'heart failure.'

'Yes,' I replied blankly. Sandra was in floods of tears as was Wilson and they were sitting tight together. I cried for all of us. I'd lost my darling, courageous, and brave wife.

Mrs Reid said her goodnights and left us to our misery.

Cemeteries had to be used for humans, but the same rules did not apply to humanimals so we decided we'd like her to be buried nearby. On Sunday morning, we all shared the digging of a large hole in the garden and laid Caroline to rest.

In the afternoon, we bought a flowering cherry tree from the local garden centre and planted it beside her. Each spring the blossom would remind us of our loss and our love.

33 NO ASTRONOMER ROYAL

A year later, the last meeting of the Catastrophe Committee was called to order by Giles Burton. 'On behalf of the PM, the Home Secretary and the entire government, I want to thank you all for the tremendous help you have been in assisting us to turn this catastrophe into a manageable disaster.

'The concepts you devised and your work with banks and financial institutions, has freed up large amounts of working capital to go towards rehabilitation of disadvantaged and fragmented families. The newly formulated insurance, property, and asset laws have allowed us to deal with complex situations and are working well. Yes, there are still matters to resolve, but in general the rules you formulated work well and will continue to improve.

'The innovative ideas you devised for wages, compensation, and training programmes for people unable to continue in their original roles also overcame many potentially difficult and aggravating individual problems. The guidelines were excellent and helped no end in redeploying skilled workers into worthwhile pursuits.

'Your plan for the humanimals to be reintegrated into the general population where practicable has also been a success. Although it's a drain on welfare resources, it's a short-term measure as many of the humanimals will have a relatively short lifespan. I'm not being callous there, simply stating the obvious. Know what I mean?

'Your suggestions about how to deal with the humans with animal minds were taken on board and discussed with the leaders of each of the main religions in the UK. With regret, they all agreed we should put them down and it was done in secret last week. You have all signed the Act and this all forms part of the secrets which must be maintained. It will eventually get out, but no one had any more sensible alternatives. A similar plan was instigated in most other countries.'

'It remains for me to say you'll all be recognised in the honours list which is also a secret for the time being.

'It's been a pleasure working with you all and I hope you can return to your day jobs, knowing you have been of great service to your country.'

Mark stood up, 'One final area remains unresolved. Do you have nothing to say about the secret project?'

'No. I'm sorry, Mark. All your ongoing good work is recognised, but it's not open for discussion, even by or within this secret committee.'

Mark slumped back into his seat. What had he wanted to say or bring to our attention? It was illegal for us to even ask the question. A lot of handshaking ensued and gradually the room emptied.

For probably the last time, I made my way out of Downing Street by the front entrance, through the famous steel gates, turned left and walked towards the station.

I was much more thick-skinned these days and ignored the workmen's wolf whistles. In fact, the one stripped to the waist was quite fit!

However, with footsteps close behind, apprehension overcame me. Was someone about to attack me? I spun around to confront them, but no, it was Mark, catching up with me.

'Slow down, Beth,' he said.

We came to a halt and moved to the side of the footpath.

'What can I do for you, Mark?'

'Well, I wondered if you could help me. Do you know anyone with a couple of greyhounds?'

He was finally ready to try to transfer Caroline into a younger animal.

'Oh, Mark. You hadn't heard? Caroline died of heart failure nearly a year ago, I'm afraid.'

'Beth, I am so sorry. I didn't know.'

'Were you going to be able to do it without loss of intelligence?' I whispered the question.

'"You might very well think that, but I couldn't possibly comment."'

We both knew exactly what the famous quotation meant.

'Thanks for not forgetting, Mark,' I said, shook his hand warmly, and we continued on our way.

My days in the corridors of power were at an end. Now I wanted to get back home and some semblance of normality in this crazy new world.

Next week, in my new day job, I'd be giving a presentation on the Betelgeuse data to a conference of more than two hundred astronomers and astrophysicists. Justin had been appointed head of Jodrell Bank and I had become the youngest head of the Royal Observatory. The post was Astronomer Royal, but the title was being changed. So instead of being the first female Astronomer Royal, I was now the first ever Official Astronomer.

A new era had begun. Strange times indeed.

34 A TIME FOR REFLECTION

Eighteen months after Mindslip, the world was a different place. Families had, for the most part, come to terms with the horror they had experienced as loved ones vanished or became different people, or even different species. Nothing would ever be the same again for those who lived through it.

Quantitative easing allowed the world's economies to adjust to the new order. It meant most countries avoided the worst effects of inflation.

The dysfunctional royal family had gone into retirement and a referendum to make Britain a republic, was about to take place. The House of Lords was to become a second elected chamber.

Betelgeuse was still the brightest object in the night sky but was expected to fade to the magnitude of Venus within a decade. A small telescope already showed a beautiful nebula. It would forever be a reminder to the world of the power of the universe and the fragility of life on Earth.

The International Space Station had been running normally for more than a year now. The reluctant astronauts, created by Mindslip, had long-since returned to Earth, dining out on, and lecturing about, their unique experiences.

Peter, the child pilot, was given special dispensation to continue his helicopter training despite his physical age and was hoping for a new career in aviation.

Angus now enjoyed a rather challenging motherhood with his extraordinary baby, who had, himself, once been a lonely, and very grumpy, old man in a care home and was never slow to voice his opinions. Somehow the two managed to avoid mutual destruction.

The Italian abattoir manager only discovered the word "HELP", which Andrea had scraped in the mud of their holding paddock, long after they'd processed all of the animals.

Of course, many people never found their close relations for one reason or another. Some had died in accidents during Mindslip, others had become humanimals, but unrecognisable as human, for instance, mice, lizards, snakes, fish, seagulls and so on, the smaller creatures even losing the ability to reason like a person.

Billions of insects died within days of Mindslip, but populations soon recovered. I often wondered about humans who had become spiders, flies, butterflies, and beetles. Would they have even been aware of what had happened? Two well-known YouTube cases of spiders weaving words into their webs had been discovered to be hoaxes, but, nevertheless, it made you think about the possibilities.

Accidental deaths and suicides accounted for almost one in five of the population, and many child minds were never repatriated with their original families. Sandra was an example. No one could ever know who inhabited her body today – she must've been somebody's child before Mindslip. A whole group of people would forever be orphans yet would know their parents were somewhere in the greater population. Even DNA could be of no help in sorting out Mindslip transfers. In other cases, where couples were no longer compatible in sex or age, relationships irrevocably broke down and they separated. So many families were torn apart in such a manner.

What about me?

I'm Doctor Beth Arnold PhD MBE[5], Official Astronomer and director of the Royal Observatory.

My day-to-day life gradually returned to a semblance of routine, but what counts as normal in the post-Mindslip world? I'm a young oriental woman, who was once married to a greyhound, father to an adult white daughter, as old as myself, and a black son who miraculously gained incredible footballing skills. Your typical family these days.

The three of us eventually made our way to Harrow one Saturday morning and tracked down the butcher's shop owned by a certain Fred and Pete. Pete was called Petra when we visited and clearly remembered Caroline's visit. I told her Cas had always wanted to thank her personally for her kindness on her awful journey from Hatfield to Guildford.

We gave her a huge bouquet of flowers which brought her to tears which, I suppose, was lovely, and we all cried for the distraught greyhound who'd sat on their step begging for pie. I told her she had no idea how much of a lifesaver her kindness had been to Caroline during her journey. Petra insisted we all have tea together to reminisce, while Fred grumbled about having to look after the shop.

At work, we spent enormous amounts of time studying Betelgeuse, but never did discover any more about what made the collision of the two radiations perform such an amazing feat as to change all living things on the planet in such a bizarre manner. In conjunction with observatories worldwide, we assessed all other nearby giant stars which might be in danger of going nova. We had no idea how it might help us survive a similar event, but no knowledge is ever wasted when it comes to learning about the universe.

---

[5] Member of the Most Excellent Order of the British Empire – a national order of chivalry

LIGO[6] obtained some phenomenal gravitational wave data from the supernova, and it was leading to the construction of an even larger detector.

Wilson's footballing expertise was phenomenal, and he'd recently played his tenth game for the English School's XI. Southampton football club had already expressed an interest in him, but I knew his ambitions lay with the glorious cockerel which resided in North London. He'd applied for the Tottenham Hotspur youth programme and had been shortlisted. I was keeping my fingers crossed.

I suppose I was most pleased with Sandra's development. Her transferor, Georgette Damay, apparently had many culinary skills and Sandra had inherited the bulk of them. During her adult-child education lessons, it became clear there was a cooking expertise burgeoning. She now had a boyfriend too and, one Saturday, she gave me a real dilemma.

'Dad. Can I ask something?'

I nodded.

'I want to ask Malcolm to stay over,' she said, looking down at her hands.

'You mean in your room?' I asked full of trepidation.

'We've been dating six months and I do love him, Dad.'

'Does he love you?'

'Ee says so.'

'Don't drop your hs.'

'Sorry. Please, Dad. I know all the facts of life and things and I'll ask him to get condoms.'

Good grief. She was only eleven, but I knew she was also a maturing twenty-five-year-old woman. I'd no choice

---

[6] The Laser Interferometer Gravitational-Wave Observatory is a large-scale physics experiment and observatory to study gravitational waves.

really and gave permission. I don't suppose I'd the right to say no anyway. Legally, she was an adult. Okay, there were still occasional childish aspects to her actions and conversations, but they were happening less and less frequently. The boyfriend seemed to be in love with her, and love is such a precious commodity in this brave new world. It separates us from unthinking beasts.

Today was a good example of how things had moved on for us all. We'd taken to having regular dinner parties with friends so Sandra could practice upon us with her new culinary creations. She was amazing and, if I came into the kitchen when she was busy, she shooed me off in no uncertain terms. Her desire was to have a restaurant and she'd obtained a job as a sous-chef under the best chef in Guildford. The results were stunning dishes in both taste and appearance.

This evening she was cooking for five of us. Wilson, however, a typical teenager, bolted whatever delicacies she prepared and got bored sitting at the table while the remaining four of us savoured her delights. Wilson tended to flit back and forth between table and sofa to continue some football management game.

Sandra's first dish was the loveliest combination of homemade pâté with grapefruit slices and delicate rocket salad. As a main course, sliced potatoes and asparagus in cream with herbs, accompanied medallions of pork. I'd chosen a rich Rioja to go with it. Dessert was an exquisite work of modern art with strands of liquid chocolate randomly trailed over a most light and fluffy lemon cheesecake, all embellished with a spun sugar crown.

We all thoroughly enjoyed the experience her skills had given us. Such a boost in confidence for Sandra too.

Later, I lay on my bed, contemplating how my own life had changed since Mindslip. I'd finally accepted that I was a woman. I enjoyed my clothes, keeping fit, seeing people looking admiringly at me. I even got a sneaky satisfaction from the wolf whistles when I was out running at the weekend. I was very attractive and was learning to live within a sensuous and beautiful body.

I turned towards the window and appreciated the fading nova light filtering through the lace curtains, providing soft, flickering, romantic illumination. His naked figure was silhouetted against the light and the bed moved as he joined me, his breath warm upon my cheek, his lips tender and moist.

'You're sure about this?' he asked.

'Yes,' I affirmed and received a second kiss.

My surrender to him was complete. Our lips met once more in the most beautiful kiss. Mouths moving upon each other's, gentle, moist, mobile, and tender, tongues tangling in the warm darkness. His arms gripped my sides, his hands behind my shoulders and the kiss continued unabated, warmer and so passionate.

My own naked limbs surrounded him, my arms and hands embracing his muscular back. My legs rose to encircle his hips.

When it finally happened, warmth and pleasure relieved my natural apprehension. The unexpectedly wonderful sensation of being opened, stretched and filled enthralled me. By far the most beautiful experience though, was the unanticipated joy of being possessed by such loving masculine strength which would once have horrified me.

'Oh, wonderful,' I whispered, temporarily escaping the kiss.

'Yes, amazing,' he replied as our lips reconnected, taking our lovemaking to a whole new level.

Coming up for breath once more, I whispered, 'I love you, Gren.'

'Love you too, Beth.'

We were losing post-Mindslip "virginity" to each other in our still unfamiliar bodies, savouring the most extraordinarily novel and exciting sensations, while our pre-Mindslip memories gave us a unique insight into what the other was feeling during this most intimate experience. Our desire for one another was complete, each truly understanding the needs and responses of the other as no couple ever could before.

The rhythm of our first intimacy grew to a crescendo of simultaneous exhilaration, our loving motions only ceasing when we were both sated, but still locked together in post-coital exhaustion.

Blissful time passed. We separated. We lay side by side, holding hands, our bodies illuminated by the shimmering nova light. We recovered our breath. We cuddled into the security of each other's arms, in awe at what had just transpired.

Gren whispered, 'Marry me, Beth.'

I didn't need to think about it. I caressed his cheek, its designer stubble, his firm jaw and answered, 'Yes, please.'

35 PLUS ÇA CHANGE, PLUS C'EST LA MÊME CHOSE

Outside the sterile room, a beautiful young woman finished counting the bundles of thousand-dollar bills stacked upon the desk top. It was surprising how little space such a vast sum of money occupied. This was the fourth operation of the day. Five a day was about the limit for one facility.

'Thank you, Mr Nash, I make it two million dollars.' She smiled professionally at him, handed over a receipt and they shook hands. 'You can wait in the lounge. Second door on the left.' She indicated the corridor.

The heavily-built individual with the bulging breast pocket, spotted a chair in reception and sat. 'I'm responsible for his security. I'll stay here, if I may.'

Mrs Weston knew it was a statement, not a request, and simply nodded. They were used to dealing with the rich and powerful. They didn't argue over why security might be critical.

There were circular windows in the doors to the sterile room. She caught the eye of her neurosurgeon husband, Sir Dr Mark Weston, and gave a nod which he acknowledged.

Inside, an ageing figure lay on the hospital trolley, his face contorted with pain. He was riddled with cancer and struggled to speak to the neurosurgeon, 'Can we please get on with this? The lack of painkillers is torturing me.'

'Yes. I'm so sorry we can't give you any drugs for the pain. It is vital your brain is not dulled for the process to be effective.'

The figure coughed, 'You have morphine ready? I can't stand this agony a moment longer than necessary.' His terminal cancer was not only in his lungs, but also throughout his torso. Every breath was like a blast of superheated steam and throbbing waves of agony were churning endlessly around his abdomen. Now he was not on any painkillers, the cancer, which had spread into his bones, made his legs ache and his coccyx was like a red-hot poker probing his lower back, making it impossible to lie comfortably in any position. Death had been held at bay only by the application of the most effective drugs. He'd almost left his transfer too late.

'We're strapping your head into position. You know you must not move at all during the procedure,' said the neurosurgeon, as two lab technicians performed adjustments to the ceramic skull framework.

'Yes, yes. Just get on with it.' The pain caused him to sound as if the cancer had personally attached its bile to every word he uttered.

Behind the patient, another man lay, already strapped into place. He was a perfect physical specimen. Six foot two inches tall, blond hair, tanned skin, muscular and handsome. He was unconscious and had the same skull contraption attached to his head. The neurosurgeon examined the affidavit signed by the recipient stating he'd agreed to the upcoming transfer. It wasn't his business to reason how or why the man had signed the release. All he needed to do was to check the document was valid and signed in the presence of two legal notaries.

Technicians wheeled the trolley holding the old man up tight against the blond giant. Using ceramic bolts, they connected the two frameworks so both heads were fixed relative to each other.

'All in place, checked and secure.'

'Right,' said the neurosurgeon, 'if you need to cough please do so before the process. During the transfer, you'll need to keep perfectly still. It'll take some time to warm up and the process will last about thirty minutes.'

'Just do it.' The wrinkled face grimaced and his forehead creased with the torment he was experiencing.

Another technician fired up the scan transfer machine which hummed.

'Thirty more seconds to warm up, sorry.'

The old man grunted, his eyes screwed up to bear the pain, desperate for the relief of the morphine he'd been promised once it was over.

'Action,' said the technician, and the machine hummed more loudly.

'We're beginning. Try not to move,' the neurosurgeon instructed.

A blue line of light formed a stripe across the top of each of the men's heads and slowly traversed towards their chins. The machine was scanning the data pattern from the old man's brain. It was passed through a computer in the corner of the room and radiated into the blond a short time later.

The whole scan took twenty-six minutes.

The neurosurgeon stepped forward and injected a heavy dose of morphine into the dying man.

After a few seconds, the man's expression relaxed and he said, 'Thank you, Doctor Weston.'

The skull frameworks were unbolted, both trolleys moved away from the machine and placed side by side. Two orderlies pushed them through the operating theatre's doors.

The heavily set man with the bulge in his jacket stood and followed them as they were taken into a recovery room where he took a seat immediately inside the door.

'More morphine, Jack,' the old man ordered.

The bodyguard jumped up smartly, pulled a kit from his briefcase, primed the syringe and injected his boss.

'Thanks, Jack. The medics always skimp,' he said and the pain lines on his face fully relaxed at last. There was even the hint of a smile, but its thin warmth wasn't reflected in his eyes.

The neurosurgeon and a male nurse arrived to examine the young man.

'All vital signs normal. I'm giving him the stimulant,' said the neurosurgeon.

The old man watched what was happening to the figure on the adjacent trolley. There was a change in his breathing and his head moved. The neurosurgeon asked him several questions. How many fingers he was holding up, what day of the week it was and many more. The dying man waited impatiently until the routine questioning was complete.

'Who are you?' he shouted at the blond giant, gasping with the exertion.

'Ken Batten. It's me.'

'You all right?'

'Fine,' he said as he was helped to his feet and sat in a wheelchair which faced the old man.

'What did uncle Robert give us for Christmas in 1952?' snapped the old man.

'A driving game. With magnets to make the car move.'

'Who did we first have sex with and where?'

'Ha-ha. Doris Parker in her dad's shed. It was somewhat hurried.'

'What is Helix worth?'

'Not as much as it should be. About one hundred and five million.'

'And its profit the year before last?'

'Made a loss of one hundred and thirty-two thousand, but the potential's enormous.'

'Should we sell it?'

'Not a chance!'

'Yes, you're me.'

'No. You're me. Ha-ha,' the young man said.

The dying man said, 'I was hoping to be the version which moved into you. Seems I was unlucky.'

'But you did. I am you. I'm sorry I have to leave you behind,' said the blond giant.

'Yes. We knew one of us would still have to die. Just wish it wasn't me.'

'Strange situation. Isn't it?'

'Stranger for me, I assure you.'

The young man asked the neurosurgeon, 'You're certain there'll be no deterioration now?'

'Yes. It was a story put around to stop the operation being performed wholesale. We've even overcome the tiny loss of IQ in the latest process.'

'Have I lost anything at all?'

'Yes. There'll be a few memories which won't have been transferred, but there's nothing we can do about that. The memories will probably still be there, but your ability to access them might be less efficient. You could have trouble remembering a name from time to time, an event or some other details, but the aberrations are unlikely to be of any great consequence and, if you recall, we suggested you made a record of all passwords and other vital information which existed only in your memory.'

'You are sure?'

'As sure as we can be.'

The old man spoke again, 'In that case, Doctor Weston, please put this version of me out of my misery.'

'I don't like doing this. A doctor's mission is to preserve life, not take it.'

'You've been well paid, and it was part of the deal,' the young man reminded him.

The neurosurgeon took a syringe and prepared to inject the old figure whose hand was now being gripped by his mental doppelganger.

'This will be quick. If you have anything else you wish to say, do so now,' said Dr Weston.

'Look after our interests and my family,' the old Ken Batten said to the young man, and to the doctor, 'Do it!'

'I will,' confirmed the new Ken Batten.

Dr Weston injected the pentobarbitone. The old man's features relaxed; lifeless eyes remained open until the nurse closed them. The stethoscope was applied, and Dr Weston confirmed death. The old man was no more than a husk and the only Ken Batten in the room was now the young blond giant.

'Call the team, Jack,' he commanded with all the authority the old man ever exhibited.

The bodyguard left the room and, shortly, a funeral team arrived to collect the body.

'Can I stand?' Ken Batten asked the neurosurgeon.

'Yes. If you are unsteady sit for a while. Some of your motor functions might not be perfect until you adapt to your new body so take care for a few days.'

He stood and took a few steps towards the door, held it open and shook the doctor's hand, 'Thank you, Doctor Weston, much appreciated.'

He proceeded along the corridor and set off on his rejuvenated life. His newfound youth should be great fun. He strode out of the building, jumped into the back seat of his Rolls Royce and they followed the hearse away from the desert medical centre and on into Benghazi. The funeral was quickly held and the anonymous ashes scattered.

Ken Batten boarded his private jet for the long flight back to the United States of America to take control of his business empire. He also had ambitions. In a few years, he would seek the Republican Party nomination. One day, he might become president.

«««o»»»

Back at the transferral centre, Sir Dr Mark Weston and his wife, Lady Julia, enjoyed a coffee break. No one who knew them in England post-Mindslip would have recognised them today. Mark Weston had transferred himself into a fit, vibrant, and handsome twenty-year-old man. His wife was now a nineteen-year-old, who could easily have graced the catwalk of the most prestigious fashion houses. They were enjoying a fabulous lifestyle and building up a fortune from their transferral business. He'd invested diversely and wisely. Their intention was to stop work next year but keep two sets of equipment in working order in their Benghazi and Norway facilities. They'd be able to live in luxury for as long as the Earth might exist.

For security and in case of accidents, Mark had purchased six thousand yottabytes (one yottabyte is 1,000,000,000,000,000 gigabytes) of the new DNA cloud storage and also had a similar amount in their electromagnetic-proof, three-thousand-cubic-metre, underground vault in Norway. His and his wife's data patterns were stored in both for safety and updated every two months. Their immortality was thus secured even if they suddenly lost their lives.

They finished their break and returned to work.

«««o»»»

The last patient of the day was being wheeled into the theatre. They both recognised him as the dying president of Dhivanda. Mindslip had dealt harshly with this dynamic, young, but tyrannical leader, transforming him into an aged cripple. Mark regretted giving this obnoxious individual a new lease of life but guessed the assassin's bullet would not be too long coming.

THE END, but look out for a follow up - HEAT

Tony's Books

Thank you for reading MINDSLIP. Reviews are very important for authors, and I wonder if I could ask you to say a few words on the review page where you bought this book. Every review, even if it is only a few words with a star rating, helps the book move up the rankings.

Other books. They include a trilogy, a series, some stand-alone novels, and some non-fiction works.

MARK NOBLE SPACE ADVENTURE SERIES

THE FEDERATION TRILOGY

STAND ALONE NOVELS

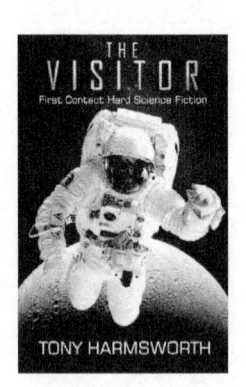

TONY'S NON-FICTION BOOKS

COMPILATIONS (Not all available in paperback)

Reader Club

Building a relationship with my readers is the very best thing about being a novelist. In these days of the Internet and email, the opportunities to interact with you are unprecedented. I send occasional newsletters which include special offers and information on how the various series are developing. You can keep in touch by signing up for my no-spam mailing list.

Sign up at my webpage: **Harmsworth.net** or on my **TonyHarmsworthAuthor** Facebook page and you will know when my books are released and will get free material from time to time and other information.

If you have questions, don't hesitate to write to me at Tony@Harmsworth.net.

Printed in Great Britain
by Amazon